Panic ...
He ...
A cart whee~~l squeaked~~ as Hunter's shopping cart pulled in behind her.

She nearly dropped her coupon envelope. He still smelled the same—like pine, hay and summer sun. His black T-shirt hugged a powerful physique that had matured impressively.

She felt his gaze rake over her again like a cold hard punch. He froze, finally really looking at her. Recognition snapped through him. His entire body went rigid. His jaw dropped and he fell silent, leaving the rest of his thoughts unspoken.

She didn't glance at Hunter as she took her receipt, turned her back and grabbed her single bag of groceries from the end of the check stand.

Don't look back, she told herself. She didn't need one last look at the man. She'd learned all she needed to in his shocked and silent stare. Not that she'd held even the faintest hope of a friendly reunion. No, not after the way they'd left things. But she hadn't expected him to look at her with horror, either....

She could still feel Hunter's gaze as she crossed the lot—a cold gaze, when it had once been so loving. Why did that hurt so much?

Books by Jillian Hart

JILLIAN HART

grew up on her family's homestead, where she helped raise cattle, rode horses and scribbled stories in her spare time. After earning her English degree from Whitman College, she worked in travel and advertising before selling her first novel. When Jillian isn't working on her next story, she can be found puttering in her rose garden, curled up with a good book or spending quiet evenings at home with her family.

Montana Dreams

Jillian Hart

Love Inspired

Recycling programs
for this product may
not exist in your area.

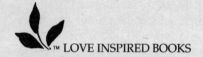 ™ LOVE INSPIRED BOOKS

ISBN-13: 978-0-373-87763-8

MONTANA DREAMS
Copyright © 2012 by Harlequin Books S.A.

The publisher acknowledges the copyright holders
of the individual works as follows:

MONTANA DREAMS
Copyright © 2012 by Jill Strickler

KEY WITNESS
Copyright © 2008 by Harlequin Books S.A.

www.LoveInspiredBooks.com

Printed in U.S.A.

Dear Reader,

Welcome to Love Inspired! We're celebrating our 15th anniversary this month, and you're invited to the party!

Love Inspired Books began in September 1997, offering readers inspirational contemporary romances. Fifteen years later, Love Inspired has never wavered from our promise to our readers; we are proud to publish short contemporary romances that feature Christian men and women facing the challenges of life and love in today's world.

In honor of our anniversary, we are showcasing some of our top authors in September. Irene Hannon, Arlene James and Lois Richer were part of the original lineup in 1997, and we're supremely blessed that they are still writing for us in 2012. Jillian Hart and Margaret Daley have been part of the Love Inspired family since the early 2000s. And newcomer Mia Ross rounds out the month. We hope you enjoy these sweet stories full of home, family and love.

As a special thank-you to our readers, each book this month contains a bonus story. Give them a try, and we know you'll find our authors the very best in Christian romance!

Thank you for reading Love Inspired.

Blessings,

Melissa Endlich

Senior Editor

I will love you, O Lord, my strength.
—*Psalms* 18:1

Chapter One

"You always were good for nothing, girl." Her father's bitter voice grumbled through the small, unkempt house. "Get the lead out of your lazy butt and fetch me something to eat. I'm gettin' hungry."

Millie Wilson straightened up, mop handle clutched in one hand, closed her eyes and prayed for strength. The Lord had to help her because she wasn't sure she could do this without Him. The call in the middle of the night, a doctor's voice on the other end of the line, her father's collapse and terminal prognosis. If only there had been anyone—anyone at all—to take over his care. "I have to go to the market, Dad."

"You should have thought of that earlier," he barked from the other room.

And I came back, why? She swished the mop into the sudsy bucket, wrung it out and scoured the last patch of kitchen floor. Marginally better, but it was going to take more than one pass over. She didn't want to think how long it had been since the floor had a proper cleaning—it would take a scrub brush and a lot of elbow grease to get out the dirt ground into the texture of the linoleum—a job for another time. Her back ached just thinking of it.

"Millie?" A knock echoed above the hum of the air con-

ditioner. A familiar face smiled in at her, visible through the
pane of glass in the door. The foreman tipped his Stetson and
rolled the tobacco around to his other cheek while he waited
for her to open the door.

"Hi, Milton. What's up?" She squinted in the bright summer sun.

"We got problems. Paychecks bounced. Again." Milton
paused a moment to gather his spit, turn aside and spew a
stream of tobacco juice into the barren flower bed. "The boys
aren't going to stand for this. They've got rent due and mouths
to feed."

"I know." Why didn't this surprise her either? She rubbed
her forehead, which was beginning to pound. "I'm overwhelmed here. I haven't even thought about Dad's finances."

"They're a shambles, that's what." Milton shook his head,
his weathered face lined with a mixture of grief and disgust.
"Work is scarce in this part of the county. No one wants to
walk away from a job right now. I know Whip is sick, but if he
doesn't take care of his workers, then we can't work for free.
Those cows need to be milked no matter what."

"Give me a day to problem solve. Can you ask everyone to
wait? I'm here now, I've been here for two hours. Let me figure out what's what, and I'll do everything I can to make good
on those checks."

"We appreciate that, Millie. I know you'll do your best by
us, but I don't know what the boys will go for." Milton tipped
his hat in a combination of thanks and farewell before he ambled toward the steps. "Keep in mind that if things don't get
better..."

"I hear you." Someone had to do the work, and it took a team
of men to do it. As Milton headed off back down the driveway,
Millie wondered if she remembered how to run a milking parlor. That part of her life seemed a world away, nearly forgotten. Probably intentionally.

"Put ice cream on that list, girl, and get a move on." In his room, Pa must have hit the remote because the soundtrack from a spaghetti Western drowned out every other noise in the house and kept her from arguing. The pop of gunfire and the drum of galloping horses accompanied her while she upended her mop bucket over the sink, stowed the meager cleaning supplies and made a mental grocery list.

Time to blow this place. She grabbed her purse and the big ring of farm keys. She called out to her dad, not sure if he could hear her over the blaring television and hopped out the front door.

"Mom." Simon looked up, pushed his round glasses higher on his nose with a thumb and held out a handful of wildflowers. "I picked them for you."

"You did?" Just what she needed. One look at her nine-year-old son eased the strain of the tough last couple of hours. Love filled her heart like a tidal wave as the black-haired boy with deep blue eyes ran across a lawn that had gone wild. Blossoms danced in his fist as he held them up to her.

Better than roses any day. "Thank you. They're wonderful. I love them."

"I thought you needed something, you know, to make you smile." He shrugged his shoulders, his button face puckered up with worry. "You've frowned the whole time, ever since you said we had to come here."

"Really? Oh, I didn't mean to. Sorry about that, kiddo." She took a moment to admire her bouquet of yellow sunflowers, snowy daisies, purple coneflowers and cheerful buttercups. "These certainly should do the trick. Am I smiling?"

"Yeah. Much better." When he grinned, deep dimples cut into his cheeks, so like his father's that it drove straight to her heart.

It was one pain that would never fade. She'd stopped trying to make it disappear years ago. There was just no use. Once, she'd loved Simon's father with all the depth of her being. Losing him had shattered her. Ten years later and she still hadn't found a way to make her heart whole.

Being back home in this little corner of Montana made her wonder. Just how much would she remember—things she couldn't hold back? She sighed, thinking of how young she'd been, of how truly she'd loved the man and, yes, it hurt to remember. She ran a hand along her son's cheek—such a sweet boy—and kept the smile on her face.

Simon was what mattered now.

"Guess what?" she asked. "I need a copilot."

"I'm on it." Simon leaped ahead, dashing toward the old Ford pickup. "Where're we goin'?"

"To the grocery store, unless you want to eat stale crackers and dried-up peanut butter for supper."

"Not so much. Can we have pizza?" He yanked open the black truck's door. The rusty old thing squeaked and groaned as he scrambled behind the steering wheel and across the ripped bench seat. "It could be the on-sale kind. Want me to see if we got a coupon?"

"That would be a big help."

She eyed the truck warily. It had been a long time since she'd driven a pickup. Totally different from her compact car and she had to adjust the seat, the mirrors and dig for the seat belt—it was buried in the crumbs, hayseed and grain bits that had accumulated in the crack of the seat over what had to be decades.

"I'm on it." Simon slipped his hand into the outside pocket of her handbag, extracted an envelope and began sorting through her coupon collection. His forehead furrowed in concentration. His cowlick stood up straight from the crown of his head in a lazy swirl.

Just like his father's.

Stop thinking about that man. She had enough to contend with without borrowing heartache. She refused to wonder what had happened to the man. The love she had for him was long dead and buried. Did he still live around here or had he moved?

It wasn't as if she'd kept in touch with anyone in the valley, so she'd never heard a scrap of the news since her father had thrown her out of the house when she was nineteen.

"Found it!" Simon's triumph was drowned out by the roar of the badly timed engine. He waved the coupon while she dug out his seat belt, too. "I hope they have the pepperoni kind at the store."

"Me, too." She couldn't help trying to smooth down the ruffle of hair, but his cowlick stayed up stubbornly.

"Mom?"

"What?" She wrestled the truck into Drive, which shouldn't be so hard with an automatic, and nosed the pickup down the driveway.

"How long do we gotta stay here?" He tucked the coupon in the front of the fat envelope.

"I don't know. I wish I did, believe me." Gravel crunched beneath the tires as she fought the pickup around a curve. "I want to go home just as much as you do."

"I miss my friends."

"Me, too."

They smiled together as the pickup bumped down the last stretch of driveway. Cows grazed behind sagging fences. Across the county road, moss glinted on the barn's roof, which happened to be missing more than a few shingles. As she cranked the steering wheel to the right hard, manhandling the rattling truck onto the pavement, she wondered just how long Dad had been letting things slide and why no one had looked her up to tell her. She may have moved out of state, but she wasn't that hard to find.

Amber fields whipped by, grass bronzing in the hot summer sun.

"How come Grandpa doesn't share his TV?"

"That's just the way he is." Her mother had a small set in the kitchen, but it was not there now. She had no idea where it went or what had gone on around here in the last ten years. One thing was for certain, a lot of things had changed. The farm was no longer top-notch, money was apparently wanting and her father? The robust man he'd once been had withered away.

"I know we've got to get by and you're not working or anything." Simon took a deep breath. "But how am I gonna watch my shows?"

"That's a good question. I'll try and figure something out, okay?"

"Okay." He stared off down the road. "Maybe we won't be here long."

"Maybe." Simon didn't know that they would be leaving only after her father died. Sorrow burned behind her eyes, which was unexpected considering how she'd once loathed her dad with every fiber of her being. She checked her rearview mirror for traffic out of habit—of course, there was none, not on this rural road—and flicked her gaze to the pavement ahead. Farmland spread around her like a patchwork quilt in irrigated greens, dried ambers and barn roofs glinting in the sun.

One more corner and they zipped past the little row of rental houses, bright with new paint, where her one-and-only love had lived. Was he still there or had he moved on to bigger and better things? Maybe he'd left town entirely—that's what she dearly hoped. The last thing she wanted was to run into him, face-to-face. Pain seared her heart, tender after all these years.

Why did it still hurt to remember Hunter McKaslin? She didn't know—it was a mystery she might never solve.

"Did you go to school there?" Simon asked, pointing toward a squat gray block building hugging the outskirts of town. The windows were dark. Students wouldn't fill those classrooms for another month.

"Yes, I did. I jumped rope in that courtyard. And see that last door right there? That's the library where I spent every rainy recess."

"It looks awful small, Mom."

"Welcome to life in Prospect, Montana," she quipped. "Where everything is small."

"This is the main street?" Simon scratched his head, looking around with a wrinkled nose and a slight look of dismay. He'd been asleep on the drive from the Bozeman airport. Milton had met their plane, a tiny prop that lurched and swayed with every gust of wind. She dreaded getting back up in the air for her return trip.

"I know it doesn't look like much, but it's the quality and not the quantity that counts," she said of the town.

"What does that mean? More is better, Mom. You know it is."

"I was talking about the people. That's what makes the difference anywhere." She swung into a lot, yanking hard on the wheel. Boy, did she miss power steering. It was all she could do to grapple the big truck into a parking space. At least she *hoped* she'd managed to fit between the lines. Who knew? She was afraid to pop open her door and take a look. Good thing there was plenty of room in the nearly empty lot. The engine shuttered to a stop, she tossed the keys into her purse and unbuckled.

A hot, dry wind puffed over her as she led the way into the store. The grocery hadn't changed much. It was still family owned, sporting fading posters in the front wall of windows, and the automatic doors gave a long pause before they wheezed arthritically open.

Just get in and get out, she thought as Simon tromped alongside her. If she hurried, then maybe no one would have time to recognize her and see what had become of her.

"I'll grab a cart!" Simon leaped forward to pick apart the wire carts and took charge of one, steering it by its red handlebar. He stopped dead in his tracks when he looked around. "This is it?"

"I'm afraid so." They were used to a large chain store in Portland bursting with selection. This little place had ten aisles—short aisles—and hadn't been remodeled since she'd left town. The fifties decorating scheme added charm, but it didn't come close to impressing her son. She smiled and rubbed his shoulder encouragingly. "Maybe their pizza selection isn't too bad. See the refrigerated cases along the back wall? Why don't we go check 'em out?"

"Okay." Leading the way like an intrepid explorer who just discovered the terrain was much more perilous than expected, Simon shoved the cart ahead of him.

"Millie? Millie Wilson? Is that you, dear?" An elderly voice quivered with excitement.

Millie skidded to a stop. Up ahead of her, Simon did, too. He turned around with curiosity bright in his dark blue eyes. So much for getting in and out of here without running into someone she knew. "Mrs. Hoffsteader, how are you?"

"Fine, just fine. I can't believe my eyes. Little Millie, all grown up. I almost didn't recognize you." The white-haired lady tapped up with her loaded cart, her cane hanging on the handlebar. Her smile turned serious. "I suppose you're back in town to help with your father."

"Yes." She nodded at Simon, letting him know to go ahead without her. Not only was the pizza case in plain view, but she was a little afraid of Myra Hoffsteader's sharp gaze. What if someone recognized Simon's dimples and dark blue eyes a shade lighter than his father's?

"Whip has his faults and he's the hardest man I've ever met, but I hate to think of anyone ill." Compassion wreathed the woman's lovely face. "It has to be hard for you, too."

"I'll be fine. Wherever I am, I'm not alone."

"No, God is watching over us all, and that's the truth." Myra's gaze narrowed, perhaps eager to bring up a certain subject. "He's still in town, you know."

"H-Hunter?" She gulped for air, nearly choking over the name she hadn't spoken aloud in so long that it felt foreign on her tongue. The one name she'd once loved most of all.

"In fact, there he is, walking this way." She nodded her silver head in the direction of the front windows where a tall, wide-shouldered man stalked across the parking lot, his Stetson brim tipped to hide the sun. All she could see of his face was the firm, unyielding line of his mouth and the square manly cut of his jaw.

Hunter. Her heart rolled slowly in her chest, flipping upside down. Hunter, here, after all this time. And so close. She stumbled a few steps back. Her first instinct was to run. She cast her gaze down the aisle where Simon stood in front of the glass doors, fist to his chin in thought.

There was no reason why Hunter would suspect, she told herself. But those words didn't comfort her. "Mrs. Hoffsteader, it's been good seeing you, but honestly, I don't want to be standing here when Hunter walks through that door."

"I understand, dear. He broke your heart." Sympathy softened her voice. "I suppose you've got a lot on your plate tending your father. That's enough adversity for a girl to deal with. You go on now."

"It was good running into you." Millie backed down the aisle, taking refuge between the tall shelves of cooking oils on one side and spices on the other. "I'll see you Sunday?"

"Absolutely. I'll keep an eye out. We're having a church picnic. Rumor has it that you are a Christian now. Be sure to come."

"I'll try." She glanced toward the door—it whooshed open, meaning Hunter was almost in sight, so she took off. No way would he recognize the back of her as she skedaddled down the aisle.

"They had pepperoni." Simon smiled, dimples flashing, holding up the box. "It's the large size, but that's okay. The coupon covers it."

"Good boy." She glanced at the price tacked inside the case, but it was hard to concentrate with her heart drumming a thousand beats a second.

"I found a coupon in there for cookie dough." Simon's gaze slid sideways to the rolls of premade tubes sitting in bright yellow packages. "It's okay if we can't afford it, but they just look good."

"Yes, they do." Impulsively she yanked open the door and snagged a roll of chocolate chip, Simon's favorite. She heard a man's boots thud nearby, a gait she'd know anytime and anywhere, it was sewn into the fabric of her being.

Hunter. His step hesitated directly behind her. Her blood pressure rocketed into the red zone. He tugged at her like a black hole's gravitational field—a force she had to resist. Her palms went slick. She slowly set the dough tube in the cart. Maybe if she didn't make any sudden movements, he wouldn't look her way. Let him go on with his shopping without noticing her. That way she wouldn't have to look him in the eye and feel her heart break all over again.

"Mom?" Simon grasped the bar and gave the cart a shove. "What's next?"

"Uh—" She stared at Hunter's reflection in the glass refrigerator case. He was tall enough to steal a woman's breath, well-built in a country sort of way—those were solid muscles beneath his T-shirt. His dark hair, still thick, tumbled over his forehead. Her fingers remembered the silken feel of those locks. If he wasn't wearing that Stetson, his hair would stick up just a hint at the crown, where a cowlick whirled.

She swallowed hard, feeling a bump against her elbow. Simon. She saw her reflection, too. Not the youthful girl she'd been when Hunter had loved her, when the most handsome man in the county had chosen her as his girlfriend. Time and hardship had worn their way onto her face. Faint creases marked the corners of her eyes, the plane of her forehead and bracketed her mouth. No, she was so not the girl she'd been.

That wasn't the reason she didn't answer her son right away. What if the sound of her voice drew Hunter's attention? She pointed to the dairy case. Simon turned the cart with a rattle and headed toward the egg cartons lined up in the next case over.

There was a thump behind her as something landed in Hunter's cart. Wheels squeaked and boots knelled on the tile. Thank the heavens above, he walked away in the opposite direction. *Thank You, Lord.*

Relief blasted through her. She risked a glance over her shoulder just as he turned down the next aisle, his attention on his shopping. Iron jaw, granite features, he'd become a man who looked harder than she'd remembered—the father of her son.

Chapter Two

Guilt wrapped around her as she faced the little boy checking the prices on the various egg cartons.

"This is the best price." Simon slipped it into the basket. "I got a carton of milk, too. The generic stuff. We don't have coupons for either of 'em."

"That's okay. We need bread and peanut butter next." And ice cream, she remembered through the rattled terrain her brain had become.

Hunter. She wanted to get a better look at him and see how deep that rock-hardness went. He'd been tough but tender in their teen years, but it looked as though time had hardened him more.

Maybe he was too harsh for anyone to reach. She didn't have to wonder if he'd married—he'd been very clear on his opinion of matrimony. *Nothing but a ball and chain for a man and misery for a woman,* he'd told her. *There's not one thing on earth that would ever make me do something that stupid.*

Sure, he'd been twenty-two at the time and embittered by his father's betrayals. She hadn't seen, until too late, how she'd been attracted to a man similar to her father—too remote and unfeeling to ever soften, a man who became more unreachable as the years went by.

Her heart broke a little walking away.

"Mom." Simon held up a loaf of bread. "Score."

"Good job." She grabbed a pint of ice cream, not bothering to check her coupons.

"Mom?" Simon clunked a jar of peanut butter into the cart. "What else?"

"Crackers." She plucked several cans of her dad's favorite soup off the display.

"Roger, captain!" Simon made a jet-engine sound as he spun the cart around and headed off for the saltines at the end of the aisle.

Her mission had changed—to get everything they needed and get out of the store before Hunter recognized her.

"Okay, we've got everything, right?" Simon dumped a box in the cart. There wasn't much there, just enough food to get them by for a couple of days. It would have to do.

"That's it for this run. Let's get out of here." She grabbed the cart by the basket to get Simon moving faster.

"Howdy there," a friendly older lady Millie didn't know tossed them a genuine smile from behind her register. "Nice day, isn't it?"

"Yes, it is." She unloaded her cart as fast as she could, breathing a sigh of relief when she dropped the last item—the cracker box—onto the conveyer belt. Simon shoved the cart through while she unzipped her purse.

"Did you find everything all right?" The checker scanned in each item with a beep. Her name tag read "Enid."

"We did." The familiar beat of cowboy boots on the tile distracted her. She resisted the urge to look over her shoulder as Hunter's quick, no-nonsense cadence knelled louder.

He was coming this way. Panic licked through her. A wheel squeaked as his cart pulled in behind her. Her skin prickled like a storm the instant before lightning struck as Hunter began unloading his cart.

At least he hasn't recognized me yet. She sorted through her coupon envelope, doing her best not to look. He still smelled the same—like pine, hay and summer sun. Her uncooperative gaze slid sideways to sneak a peek. A black T-shirt hugged his powerful physique that had matured impressively. Muscles rippled as he dumped paper plates, paper towels and hamburger buns onto the conveyer, working fast, concentrating solely on his task. Not a man to look around—the Hunter she'd always known.

"Oh, I have coupons," she told Enid and handed over the cluster.

"Okay, deary." The older lady sorted through them before she scanned them in, one by one.

Hunter's foot tapped impatiently. He'd finished unloading his cart. She could feel him standing behind her, radiating heat and pent-up male energy.

Every breath she took was torture. Knowing Hunter, his mind was probably somewhere else. Maybe he wouldn't notice her, or—did she dare hope?—recognize her. Was that too much to ask?

"Sorry, deary. This one's past date." Enid handed over one of the coupons.

She feared the attention would draw Hunter's scrutiny. Her hand shook as she took back the coupon. *Please, don't recognize me,* she prayed.

"That'll be seventeen oh three."

Her hands shook so badly that she had trouble pulling out dollar bills. It took a beat before she realized her budget had been fifteen dollars. She searched through her change, but didn't have it. Heat flooded her face. "Uh, can you take off the box of crackers?"

"Sure thing." Enid kindly took back the box and beeped it over the scanner.

"Oh, for goodness' sake." Hunter flipped two dollars onto the conveyer belt. "Enid, take it. I'm done with waiting—"

She felt his gaze rake over her like a cold hard punch.

He froze, finally really looking at her. Recognition snapped through him as his entire body went rigid. His jaw dropped, leaving the rest of his thoughts unspoken.

"Hi, Millie," someone called out from behind his big hulking presence. Hunter's brother, Luke, peered over to smile at her. "Good to see you in town again. How's your dad?"

Hunter kept staring at her blankly, stiff with shock. She couldn't help maneuvering a little, trying to hide Simon from him. It was easy to lift her chin, holding on to her dignity for all she was worth and push away Hunter's two dollars. They lay awkwardly on the conveyer belt, their crumpled ends ruffling in the breeze from the air conditioner.

"Dad's holding his own, but it's bad, I guess." She bowed her head to count out her money. "They caught it way too late to do anything."

"Word has gotten around. The whole congregation is praying for him."

"Thanks, Luke." She handed exact change to Enid. "If anyone needs prayers, it's my dad. It was nice seeing you."

She seized her receipt, turned her back on Hunter and grabbed her single bag of groceries from the end of the check stand. Back straight, she followed her son to the rows of carts near the door.

Don't look back, she told herself firmly. She didn't need one last look at the man. She'd learned all she needed to in his shocked and silent stare. He'd been traumatized seeing her—they shared that in common. Not that she'd held even the faintest hope of a friendly reunion. No, not after the way they'd left things. But she hadn't expected him to look at her with horror either.

"Mom, I'll carry that." Simon left the cart neatly with the others and tromped over to take the groceries from her. "Is there any chance Grandpa has neighbor kids my age?"

"I have no idea. I'll give Myra a call when we get home. She knows everyone around here." Her feet may be carrying her forward, but her mind remained with the man dressed in black. She could feel Hunter's gaze as she trailed her son into the ovenlike heat of summer.

Suddenly aware of her wash-worn clothes and the hair she hadn't fussed with before leaving the house, she headed toward the truck. She could still feel Hunter's gaze as she crossed the lot—a cold gaze, when it had once been so loving. Why did that still hurt so much?

Their first meeting could have gone worse. She dug the keys out of her purse. *Thank You, Father, for that.*

Millie? Hunter couldn't get over the shock watching her walk away. Millie was back?

"Hunter, move along, we're waiting." Luke nudged his brother, his tone teasing.

Fine, he deserved that. He hadn't meant to be impatient; shopping always put him in a mood. The automatic doors opened and closed. Millie and the child were out of the building but not out of sight of the long front windows where a rusty, thirty-year-old Ford waited for them. It had taken a while to recognize her because she'd changed so much.

"Are you all right?" Luke asked, kindly, always a good brother.

Hunter cleared his throat and gave his cart a shove forward. He wanted to look unaffected, as if seeing Millie didn't bother him one bit. He was tough. No woman was going to bring him to his knees. He'd learned a long time ago the best way to protect yourself from a broken heart was not to have one.

Not that that was the truth, but he didn't have to admit it, did he?

Because he didn't trust his voice, he said nothing and faced Enid with a nod. Maybe Luke would get the hint and go back to talking with his girlfriend. Over the beep-beep of the scanner he watched Millie disappear behind the far side of the pickup—probably getting the door for her kid.

That kid. Agony tore through him at the thought of Millie's child. No, he couldn't think about her married to another man. Too painful. As he swiped his card and punched in his PIN, his gaze stayed stuck to the window.

Millie. She stepped into view, far from the bright, sunny girl he'd loved so deeply that she outshone everything in his life—every other thing. There had been only her, beautiful and precious, and his great overwhelming love for her.

"That'll be eighty-seven dollars and forty-six cents." Enid punched a button and her cash register spat out his receipt. "Would you like paper or plastic?"

"Whatever." He didn't care—he'd forgotten the reusable bags again. He hardly noticed the box boy moving in to bag his purchases. All he could see was Mille climbing into her dad's rusty old pickup. What had happened to the bounce in her step? To her wide, beaming smile that made everyone around her smile, too, unable to help themselves?

"Out of the way, you're holding up the line." Judging by the laughter in Luke's voice, he was enjoying this.

"I don't want to get back with her if that's what you think." He rolled his eyes, glad Luke couldn't read his thoughts. Millie, on her own, with a child? Nothing angered him more than a mother on her own struggling to pay for groceries. Where were the fathers? Why weren't they better men? A man takes care of his family, that's the way it was supposed to be.

Sure, it was an old issue with him. It brought back memories of how hard their dad had been on Mom. Never reliable, always out gambling or drinking, always shirking his responsibilities. Hunter's guts twisted up thinking Millie's life obviously hadn't turned out much different. There hadn't been a wedding ring on her left hand.

He'd checked.

"I'll see you back at the ranch." It wasn't easy to unclamp his jaw. He took charge of his cart and steered it toward the automatic doors. Out of the corner of his eye he watched Millie—

still slim and graceful—hop onto the seat. When she closed the door, he lost sight of her. Too much glare on the side window.

She wasn't going anywhere in that truck, or didn't she know it? He frowned, arrowing his cart at his vehicle, parked two spaces away from the rusted heap Whip Wilson should have junked long ago. While Hunter was sorry the man was dying, he should have at least told his daughter about the barely working transmission. Whip had never been a good dad either.

Not your business, Hunter, he told himself passing by at top speed. The cart rattled and bucked in protest, but minding his own business turned out to be impossible. Behind him, the rusted pickup's engine coughed to life, pistons misfiring. He yanked the cart to a stop, wedging it against the side of his truck so it wouldn't roll away. Disappointed in himself—a truly tough man, one who was completely over a breakup—would put his groceries in the truck and drive away.

But did he?

No, you are a fool, Hunter McKaslin. His feet took him around to the driver's side of Millie's truck. She'd rolled down the window, concentrating so hard on trying to figure out what was wrong, frowned brow, pursed lips, and he made himself like steel. Not going to notice how pretty she was.

Surprised, she jerked in her seat. "Hunter. You about gave me a heart attack. What are you doing sneaking up on me?"

"I wish I knew." He leaned his forearms against the hot metal door, peering in at her. "Guess Whip should have told you the truck doesn't have Reverse."

"What do you mean? It says *R* right here on the gearshift." She blew out a huff of frustration. "Of course it has Reverse. It just doesn't want to go *into* Reverse."

"Whip's been driving around without Reverse for a good year." Hard times had come to the Wilson spread, where Hunter had started working right out of high school. While he wasn't fond of Whip, the old man had taught him a lot about running a successful dairy. He was sorry for the Wilsons' misfortune.

"You'll have to keep that in mind next time you're parking. Want me to give you a push?"

"No." The word popped out, showing Millie's stubborn side, which still drove him crazy. He gritted his teeth until his molars hurt.

"Just put it in Neutral and make sure the parking brake is off." He shoved away from the door, turning his back on her protests. Did she think he liked this either? No, not one bit. His heart felt ripped open looking at her, but he held himself as hard as stone. Maybe that way he wouldn't feel the pain or the loss.

Or the fact that some other man's son sat beside her, looking at him with owlish eyes.

Don't think about the kid, he told himself, lock-jawed. Millie's face drew him—pinched and worried behind the glass. He couldn't seem to tear his gaze away from the wide blue eyes a man could fall into or the sweet set of her mouth that no longer smiled. His chest felt tight and achy wondering why.

Not your business. He planted his hands on the hood, braced his back and put some muscle into it. The truck eked backward a few slow inches before it gained momentum. Through the window shield, the dark, sleek cascade of Millie's hair flipped as she looked over her shoulder, one slim hand on the steering wheel.

"There." He let go, stepped back and watched the decrepit vehicle roll a few more feet. "Good luck with that truck."

"Thanks, I need that and a whole lot of prayer." She studied him through the window frame, the breeze tossing the ends of her soft hair.

She was definitely changed from the Millie he'd known a decade ago. A stab of grief settled deep in his chest for the girl she'd been, the laughing girl who he could no longer see in the serious-eyed woman. She nervously folded a flyaway lock of rich brown hair behind one ear.

"You didn't have to do that, you know." Her chin went up

in either a show of stubbornness or a statement of pride, but her expressive eyes shone with hurt.

This wasn't easy for her either. That helped. He shrugged his shoulders, trying to let go of the stress and the old wounds between them. "Prayer, huh? The Millie I used to know didn't pray."

"I do now." She dipped her chin as something private and vulnerable passed across her face, and he wondered at it. He opened his mouth to ask her what had happened, but instinct held him back.

Wouldn't that open a can of worms, one he wasn't interested in? Millie had been the one to leave him. She'd broken it off. She'd fled him, obviously for someone better. He tamped down the strike of agony and kept his eyes on her—only on her—and not the boy sitting beside her. She'd obviously left him for another man, just as her father had said.

"I'm a praying man these days. Surprises you, right?" He tossed her an easy grin, one that said he wasn't hurting and that he didn't care one whit that she'd left him. Not true, but a man had his pride.

"Absolutely. I would never have guessed independent, trust-no-one Hunter McKaslin would become a man of faith." A hint of a smile, and only a hint, touched the corners of her mouth.

"Miracles do happen."

"Guess you're proof of that." No twinkle gleamed in her eyes. Only the faintest warmth of humor touched her voice, which had once been so bright.

Only hard times could do that to someone. He steeled his spine, fighting the natural need to care about her. An old habit, that was all. It didn't mean a thing. Just like it didn't mean anything wanting to go to her and try to brush the worry off her face. He jammed his hands in his pockets instead. "I'm sorry about your father. He isn't an easy man."

"No, he isn't."

"But he taught me what I know. I wouldn't have a successful dairy if it wasn't for him and Milton." He swallowed hard, warring with himself. The smart thing to do was to tip his hat and walk away and pray he never saw the woman again. But was it the right thing to do?

"Oh, you did get your own dairy?" She tipped her head slightly, and a sleek dark lock of hair tumbled from behind her ear and back into her eyes. She shoved it away impatiently and the corners of her mouth turned upward into a genuine smile. "Hunter, I'm so happy for you. It's what you always wanted."

"Luke and I run it together." He heard the rattle of a cart and the murmur of voices. When he checked over his shoulder, he spotted his brother and his girlfriend emerging from the store, pushing a loaded cart. "I've got to go. We're having a family barbecue."

"Sounds like fun. I got an email from Brooke last week that I've been meaning to answer, but no time." She gripped the steering wheel tighter. "I hear she got married."

"She did. I'll tell my sister you said hi." He took a step back, chest swelling with a sense of loss he couldn't explain. There had never been any might-have-beens when it came to him and Millie. She hadn't wanted him.

Not that he could honestly blame her for that, not completely. She'd needed what he hadn't been able to give—and never would. "Let me know if Whip needs help. Word has it he's not up to managing the dairy."

"Thanks, but I've got it." The smile vanished, her chin went up and pure hurt shone in her eyes. The echoes of that hurt filled him as she put the truck in gear and drove away, the engine misfiring.

"Hey, are you okay?" Luke called out.

"Yeah, fine." He waved away his brother's concern, doing his best to hide his sorrow. Some things weren't meant to be—he and Millie were one of them.

Chapter Three

"Who was he?" Simon asked as the truck backfired, the sound echoing like a gunshot along the peaceful town street.

"You mean the man who gave us a push?" Her pulse stuttered but she tried to pretend it hadn't.

"He was real strong. Think I could shove a whole pickup like that? Probably not." Simon squirmed on his seat, restless and full of little-boy energy. "I liked his hat. No one wears hats like that in Portland. Not that I've seen."

"Me either, but they're everywhere around here. See?" She pointed in the direction of the sidewalk where a Stetson-wearing man headed into the dime store. "Everywhere."

"My head would get really hot."

"Mine, too." She couldn't help smiling, a genuine one this time. Her pulse evened out as the sputtering truck took them farther away from Hunter.

He'd changed so much since she'd known him last. He'd matured, looking like a dream in a Stetson. It seemed as if he'd mellowed a bit, too. Time had definitely improved him.

Not that she was interested. No way. It hurt too much. She slid her gaze across the bench seat to where her son sat, gazing out his window, taking everything in. It hadn't been an easy decision not to tell Hunter about his son. Through the years guilt continued to claw at her, but she'd done what was best for Simon.

She knew there was a problem the instant the farm came into sight. A thousand Holsteins stood in a gigantic black-and-white cluster at their pasture gate, mooing. She lifted her foot from the gas pedal, and their combined chorus made enough sound to drown out the truck's backfire.

"Mom, what's wrong with them?"

"They're waiting to be milked." That didn't seem to be the problem, though. The lack of farmhands did. She pulled onto the shoulder of the road. Only one vehicle sat in the shade of the barn—Milton's old, battered truck. Had everyone else gone?

"I'm sorry, Millie." He stepped out of the shadowed doorway, lean shoulders slumped. "This time was just the last straw. I got the boys to agree to come back when you can cover their checks *if* they haven't found other jobs."

"How long has this been going on?" She opened her door, stepping away from the truck so Simon wouldn't overhear.

"For the last six months. Whip hasn't paid us on time. The checks don't clear. It takes most of a month to make good on 'em, and then it starts all over again."

"I can't blame them. I'd walk off, too." She didn't add that she'd had the experience of holding a worthless paycheck in her hands followed by a long stint of unemployment. It was a hollow-stomached experience she wouldn't want for anyone. "Thanks for staying, Milton. I appreciate it."

"No problem. The thing is, I can't milk all these cows on my own. I'm gonna need help."

"I know." She blew out a sigh. "Is there anyone you can call in?"

"No one who will come without cash in the bank. Your pa has burned a lot of bridges over the past few years. He's gotten old and cantankerous." He winked to soften the truth. "I'll make a few calls and see what I can come up with."

"Thanks, Milton." She checked on her son, still buckled up,

craning his head to get a good look at the cows. Their udders were full, they had to be milked and couldn't wait. "I'll call you as soon as I can about the money."

"All right." Milton strolled away. Spotting him, the cows mooed harder, making so much racket that she couldn't hear herself think.

Simon watched her with wide eyes as she climbed behind the wheel. The door didn't shut on the first try. She had to give it a good slam before it caught. No matter what, the cows had to be milked. Just one more thing to add to her list, which was getting very long and overwhelming.

I'm trusting You, Lord, that this is all going to work out. She didn't know how, but she had faith. She gave the pickup some gas, yanked hard on the wheel and bumped across the county road and up the driveway. Clouds of dust rose up behind her, fogging the air and cutting off all view of the barn in her rearview mirror.

It had been a long time since she'd worked in the dairy and her skills might be a little rusty, but that was okay. She'd look at the books while she fixed supper and afterward head down to the barn to help Milt.

I can't believe I'm back, she thought. *Right back where I started.* She'd grown up miserable here, but it surely had to be different this time. It wasn't as if she were staying.

Leaving was nonnegotiable. And if Hunter's face filled her thoughts—high cheekbones, straight blade of a nose, magnetic deep violet eyes—then that was all the incentive she needed. That man had torn apart her heart, leaving nothing but pieces. He wasn't going to do that again. And that's exactly what he would do if he ever found out the truth.

"Mom?" Simon's voice bumped along as the truck bounced over ruts in the driveway. "I can help with supper if you want. I know you've got a lot to do."

"Why, I'd appreciate a helping hand." That put a smile on her face. "You can be in charge of the pizza."

"I'm good with pizza. But I sorta heard what that man said. I could help with the cows, Mom. I know I could."

"I don't want you having to work in the barn the way I did when I was your age." She swung the pickup across the edge of the lawn and circled around, nosing it toward the driveway before shutting off the engine. It coughed to a slow stop. "I'm sure God has a plan in mind. Don't worry, it will all work out."

"Okay." Simon unbuckled. "Mom?"

"Yeah?"

"Bein' here's not so bad. I just want you to know you're not alone." He dropped to the ground and manhandled the grocery bag off the floor. "I'm gonna help you. You left your friends behind, too."

"Thanks, kiddo." She let the Montana breeze blow through her hair as she gave the door a good slam. Judging by the shape everything else was in around here, she sure hoped the oven worked or supper would be quite a challenge.

Hunter barely heard his cell ring over the noise. Whenever his family got together, noise was a given. He left his sisters talking at the picnic table over their desserts and hiked across Luke's back deck to get a little privacy. He shouldered through the back door where there was bound to be some quiet. "Hello?"

"Hunter? Glad I caught you." Milton Denning's voice crackled over the line. Sounded like he was in the barn with the roar of machinery in the background, making him hard to hear. "Don't suppose you're lazing around with nothin' going on by any chance?"

"Me, lazing?" He glanced out the kitchen window where his family—brother, sisters and half sisters—roared in laughter about something. Something obviously hilarious. "What's up? Are you running low on milk replacer again? I got a bag you can have—"

"Thanks, but that's not my biggest problem, not right now."

Milton's words rumbled with severity. "I'm in the middle of milking without a single hired man."

"Milking?" He glanced at the clock. "Shouldn't you be done with that by now?"

"Yep, and I'm not even halfway through—" The phone cut out on Milton's end, leaving only static and crackle. "—just the two of us—be past bedtime when we finish up if I don't get more help."

"This wouldn't have something to do with Cal stopping by looking for work, would it?" He leaned against the counter, his thoughts drifting to Millie again. He gritted his teeth, trying to banish the woman from his mind. "I suppose it's inevitable your men would try to find another position knowing Whip's condition."

"That's not it. Money trouble. I can't afford to pay you, but we can work something out. Maybe trade man hours or something." Milton blew out a frustrated breath. His phone crackled again. "—I need help tonight. I'm too old for this. Should have retired years ago, but I saw how Whip was. He's been sick for a long time, he was just too stubborn to admit it. Someone has to look after the cows and fight for the hired men."

"The thing is, it's almost my bedtime." He glanced at the clock above the stove. Seven-eighteen. "I'm up at four for the morning milking."

"I know what I'm asking, but I'm struggling here." Milton's tone stung with wounded pride.

That had to be a tough thing for a hardworking man to admit. Hunter blew out a sigh, did his best not to let the image of Millie into his mind, the one of her standing in line counting coupons, looking too thin and poor and worn-down. He couldn't stop the lurch of his heart, just like he couldn't stop hurting for her.

So, her plans hadn't worked out. It surprised him his bitterness had gone, leaving only regret in its place. Unaccustomed to the ache dead center in his chest, he pressed the heel of his hand there and rubbed.

"Sure, I'll come." It wasn't as if he'd have to see her. She wouldn't be in the barn. Millie had Whip and her son to take care of—best not to think about the boy—so she'd be busy up at the house. It would be just him, Milton and the cows. "Let me tell Luke. I'm guessing he'll want to volunteer to help you in the morning."

"What? Why, that would be Christian of him. Of both of you." Milton swallowed hard. "You don't know what this means."

"Hey, remember when I hired on at Whip's place? You showed me the ropes. You taught me everything you knew about cows. This is the least I can do for you." Hunter disconnected, pocketed his phone and checked the window again.

Judging by the way everyone was gaping and pointing at him, Luke had likely told them about his run-in with Millie. Great. He rolled his eyes, shouldered through the door and hiked up the walls around his heart. No way was he letting anyone know, even those he loved most, exactly what having Millie back in town meant. Pain seared with each footstep he took toward those hopeful faces.

"We just heard the news." His half sister Colbie preened from the picnic table.

"And now he gets a call and he's going out. Look at him." His sister, Brooke, gave a flip of her dark hair, violet eyes warm with optimism. "Those are his truck keys."

"Milton has a problem at the barn." Best to act cool, as if he didn't know what on earth they were talking about. He glanced past Colbie and Brooke to where his brother sat beside the twins, who were the youngest of the group. "Luke, I told him you'd pitch in come morning. He's alone over there."

"With all those cows?" Luke's brows shot up with concern. "Tell him I'm in."

"Good." Best to leave before they bring up Millie again.

Nell, their dear old dog, lifted her head off her paws, her eyebrows quirking with a question. She was a good herd dog, but she'd already put in her work for the day. "Why don't you stay here, girl, and keep an eye on all those troublemakers?"

She panted in agreement. He stroked her head on his way by her bed on the edge of the deck.

"Hey, Hunter!" Luke's voice sailed across the yard on a warm wind. "Say hi to Millie for us."

"Yeah, say hi!" the sisters chorused.

"That would be hard—" he quipped "—as she wants to see me even less than I want to see her."

He turned on his heel, his boots crunching in the gravel as he headed to his own little house sitting at the end of the driveway. So, his family thought there was a possibility of a reunion? Really? Didn't they know him by now? Through all the years he'd been a bachelor, including the long decade Millie had been gone, had he once taken an overt interest in a lady?

No. Because he knew where romance led. He knew that love ended. Sure, a marriage may survive, but love? It was too fragile to last. That was the plain and simple truth and nothing on earth could ever convince him differently. He'd seen it in his parents' marriage and in his own life, thanks to Millie.

Agony shot through him with a crushing intensity that stopped him in his tracks. He pressed his hand to his chest again, reeling with the pain. If he didn't know better, he'd fear it was a heart attack, but it was simply the old death throes of the love he'd once had for Millie, remaining like a ghostly pain long after the wound was healed.

A little help, please, Lord. He reached out in prayer, hoping the Father above would understand. Hunter opened his truck door, climbed onto the seat and turned the engine over. It hummed quietly as he whizzed down the windows to let out the heat. He knew God had a plan in bringing Millie back to the valley. Her father was dying, and she had issues with her father that she deserved to have resolved before he passed on.

Hunter didn't begrudge her that. He alone knew how hard the man had been on his daughter.

But that didn't mean Millie's path had to cross his ever again. Hunter slid the gearshift into Reverse, swung around and nosed down the hill. His family called out to him as he rumbled by, and he did his best not to hear their "helpful" advice as he waved. Thankfully, he left them behind in a cloud of dust when he pulled onto the county road.

No, with Millie in the valley again, his options were clear. Avoid her. That was his new goal in life. He couldn't go walking around in this kind of torment. He drew a shallow breath, hardly able to get air with the pain pushing in on him.

He could use the crowd at church as a barrier between them. He could send Luke to town for groceries. And as for this evening, he'd keep to the barn with Milton and everything would be all right. Problem solved. If he played it right, he'd never have to see Millie again.

When he reached the Wilson dairy, things were just as he'd expected. The rusty pickup Millie had driven to town was parked neatly at the house across the road. Lamplight shone in the windows. No doubt she was there, finishing dishes or maybe watching TV with her son. No need to worry.

He pulled beside the barn and cut the engine. The hot evening air met him. A giant herd of cattle lowed the moment they saw him. Their unhappy bellowing followed him as he stalked away from the truck.

A shadow moved in the dark depths of the barn. Milton, probably come to say how relieved he was. Hunter tugged down the brim of his hat. The slanting rays made it hard to see who stepped out of the darkness to greet him.

"Hunter McKaslin." Millie burst into the sunshine, burnished by it. "What are you doing here?"

"The bigger question is why aren't you over at the house?"

"Because Milton needs help. That's why you're here." She

nodded, as if putting it all together. "That's why he didn't tell me who he'd put calls in to, and for good reason."

"Don't get worked up. I know that look—"

"What look?" She glared, like a warrior woman ready for battle.

"Glaring eyes. Chin tipped up so high you can barely see me over your nose." He planted his hands on his hips. "It won't do any good to try and get rid of me. I gave Milton my word."

"He doesn't need your help."

"You mean, *you* don't."

"You've helped enough." The earlier humiliation at the grocery store returned. He'd been a witness to the fact that she'd been unable to pay for all her groceries, and that he'd given the truck a push still rankled. "I can't be obligated to you. You get that, right?"

"Doesn't change my intentions."

"How would you feel if the circumstances were flipped? What if you needed my help?"

"Darlin', I'd never accept a woman's help."

"And I can't accept yours. This is too much. You know full well I can't pay you."

"That's right." He squared his hat on his head. "I'm not doing this for money. I'm here for Milton, not you."

"Oh." A slap couldn't have stunned her more. She should have known. Humiliation swept through her, remembering the days when Hunter had shown his sweet side always doing for her, always helping. Crazy that she'd just assumed…well, of course things had changed. "Sorry."

"If I run the second carousel, can you keep up?" Brash, Hunter shouldered past her toward the door.

She nodded, listening to the beat of his boots against the cement and wishing she was anyplace but here. Being beholden to the man was going to be a bitter pill.

"Don't worry, Freckles." His voice rumbled low with a nostalgic warmth. "You'll hardly know I'm here."

Why did her pulse skip at the hint of his grin? "That's what you used to call me when we were…"

"Close?"

"I was going to say in love." She shrugged. "Water under the bridge."

"I'll say." He shrugged a what-can-you-do? "I'll take the present over the past any day. How about you?"

"Absolutely. The past is a bummer."

"Then we'll leave it floating down the creek with the current. How about it?"

"Sounds good. It's probably heading toward the ocean about now."

"Or floating on the tides to Fiji. We were a long time ago, Millie. I say we forget about it."

"Agreed. Thanks for coming."

"It's what we do around here, neighbors helping neighbors." He paused at the doorway, half swallowed by shadow. "No thanks necessary."

"The thing is, I don't see any other neighbors rushing in to help."

"No, Whip likely broke their good will long ago. He's a hard man, but he was hardest on you. That was never right."

"Doesn't that fall into the category of the past?"

"I'm just sayin'." Hunter's iron jaw softened, perhaps a momentary weakness. "Get back to the wash-down. If Milton knew I was standing around shootin' the breeze when I ought to be working, he'd have my hide."

"Tempting to say you'd deserve it."

"No doubt." An almost-smile curved the chiseled line of his mouth. He disappeared through the barn doors, leaving her alone in the sunshine.

A cow's moo started the rest of the herd lowing, a loud bawling that shattered the evening's peace. Shaking her head, she headed inside. Hunter McKaslin back on the Wilson farm again. How about that? She dearly hoped it was *not* a trend.

Having him around here all the time? Could not happen. No way, no how. There was one piece of the past she couldn't banish down, and it was sitting inside the house with Dad, watching spaghetti Westerns.

Chapter Four

Hard not to notice her, but as he unlatched the gate to send the batch of newly milked cows into the runway, he was able to keep the past downstream under the bridge. The faster he got this work done, the quicker he'd be home.

Milton's radio squawked and Hunter braced hearing against the faint cadence of Millie's gentle voice. Crazy how such a soft sound could carry above the hum of machinery and the clatter of hooves on concrete. The next batch of cows, freshly scrubbed down and shining clean clamored down the carousel, into place. A bold animal grabbed hold of his sleeve with her lips and tugged playfully.

"Hi, cutie." He hit the lever, grain spilled into troughs and the cows dug in, eating contentedly. He turned his back to Millie. A smart man would pay her no mind. After he walked the line, made sure the connections were good, he left the carousel to check on Milton.

"Whew, this is the last batch." The older man swept off his hat. "Just in time, too. I'm run ragged."

"It's a lot for one man alone."

"Millie helped. She's as good as two men when it comes to work."

"Yeah." He had to acknowledge that, but he wouldn't say

what was on his mind. It wasn't right how hard Whip used to work Millie in her youth. It wasn't right to expect the same of her now. There she was, hosing down the waiting pen, stopping to spray bleach. She grabbed a long-handled broom to scrub down the concrete. Still a hard worker. "I like to think I cut down your workload some."

"Only a small bit. Hardly noticed you were here." Quick to kid, Milton swiped sweat from his brow. "Can't believe it's only nine o'clock. Thought for sure I'd still be at it. You're a good worker, too."

"I had a great supervisor once."

"That so?" A smile wreathed Milton's face. "Good to know. Never thought I could make a difference in that hard head of yours."

"Miracles happen. Why don't you call it a night?"

"That'd be foolish, as the work isn't done."

"I'll finish up. Go home."

"Not sure I can trust you to do things right."

"You're not foolin' me." Hard to hide his fondness for the man who'd taken him under his wing long ago. "I got this. Get going."

"Guess it wouldn't hurt. Millie's here to keep you in line."

Right. Millie. Being alone with her would be a problem. He waved Milton off. "I'll see you tomorrow."

"Tomorrow?"

"For the evening milking. Don't think I'm not in this for the long run."

"That's real neighborly of you." Emotion brightened the older man's eyes.

"It's no problem." He walked the carousel detaching suction cups, listening to Milton's boots drum away into silence. Millie, just out of sight. The splash of water and the rasp of the broom reminded him she was near. Too near.

So much for his plan to avoid her.

What he needed was a temporary plan for the interim, until he could go back to steering clear of her.

"That's it, girls, you're done." He opened the gate, freeing the cows. But did they leave? No, the first animal in line lipped his hat brim, so he rubbed her nose. "Go on, get some fresh air."

The bovine batted her long lashes before ambling down the ramp. The others followed her, docile and placid, although more than a few of them expected a pat or two before moving on.

He left the door open to the wind, fragrant with mown grass. Late evening's peace had settled in with long shadows. A few larks sang on the fence rails and as he circled around to check on the second carousel he smelled something else on the wind. The acrid scent shot alarm straight through him. A wildfire?

But, no, one glance outside told him all was well. Green grass, grazing cows, a few deer wandering across the meadow. No black smoke, no roiling flames anywhere.

"Hunter, you don't smell smoke, do you?" Millie's hose cut off. Her boots tapped closer. "Tell me you didn't light up in the milking parlor?"

"I quit smoking after you left." Ran off on me, he didn't say because that was water under the bridge. He sniffed, following the scent. "It's coming from the barn."

"No, the smoke alarms would be going off." Her forehead scrunched, as if she had second thoughts about that and shot past him.

Right. They would be going off if they were properly maintained. It didn't take an expert to glance around this place and see maintenance wasn't a high priority for Whip.

He followed her, fighting a bad feeling in his stomach. He dashed past the office and into the main barn. Smokey air, cloudy gray, confirmed his worst fears.

"It's in the hay mow." Millie stormed down the aisle, pitchfork in hand.

He grabbed an extinguisher off the wall, prayed it was in working order, and followed the crackle and roar. Orange light licked from between two bales, one of a thousand stacked bales that ran the length of the barn. Buried in there somewhere, heat had built up and made fire.

"We're not too late. We had better not be." Headstrong, she jumped in with her pitchfork, ripping away smoking bales with the pitchfork's tines. "I'm not going to lose this barn. No way. Not today."

"I like your determination." He tucked the extinguisher in the crook of his arm and shot retardant into the heart of the fire. "It suits you."

"Losing is not an option."

"You keep saying that." Instead of dying, flames writhed higher, snapping and popping as they consumed the tinder-dry fuel at an alarming rate.

A few minutes more and it would be out of control. They realized it at the same time. Their gazes locked, adrenaline pumped into their veins. She already had her cell in hand, punching in 9-1-1, as he kicked away a few bales of untouched hay to stair-step up the stack. Heat licked his face as he emptied the canister.

Still no good. Smoke doubled, turning black and thick. He coughed, barely able to see Millie through the haze.

"They're coming!" Her shadow moved closer. A pitchfork's handle materialized out of the smoky cloud and he seized it. He held out his hand, felt her smaller, softer one grab hold and ignored the sudden kick in his cardiac area. As long as he didn't think about his heart then he could deny all feelings. One tug and she landed on top of the stacked hay, coughing, too.

He yanked the collar of his T-shirt over his nose and got to work. No words necessary, which suited him just fine as they worked together separating the fire from its fuel. He wished he wasn't aware of every stab of her fork and every pitch of hay. He especially didn't want to notice the lean, elegant lines of her arms as she worked, or the soft tendrils escaping her ponytail to frame her heart-shaped face.

Don't think about her face. He clamped his molars together and kept pitching. Suddenly her face was all he could think about. The slope of her nose, the adorable little chin, the satin feel of her skin against his hand.

His cardiac region squeezed hard. No doubt about it, being close to her was a bad idea. Fine, so he cared for her. Hard not to like the woman she'd become, so strong, serious and determined. With her delicate jaw set, purpose carved into the flawless curve of her face, she stood boots braced and confident, pitching hay with military precision.

"I found it!" Millie's pitchfork held fresh flames and hay turning to ashes. "It's down in here, but how deep is it?"

"Hold on." He dropped to his knees, heedless of the heat and the ashes raining down on him and grabbed the hem of her jeans. He covered it with both hands and heat seared through his gloves. Just a spark, nothing serious, but when he let go of the denim a chunk was missing. A black scar on her boot told him he'd caught it in time.

"Thanks, Hunter. I didn't even realize." More forgiveness shone in her eyes.

He hadn't realized how much he needed to see it. He took the pitchfork from her and emptied the burning bits back onto the stack. Anywhere he threw it would start a second fire. "We can't fight this with two pitchforks. It's growing too fast."

"I know, I know. But I can't just let it burn."

"I'm thinking." Heat drove him back, and he tugged Millie with him.

Getting down proved tricky. The fire roared, licking and popping, shooting red-hot embers into the air. He batted them away from his head and Millie's face, took her hand and led the way down, kicking out footholds as he went. By the time his boots hit the floor, the fire doubled. Flames spat at him. Red-hot ashes swooped in the air, landing on the tinder-dry hay and igniting another patch.

"It's no good." He leaned the pitchfork against the wall. "Get out of here, Millie."

"No. What about the milking parlor and the office? They'll burn if the barn does." Something landed on her head. A red-hot ash. "You should go. There's too much smoke—"

"Here." He brushed the scorching ember out of her hair. Tender, when he could have been rough. "Do you really think I'd walk away?"

Guilt hit her like a hammer. She knew he wasn't talking about the past, but she couldn't help remembering her worst fear. That if he'd known the truth, he would have done just that. Abandoning her when she'd needed him the most. She choked on smoke and lost sight of him.

Keeping low, trying not to breathe in the black air, she raced to the loading bay, put her shoulder and weight into it and dragged the heavy wooden doors on their protesting wheels. The side of the barn opened, giving the smoke more places to escape.

"Mom, you're okay!" Simon skidded to a stop in the gravel. "I called the fire department, but I didn't know where you were."

"Stay back, Simon. Go back to the house."

"No, I'm gonna help."

"You'll help by staying out of the way, kiddo." She grabbed her pitchfork and started pulling down burning bits of hay. Heat seared her face and burned her lungs. She had to shout over the fire's roar. "It's too dangerous here for you."

"But I—"

A boom exploded from the other side of the stack. The back-fire of an ill-tuned engine, she realized, startled. She grabbed Simon by the shoulder and marched him out of the way, across the road and onto the knee-high lawn. "Stay here. I need your word, Simon."

The boy nodded, too engrossed watching the fire to speak. The distant wail of sirens accompanied her across the road.

She watched hay bales topple onto the concrete. Wild, the fire writhed like a monster, blackening the rafters and twisting in protest as the stack's end cap tumbled into the gravel, raining flame and red ashes. She caught a brief glimpse of Hunter behind the wheel before the swirling smoke cocooned him and the tractor squealed into Reverse.

This was crazy, he really should get out of there. This wasn't his battle, but she appreciated him for it. She grabbed her pitchfork and slipped around the inferno. Too many ashes were falling onto the haystack and igniting, causing a greater hazard. She had to get to them now.

By the time she'd scrabbled up the side of the remaining stack, little infernos had ignited everywhere. There were too many. Maybe it's time to let the barn go. The tractor's engine roared and more crackling bales gave way at the ramlike punch of the tractor's bucket. She caught sight of Hunter shifting into Reverse, covered with soot and brushing burning hay off his forearm. Sparks rained on him, incinerating chunks tried to land on him and still he made another go at the fire.

Definitely time to admit they were outmatched.

"Step back, missy." A voice spoke behind her. Milton drove his pitchfork into a patch of burning hay. "We've got a barn to save."

"We?" Through wisps of smoke, pickups pulled to a stop across the road. Men leaped from them, shouting orders.

"Hunter called on his cell," Milton explained, pitching the flames and hay outside onto the gravel. "I turned around and called a few neighbors. Don't worry, we'll get this licked."

Emotion pricked her eyes and she had to turn away. Hunter. Why did everything always come down to him? She watched him behind the wheel, in control, lowering the bucket to scoop burning debris away from the remaining haystack. So close she could see the heat reddening his face and an angry burn on his arm.

Her only goal in coming here had been to avoid him. Impossible. Somehow she was going to have to figure out a way to deal with him. She risked a glance across the road, where Simon sat next to Whip. She caught the nasty gleam in her old man's eyes. He was the sole keeper of her secret.

The problem with secrets was that they rarely stayed truly hidden.

This one had to.

"I told Whip that hay was still a mite too damp." Milton looked worse for wear as he sat on the bumper of the fire truck, letting Jerry, the volunteer fire marshal, patch him up. "But no, he wanted the men to stack it. Wouldn't listen to me. You know how he gets."

"Everyone knows how he gets," Jerry assured him.

"You put up hay that isn't totally dry, those damp spots build up heat. On a day as hot as today, it can ignite." Milton sent a stream of tobacco into the ditch. "Truth is, those were some tough days with Whip sick and in pain and takin' it out on us. Not sure the men stacking the hay cared much, and I was busy jury-rigging the water pump, so my hands were full."

Hunter nodded, leaning against the fire truck's fender. No doubt working conditions had been tough here for a while and considering his obvious financial problems, Whip hadn't wanted to pay the hands an extra day's work to wait around for the hay to dry. He took a moment to notice the peeling paint and the missing shingles. While he'd worked in this barn after high school, he and Whip had parted ways long ago, before Millie left. He'd never had much respect for a man who treated people the way Whip did.

"The fire's out, we've mopped up, but you'll have a big cleanup." Jerry gave Milton a pat on his arm. "You make sure Doc Littlejohn takes a look at that tomorrow. Hunter, you're next."

"I don't need patching up." A few blisters were nothing to worry about. "Did you take a look at Millie?"

"First thing. She refused, too."

"I'm not surprised." That woman could take stubbornness to new levels. He'd nearly had heart failure seeing her climb the stack, standing in the rafters surrounded by flames. Not that he didn't admire her for it. "If we're done here, I'm heading home."

"That's what I'm gonna do." Milton staggered to his feet. "It's way past my bedtime."

"Nearly midnight. Sleep tight, Milt." Hunter followed the light of the moon to the open barn doors, where the volunteers rolled up the last fire hose. The dank smell of smoke and charred hay overwhelmed him as his boots hit the floor.

A close call. No doubt about it. He wandered down the aisle past vacant stalls to the fall of light from the office door. The wise choice would be to hop in his truck and head home, but he had to check on her. Some habits were hard to break, regardless of how bad they were for you.

"Okay, I'll be there in a bit." Nothing was prettier than Millie's voice soft with affection as she talked into a handheld radio. "Just close your eyes and think of home."

"But there's funny noises in the wall." The boy's words crackled across the two-way.

"It's nothing to worry about. Think of being able to play with your friends again. What's the first thing you're going to do when we get back?" Leaning against the wall, she smiled over at him, gave him an in-a-second look.

He nodded, message received, and stayed in the hallway. He jammed his hands in his pockets, just glad to see she was all right. Well, relatively all right, as she was streaked with soot and her T-shirt riddled with little burn holes. What was she doing refusing medical treatment?

"Then just think about Alexander's tree house and going back to school with your friends and you'll fall back to sleep, kiddo."

The boy's sigh rasped from the speakers. "I'll try."

"Good boy. Call again if you need me." She set the hand unit on the battered wooden desk. Heaps of paper, junk mail and bills with red past due stamps were piled as high as the cracked computer monitor. Millie shook her head at the mess and focused on him. Big blue eyes full of gratitude. "You. Not sure what would have happened if you hadn't been here."

"Anyone around here would have done the same thing. No biggie." He didn't want her feeling beholden to him. That was a recipe for disaster. "Just wanted to check on you before I head out."

"I'm glad you did. I owe you a huge, ginormous thanks." She pushed off from the wall. "What you did tonight—"

"Forget it."

"I can't. You could have been badly burned. The entire stack could have come down on you."

"I used the bucket as a shield. Not my first time knocking down a fire." The air in the room vanished. He pretended it didn't. "Had a big wildfire last summer. Most neighbors were out fighting it by hand. We stopped it before it got a hold and ripped through every field and barn in the valley."

"Why am I not surprised? You were on the front line leading the charge, weren't you?" She eased in, smelling of charred wood, smoke and faintly of lilacs.

Lilacs. That jogged his memory, flashing him back a decade. Easy to remember standing right here in this barn, with the haze of midsummer sunshine and the horses huffing softly in the doorway, waiting to get going with the trail ride. How he'd taken his time, laying his hand against the satin softness of her cheek, his pulse kicking double time, gathering up enough courage to kiss her. His chest squeezed, wringing out an old drop of affection. Affection he'd be a fool to give in to.

"Better go. I've got an early morning."

"It *is* technically morning. You're not going anywhere until I take care of those burns."

"They're fine."

"Don't even try that on me." She opened a squeaky cabinet and hauled out a flat gray box. "Not sure how up-to-date this is."

"It looks like World War II surplus."

"Tell me about it. The cobwebs are a little worrying." She swiped them off and opened the tin, shoving aside the pile of paper on the desk to make room to set it down. "There are a few cans of pop in the fridge, if you want to get them."

"Now that does sound good." He was parched from the inside out. The rumble of the fire truck faded, the men were gone and he and Millie were truly alone. Not sure he was comfortable with that. He yanked open the ancient refrigerator and let the cool wash over him before grabbing two cans from the shelves.

"Here." He popped the tabs, set Millie's down next to the first-aid kit and breathed in the sugary scent of grape soda. "Guess Milton won't mind. We haven't broken into his stash in ten years."

"It's no good, Hunter. I know you always sneaked in and replaced the bottles." She pushed out the desk chair with her foot, giving him a look that said *sit*.

He'd learned not to argue with that look, so he hunkered down. "It was only fair. Milton's a good man. He's stuck by your dad a long time."

"Not an easy feat, but bless him for it." She dabbed a cotton swab along his brow. "I hear from your sister that Luke has a serious girlfriend."

"Don't know how serious she is, but he's smitten. I didn't know you and Brooke kept in touch."

"We reconnected over the internet a few years ago. Judging by your tone, you don't approve of this girlfriend?"

"Does that really surprise you?"

"No." She swabbed a clear balm onto his forehead. "Apparently your opinion on love and marriage hasn't changed a bit."

"Nope." He gritted his teeth against the sting. There were

tons of things he ought to say about Luke falling for a city girl, about love in general, about how he'd never make the mistake of handing his heart over to a woman. But did the words come? No, the ones that would reassert their differences and the rift between them lay mute on his tongue. What did come out? The one thing he never should ask. "How long have you been divorced?"

"I never married Simon's father."

While he winced at the boy's name, the sadness in Millie's eyes hurt him more. "I—I didn't know. That had to be rough on your own."

"Being a single mother isn't easy." She knelt in front of him, attacking a quarter-sized burn on his forearm with a cotton ball. "But I made it through. Simon was the best gift I've ever gotten. Hands down, the best."

"What about the father? He doesn't help with child support?"

"Why are you asking?" Her jaw snapped shut, she lurched back, stalking out of his line of sight. "I thought we agreed not to bring up the past. It was your idea, and here you are, bringing up the past."

"Sorry." Probably a sore subject, he realized. No marriage, raising a child on her own, had the man abandoned her? Anger roared through him like a riptide, taking him under. She had it hard. Coming here had to make it harder. "You're down on your luck, Millie."

"Maybe. Maybe not. Either way it's not your business."

"True, but I can't help seeing what I see. The coupons. The crackers you couldn't afford to buy."

"Again, not your business. Because you're asking, life has been a bit of a challenge lately, but things are going to turn around any minute now."

If anyone could will it to happen, then Millie could. She looked a mess—a cute mess. "You're finally going to have to give up on that old T-shirt. How old is it anyway?"

"I picked it up at a thrift store, so no way for me to know." She returned with a cotton swab and a bandage.

"You shop at thrift stores?"

"Nothing wrong with that." Chin up, pride intact, her eyes shadowed with sorrow. "We get by. I lost my job a while back, so things have been tight."

"How tight?"

"Not your business, bud." Millie had always been the strongest woman he'd ever known. She crouched before him. "Life has its ups and downs. This is one of those downs, but not for long."

"But the father, shouldn't he be helping?"

"I don't want to talk about him." Her gaze fastened on his like a slap.

"Curious, the man you left me for left you."

"What did I just say?" Honestly. He was going to notice her hands shaking if she didn't change the subject. "What about you? You're over thirty and have no one to love. No one loves you. How's your philosophy working out?"

"Just great. No one to hurt, no one to hurt me. That's all love is in the end, one big pile of hurt." But the bravado he'd sported ten years ago was gone. He swallowed hard, taking a moment to pause. "It's what I tried to save both of us from."

"It didn't work for me." She'd been the foolish one, falling so far in love with a man who didn't love her in return. He'd likely never love anyone. Really, she felt sorry for him. As hard as he fought not to make his father's mistakes, he was just like him, alone, driving everyone away who wanted to love him. "I got Simon out of the deal, so I'm good. I'm grateful."

"You're grateful for the one big pile of hurt?"

"Absolutely." Life was an unfathomable mix of pain and joy, but it all came down to what you focused on. She tore off the wrapping and slapped on the bandage, pressing to make sure the adhesive stuck.

The warm texture of his skin reminded her of all the times

she'd been this close. Holding hands and laughing, giving him a lick from an ice-cream cone and sharing whispers, all memories she didn't want. Memories she could no longer look at. He used to be her dream.

"Mom." Her son's voice crackled across the old two-way. "Mom, the noise is getting louder."

She had a new dream now. She grabbed the radio. "I'll be over in a few more minutes, okay?"

"Okay."

She wasn't surprised to hear the scrape of the chair as Hunter rose or the laid-back drum of his gait on the floor. Shadows clung to him. She didn't know how long she could keep this up, but thankfully he grabbed his hat, tipped it to her and left without another word.

She dropped into the chair, breathing hard against a mix of emotions she was too exhausted to deal with. Mostly fear. Mostly relief he hadn't guessed he'd been the one who wasn't interested in his own son. Never once had he checked on her. Not once had he returned her calls.

She'd been six months pregnant when she'd given up hoping he would come back into her life. She'd gone on alone—to give birth, to make a new life and to raise her son.

Her son, not his.

Listening to his boot steps fade, she knew she'd made the right decision. He hadn't changed. She took a long swig of soda and savored the sugary sweetness one moment longer. She heard the rasp of the barn doors closing, Hunter doing her work for her on his way to his truck.

She grabbed the radio, slipped out the office door and crossed the road, where a single light burned from Simon's bedroom window. She didn't look back.

Chapter Five

All anyone could talk about was the fire. Hunter measured milk replacer into the bucket, doing his level best to ignore the incessant ring of the barn phone. He'd hardly slept for the four or so hours he'd been in bed, thinking about Millie—and not wanting to think about Millie. She was stuck in his head against his will. She still smelled like lilacs, her soft dark hair as bouncy and untamed as ever and she could make him feel, when all he wanted was to keep his heart like stone.

"Got a good look at the fire scene." His brother burst through the doors. "That was some job you did. Kept the whole place from going up."

"You would have done the same thing, I was just the one there, that's all." He turned on the hot water tap and stuck his finger in the stream, waiting for it to run warm. "God was with us on that one."

"Sure. That indifferent tone can't fool me."

"Fool you? Luke, you're already ten times a fool for falling in love with a city girl."

"Hey, she says she's in love with me, so I'm in good company."

"Grin any wider and you'll break something." He aimed hot

water into the bucket. "You're happy now, sure, but just wait. Heartbreak always follows."

"Not necessarily. Some loves don't end."

"The romantic kind usually does." Something stabbed him in the heart, some lame emotion he didn't want. "Got to feel sorry for Millie, a single mom struggling."

"I did a little recon and asked Brooke to spill what she knew. Millie was laid off nine months ago. She worked as a receptionist, but companies aren't doing a whole lot of hiring these days."

"You'd think she could find something."

"I'm sure she will, but right now she's got Whip to deal with and all his problems." Luke flipped through the storage closet.

"Think there's any chance she can hire back Whip's milking hands so you and I don't have to help her?" He shut off the faucet, gave the batch a stir and dumped it into the two waiting bottles.

"Nope. Millie says she's worked the books backward and forward and there isn't a cent until the milk check arrives." He pulled out a box of mousetraps and set them on the counter. "Told her you and I would help where we could. She's got a few other problems. Thought we could donate some supplies."

"Wouldn't hurt." It couldn't be easy for her coming home. No good memories waited for her inside her father's house, which hadn't seen maintenance in a long while.

"Give me those." Luke grabbed the bottles. "I'll take care of feeding the calves."

"Good, then I'm heading to church. Looks like I'll be able to make it to the service early after all." He grabbed his truck keys. "Maybe I can help with some of the picnic setup."

Luke studied him with a frown. "I know what you're doing. You're trying to avoid her."

"Who?" Best to act clueless, pretend the woman wasn't stuck in his mind like glue.

"Who else? C'mon, Hunter. You never fell out of love with her, if you ask me."

"I'm not asking you because you would be wrong. I don't have any old feelings for the woman." He grabbed his Stetson. "Just relief I dodged that bullet."

"You never were going to marry her?"

"I never meant to get so serious with her. I recognized my mistake too late. It won't happen again." She'd gotten past his defenses and made him open up. She made him care. That was what kept him from REM sleep last night and what ate at him as he held up a hand in farewell and turned his back on his brother.

What he needed was to keep his distance. Filling in at the Wilson dairy wasn't going to accomplish that. But what was he gonna do? Leave her hanging?

A friendly "woof!" broke into his thoughts. His border collie streaked after him, eyes bright with excitement.

"Okay, hop in, but I have to warn you, you'll be spending an hour waiting for me. Plus, I'm not great company."

Nell didn't seem to mind as she leaped into the truck and plopped down on the passenger side, grinning toothily.

The problem with heading to town was that it took him through the Wilson property. The barn seemed empty, with doors open to let in the hot dry air. He swung around to glance at the house, shuttered up tight, and spied Millie climbing a rickety ladder. Why his foot hit the brake, he couldn't say. Call it an instant of insanity.

He pulled into the driveway, cut the engine and willed himself not to care. He was being neighborly, that's all. "That ladder is about to topple over."

"No, because I've got the short leg propped on a brick and I'm leaning to counterbalance it." Millie gingerly climbed onto the crumbling roof. "See? Now I only have to worry about getting down."

The woman had always been like this. He shook his head, held the door open for Nell and tried to ignore the arrhythmia galloping away in his chest. "Why did you get up there in the first place?"

"Looking for cracks. Why are you here anyway?" She swiped satiny strands of dark hair that had escaped her ponytail. Dressed in a light blue top and worn jeans, framed by cotton clouds and forested hillside, she was still the prettiest girl in the valley.

"I was on my way to run a few things to church, but then I spotted you. Luke told me about your mouse problem."

"*Mice* problem. It's crazy. We were up all night listening to the scrabble of little mouse feet climbing the walls."

"Sure. You've got fields behind the house. The field mice head for the barn at night, looking for grain. When they come across the obstacle of the house they climb up and over it."

"That's a disturbing image." Millie shivered. "Bleck. Why don't they just go around?"

"Can't answer that because I'm not a mouse. Why isn't Milton helping you?" He hiked to the ladder and wrapped his hands around a rung. Tested it. Too unsteady for his liking.

"Are you kidding? You really have to ask?" She flicked her ponytail over her shoulder. "He's exhausted after the fire last night. He'd been up at four for the milking. The poor man could barely stumble home."

That worried him, and he was trying not to get involved. "Have you considered selling?"

"Me? Sure. It was my first thought. But this property is in Dad's name and he says no."

"Figures." He frowned when Millie disappeared from his side. Tiny bits of designating shingle rained down on him. The barn wasn't the only thing in a state of disrepair.

"Call this another dumb idea," he told Nell. "Stay. That's a good girl."

The dog sat politely, eager to please as he put his boot on a rung, sent up a prayer and left the ground. The ladder hopped to the right, he leaned sharply to the left to counterbalance and kept climbing.

Millie's squeal launched him over the top rung and onto the rotting roof. She sat down hard on the peak, hand to her chest. "A bat. I surprised him. He was sleeping. I was—" She shuddered. "Ick. There's a reason I like Portland."

"There has to be a bat somewhere in Portland. Chances are."

"I know, but I've never had to personally have one fly at my face. Wow, I do not want to do that again."

"Then stop upsetting sleeping bats." He trekked up the slope, not shocked by the enormous crack between the chimney and the roof where flashing should be. "The attic could be full of them. And mice."

"I do not like crawly things." She shivered again. "Milton suggested poison, but I don't want that in the food chain. Think of the owls."

"Know what you need?"

"Yes, and I'm just going to have to buck up and do it. How many spiders do you think are in the crawl space?"

"Crawl space?" He thought of the box of mousetraps Luke had set aside for her. Likely wanted to put them in the crawl space just in case some of those mice were residents. "Probably not a bad idea. Better to set traps in the house near the food. What I meant is there's a better solution than traps."

"What could it be? To fumigate? Knock down the house with a bulldozer?"

"I'm not saying that wouldn't work, just that there's an easier option." Gazing into her blue eyes alight with humor made his resistance fall. It always did. He'd been a doomed man the instant he'd pulled into the driveway. "I'll give the pound a call."

"I'm not sure I can take on a new pet right now. Big plate. Too much on it."

"I'm talking about their barn cat program. I'll ask Brooke to pick out a couple cats after church and drive them up here. How about it? All you have to do is feed them."

"That is a brilliant idea."

"See? I'm not so bad."

"I never said you were." A hint of a smile touched her lips.

There it was, the reaction to her he had to avoid. He jerked away and eased down the slope of the roof a few steps. With enough distance between them, he felt safer. He breathed easier. This was the way it had to be.

"You are such a man. You took off the bandages."

"They got in my way."

"Then let me patch you up again." Concern played in her voice, nothing more.

That was the problem with Millie. She was a good woman. Her heart had always been in the right place. A hard ball of regret dug in deep somewhere between his stomach and his liver. "No way. I'm too tough for bandages."

"And what about infection?"

"Too tough for that, too." Last night she'd been a breath away, tending to those burns. His mistake had been letting her. Not gonna do it again. "What about you? Red skin, a few little burns. You didn't head to the doctor either."

"I wasn't as close to the fire as you."

"You were close enough to burn off some of your hair."

"Is it sticking up?" Figures. She stood up, dusted herself off and kept a wary eye on the crack beside the chimney. No more bats flying at her head, please. "I'm focusing on one problem at a time. The cows, the barn and mice."

"Having a cat around ought to help."

"It's a good solution." Hunter's solution. Last night had been proof of how easy it was to let him come to the rescue. To lean on him for anything, even a little harmless help, was a dangerous step. "I see you eyeing the ladder. Let me hold it for you."

"What I can't believe is that you risked climbing it."

"I'm pretty quick. I figured if it started tipping, I'd jump into the rhododendron bushes to break my fall." She tapped one finger to her forehead. "I'm no dummy."

"No, but really optimistic."

"Someone has to be. Otherwise how could I stay here?"

"Hard to argue with that." He angled onto the rung and stared climbing down. "How is Whip treating you these days?"

"Better than he used to. He's downright complimentary."

"I heard you have home care coming in to help?"

"I couldn't do this without them." To avoid the magnetic pull of the man, she gazed at the grounds. Wildflowers bobbed in the pasture where her horse used to graze. Empty, the grass had grown high, crisping beneath the hot summer sun. She spotted the broken trail Simon had made through tall grasses. Following it, she found him kneeling beside the minuscule but trickling creek, probably watching a few tadpoles scurry in the water.

"How are you juggling Whip's care with farm work?" On the ground, Hunter gazed up at her, waiting for an answer.

An answer she didn't want to give him. "It's been a piece of cake."

"Yeah, right." He might not buy it, but at least he didn't offer to help. That was sheer relief as she gripped the ladder, did her best not to look down when she set her foot on a rung.

"I've got it. I won't let you fall."

"If only I could believe you." She wasn't completely kidding. He had no idea how much he'd let her down ten years ago. She eased down rung by rung, aware that every step she took brought her closer to him.

She gulped when she climbed down between his arms, trying not to bump into his chest. So close, she could feel his warmth. Air stalled in her lungs, her feet hit the ground and he moved away.

Thank heavens. She breathed again, pretending she wasn't affected in the least.

"Let me give you some advice and don't take this the wrong way." He hefted the ladder, tipping it away from the house. "You never could take my advice."

"You know my philosophy. When it comes to advice, consider the source."

His laughter rang, a welcome sound. He eased the ladder onto its side, bringing it to rest behind the rhododendron bushes and out of sight. "Forget this is here, okay? Don't use that thing. It's a hazard waiting to happen."

"Obviously, but how else was I going to get on the roof?"

"Really? That's your reasoning. See, this is why you always drove me crazy."

"I drove *you* crazy?" She laughed at that. "Wasn't it the other way around? What about you? You climbed the ladder, too."

"We're talking about you. Don't worry about the flashing. I'll have Luke come take care of it. He may want to bring a few shingles, too."

"No, that's too much. You both have helped enough. The roof is fine the way it is. It's summer, it's not like there's going to be a snow pack accumulating up there."

"What about the bats?"

"If they're getting into the attic, then the solution is simple. I won't go in the attic."

"Can you sleep tonight knowing they're in the same house as you are?"

"Ah…" That moment of hesitation gave her away. "Totally. Without a doubt."

"Sorry, not fooling me."

"I wasn't trying to. I don't want you to feel obligated. You and me, well, let's just say you made it clear long ago. And honestly, I've been on my own a long time. I'm used to taking care of my problems and I like it that way."

"Got it." He clenched his jaw tight, seeing just how idiotic he'd been in stopping to help. And why? Not because he cared, but because he felt sorry for her. That was it. Being trapped here with her dad had to be tough. "You're right. This was a big mistake. I was trying to do the right thing. Being neighborly. That's all."

"I appreciate it. More than you know." Washed in sunshine, she couldn't look more sincere. "But you and me together, isn't this weird? I don't want to blur the lines."

"Sure, right." He whistled to Nell. "Won't happen again."

"I don't want to take advantage of you, Hunter. I don't want you to ever think I'm playing on old feelings."

"Believe me, there are no old feelings left." Those words slipped out before he could think them through, defensive and cold. All he'd wanted was to salvage his pride and hide what was bothering him. But he didn't mean to be so harsh. He watched her wince, heard her intake of breath and wished he'd been gentler. The wad of regret lodged in his gut didn't budge. "What I meant—"

"I know what you meant. You were always good at telling the unvarnished truth." Her chin hiked up, her lips compressed and she was someone he no longer knew—a strong woman, without a hint of the girl she'd been. "Have a good day, Hunter. Thanks for the suggestion of a cat."

"I'll have Brooke call you." Did he try to repair the harm he'd done, or did he walk away? And if he tried to apologize, how did he find the words? He hadn't known how to say what he meant in the first place. He opened his mouth trying to figure it out when the sound of footsteps stopped him.

Her son trudged into sight from the field behind the house, a bouquet of wildflowers fisted in one hand. Millie stepped in, shielding the boy from his line of sight. As if she feared he'd say something else hurtful.

"Simon, in the house and wash up, kiddo. I've got to think about lunch."

"I got these for you. Thought you could use 'em."

"Have I been forgetting to smile again?" Millie accepted the handful of flowers. "I've got to stop doing that. Is this better?"

"Sorta." The kid pushed his glasses up his nose and zeroed in on the stranger in the yard. "Hi. You really could drive that tractor, you know, at the fire? I watched you last night."

"Thanks." He tried to ignore Nell's friendly panting, begging to be released so she could run over and adore the boy with kisses and wags. He didn't give the signal. "I see you found the creek."

"Yep." The boy glanced down at his muddy shoes. "I like your dog."

"Her name is Nell." He almost gave Nell the command, but a car slowed on the road, signal blinking. Must be a home-care worker come to help with Whip. Must be a sign from above saying time to go. "C'mon, girl. In the truck."

The dog sighed, the boy's shoulders slumped and Millie stepped in front of her son again, looking relieved. Worried eyes, pinched forehead, biting her bottom lip, he knew exactly what those signs meant. The one thing he hated most of all was Millie's unhappiness.

"See ya around," he called out, opened the truck door and waited for Nell to hop in. His gaze found Millie one more time. "I'm sorry."

"I know." She nodded, already forgiven him.

Maybe she understood him better than he'd ever thought. He settled behind the wheel, started the engine and waited for the nurse to park before he backed down the driveway. When he looked up, Millie stood in the shade of the porch, watching him go.

She didn't wave goodbye.

Chapter Six

"Millie, dear, glad you made it for the service." In the churchyard, elderly Myra Hoffsteader grabbed her by both hands and squeezed. "It does my heart good to see you here. Wasn't sure you could make it."

"I meant to give you a call, but things got a little crazy at the dairy." She put an arm around Simon, shielding him from Myra's razor-sharp scrutiny.

"Understandable, considering. If you need someone to chat with or just a few minutes to escape for a cup of tea, you know where to find me. My, that's a handsome son you've got."

"I sort of like him." Alarms went off, clanging in her stomach. Time to skedaddle. The service had just let out, most people hadn't noticed when she and Simon slipped in at the last minute and sat in the back. It was probably best to escape before anyone else got a good look at her boy. "I'll drop by, I promise. Not sure when, but I promise."

"Sounds lovely, my dear."

She steered Simon across the lawn toward the street, where she'd parked Dad's old truck along the curb because she didn't dare risk the parking lot without Reverse.

"Mom? There are kids over there. Do you suppose any of 'em live near Grandpa's house?"

"We can find out."

"I know you've been busy." Simon's hand slipped into hers. "I said an extra prayer in church, you know, because I think you really need one."

"Thanks, kiddo. I said an extra prayer for you, too." She yanked open her door, her mind on the to-do list she'd made late last night when she was supposed to be sleeping and dropped her purse on the seat. Only then did she notice the disaster.

The street had been clear of cars when she'd parked here, five minutes before church. She wasn't the only latecomer who hadn't bothered with the parking lot. A brand-new minivan hugged the curb in front of her dad's rusting heap of a pickup. Another one had wedged in behind her.

"Uh-oh." Simon pushed up his glasses with his thumb. "We got trouble, Mom."

"Looks like we're stuck. Big time."

"Too bad I can't push it into the street like the Stetson guy." Simon's mouth scrunched up as he concentrated, as if determined to find a solution.

The solutions weren't ideal. They could walk the mile and a half home. She could ask Mrs. Hoffsteader to drive them, but Myra planned to stay for the picnic and she didn't want to interrupt the older woman's fun. Her third option would be to hunt down Luke, but then Hunter would know.

"Looks like you're in a bind." A deep, vibrant voice as familiar to her as her own rang out. Boots drummed to a stop behind her. Hunter. "Let me guess. You parked here first."

"I did. These minivan drivers had the entire street. *Both* sides of the street. And they had to park here. There's no one else parked anywhere. Look." She gestured up and down the lane. Honestly. "This isn't my fault."

"Maybe it's a sign." His eyes glittered with humor.

"A sign I should spring for a new transmission?"

"It would be a waste of money. The truck should be junked."

"I'm not arguing, but it's my only source of transportation."

"Then there's one solution. Stay for the picnic."

"No. I've left the nurse's aid alone with my dad for about as long as I dare. She's probably ready to run for the hills and never come back."

"No one could blame her, but it's her job to stay. Maybe she slipped him something to make him sleep." The way he stood framed by leafy green trees and the brilliant green of the churchyard and kissed by the golden rays of the sun, he'd never looked better. With his wind-tousled hair, the tailored drape of his suit emphasizing his linebacker shoulders and lean athlete's power, he seemed every inch a rugged Montana man. He cracked a hint of a smile, and the dimples cutting in his lean cheeks broke the moment.

Simon's dimples.

"You're stuck here." Hunter strolled closer, grabbed her purse by the strap and held it out to her. "You might as well enjoy it."

"You could give us a ride." She gulped, not sure if she was brave enough to put Simon in the same pickup as Hunter. Too close for comfort. That close, maybe Hunter might see what she saw in the boy every time he grinned. No, she needed a better option. "Why don't you hunt down Luke and talk him into taking us. I'll make you guys a loaf of banana bread if you do."

"Bribery. Do you honestly think it would work on me?" He shut the truck's door, which creaked rustily.

"No, but it was worth a try. I'm desperate here."

"No need to be. Stop worrying about Whip. He's fine. You don't have to take care of everyone every minute of the day. Stay, kick back, enjoy the picnic and catch up with folks for a while.

"There are people I'd love to see again, but—" But wouldn't they take one look at Simon and guess the truth? She circled around the truck, held out her hand to Simon and hopped onto the sidewalk. "Maybe we'll stay for the next picnic."

"Where are you going?"

"Home."

"You're walking? It's like ninety-seven degrees in the shade. If this is about what I said when I was over at your place, you know I'm sorry."

"I know. And that's not exactly an apology, by the way. Not that I need it, but just so you know. In case one day a woman takes a liking to you and you have another chance at a relationship."

"We both know that's not likely to happen."

"Just trying to be helpful."

"You're trying to distract me." He planted his hands on his hips, standing in the middle of the lane with his dark tie loose around his collar. "Let me try it again. I'm sorry, Millie. I shouldn't have said it like that, as if you'd never mattered."

"I just think it's better if we, well, keep our distance. We went our separate ways a long time ago." She spun around, her dress hem gave a little swirl. She shaded her eyes with one hand, staring up the length of the street. "Admit it, you want the same thing, too."

"What I want is for you and your kid to avoid sun stroke."

"We'll stop at the grocery on the way home, pick up something to drink. We'll stay hydrated."

"You always have an answer for everything. That drives me nuts, you know that."

"And it gives me great pleasure." Perhaps too much. How fun was that. It was the least he deserved, right? "I have another idea. You could give me the keys to your truck and catch a ride home later with Luke."

"Deal." He reached into his pocket, striding closer.

"Throw them here."

"I'm not throwing them." The strike of his shoes and the rhythm of his gait were two more things that hadn't changed about him. He came closer, driving panic straight through her. "You're still stubborn. Think about your son. There are races and prizes and a penny hunt after the barbecue."

"What's a penny hunt?" Simon let go of her hand.

"Talk your mom into staying and you'll find out." Hunter paused in the middle of the sidewalk, trapped by the shadows, and eyed the boy. "You must have figured out a way to talk her into things, not that I ever had any luck with it."

"I've been pretty successful."

"You'll have to tell me how you do it."

"As if." She stepped between man and boy. Father and son. Guilt crushed her. "Fine, we'll stay for an hour, but that's it. We leave on the dot."

And hopefully the minivans will have moved by then.

"I know what you're thinking, and don't count on it." Hunter moved in, smelling wonderful, like soap and sunshine. "This is a daylong event, so chances are those vehicles are staying put."

"Maybe we could figure out who owns them?"

"Just go with the flow." Hunter pressed his key ring into her hand. The brush of his skin ignited a spark that raced straight to her heart, to the buried memories she'd thought were lost for good.

They came to life like gifts from the past, like blessings from heaven. Sweet, gentle kisses. Tender gestures. His thoughtfulness. Buying her a horse when her father refused to let her spend her savings on one. Fixing the family car every time it broke down. Showing up for a date with flowers in hand and romantic dinner plans, then spending the evening doing barn work with her because her dad refused to give her permission to go. How afraid she'd been at the time, that Hunter would dub that the worst date ever and dump her.

He hadn't.

"Millie? I've been looking for you." A woman's voice rang with excitement, startling Millie out of the past and into the present.

She blinked at a car idling in the middle of the otherwise empty street, windows down. She recognized Hunter's sister. "Brooke! It's you! You look great. Incredible."

"True love will do that to a girl." The sedan's door swung open and Brooke launched out, arms wide. "How are you doing? I stopped by your dad's house. The nurse lady said you were here."

"I didn't realize—" She wrapped Brooke in a hug. A decade had passed since they'd been face to face, and yet it seemed no time has passed as she took Brooke by the hands and studied her. Still gorgeous and as sweet as ever. An impressive wedding set glittered on her left hand, but it was Brooke's smile that dazzled the most. Incredibly good to see her friend happy. "The cats! Did you leave them at the house?"

"No, they're in the car. The yowling has finally stopped. Right, Brandi?"

"Yes, but who knows for how long. They are starting to look around in their carriers—" An angry, earsplitting feline wail drowned her out.

"Poor things, they've got to be scared, but they're going to a good home. They'll find that out soon enough." Brooke turned her attention to the boy. "Is this your son, Simon?"

"Yep, that's me." The boy squinted at her, curious. "Who're you?"

"I knew your mom when she was dating my brother." Brooke patted Hunter's arm. "You look pretty shocked. Believe me, everyone was. Not a single soul in this valley could figure out how my gruff, lackluster brother—"

"Lackluster?" Hunter arched an eyebrow.

"—could catch a girlfriend like your mom." Brooke thoughtfully studied the boy.

DEFCON one. Major emergency. Millie seized Brooke by the shoulder and spun her toward the car. "Show me those poor cats. They sound terrified. We should take them home."

"That's the plan." Brooke opened the passenger door. "Out, Brandi. I'll take Millie, we'll get the cats settled and be back in time for burgers."

"Awesome." A platinum-blond sweetheart with violet eyes

bounded out of the backseat. She was adorable, the way a little sister should be, and somewhere in her twenties. "Finally, I get to meet the infamous Millie and her son. Hi, son."

"Hi." Simon waved.

Millie's heart stopped. Again. "And you're the twins I hear about. Well, one half of the pair. Where's Brianna?"

"She's back in Bozeman working an afternoon shift at the bakery." Brandi stopped, listening. "Hunter, Luke's calling you. Do you hear him?"

She certainly couldn't, as it was nearly impossible to hear much over the loud, *whop-whop* of blood pounding in her ears. Any moment one of the sisters, or even Hunter, would take a second look at Simon and see the truth. What would that do to her son to come face-to-face with the man who hadn't wanted him? The man who'd said he would never have it in his heart to love a child?

"I gotta go." Hunter seemed a little relieved to have a reason to escape. "See you later."

Whew. At least he hadn't figured it out.

"Mom, we stay, right?" Simon gulped, gazing longingly across the road to the church's front lawn where a game of soccer had started up. Kids about his age kicked a ball around, their laughter and shouts peppering the air.

She knew he was lonely. He was a kid. He should play, and he needed friends. But how did she protect him from prying eyes?

"Hey, you go with Brooke and he can stay with me." Brandi flicked a pigtail over one slim shoulder. "I start my student teaching in September. Because they've left me in charge of a classroom full of kids, I think I can handle just one until you come back. What do you say, Simon?"

"Sounds good." He swiveled his pleading gaze to her. "Okay, Mom?"

He wanted it badly. How could she resist those Bambi eyes?

As for her worries, was it possible that if Hunter's family hadn't noticed by now, then no one would? So far so good, right?

"Okay, but you stay with Brandi the whole time."

"Thanks, Mom!" Joy wreathed his face, his dear, dear face. Love filled her like a supernova, too impossibly great to measure. He grinned at Brandi, who smiled back and hopped onto the curb, waiting for him to join her. They walked together across the grass, heading for the soccer players.

"He'll be as safe as could be with her." Brooke bounced back to her idling car. "She's great with kids and completely responsible."

"I didn't doubt it for a second." No, that was absolutely not the problem. She might not know Brandi, but she'd heard about her from Brooke and from Hunter. Brandi and her twin, Bree, had grown up with a different mother west of Bozeman, where the girls lived now in an apartment of their own near the campus.

"C'mon, let's introduce these cats to their new homes." Brooke held the back passenger door open. "A word to the wise. Do not put your finger through the slats in the crate. You'll get swiped."

Millie settled on the seat, going slightly deaf from the caterwauling from the irate felines. She caught a glimpse of a green eye and a fluff of gray fur before the animal hissed and spat at her.

"Don't worry. You'll like living with us. I promise. You won't go hungry anymore." When her father passed on and she sold the farm, she would make sure the new owners vowed to look after the pair.

The second cat continued to yowl as Brooke slipped behind the steering wheel. "Sorry it's a little loud in here."

"The good news is that it's a short drive."

"Amen." Brooke fastened her seat belt and they were off.

Millie glanced out the window, twisting around to watch Simon join the kids at the soccer game. Brandi dutifully stood by on the sidelines along with a few moms, chatting away. Millie's last glimpse was of how happy he looked, charging after a ball, surrounded by kids his own age. Then Brooke's car wheeled around a corner, taking him from her sight.

She'd forgotten about the key ring clutched in her hand and she studied it now, wondering about the man. Hunter didn't want family ties. He didn't believe in love. What other decision could she have made?

"You had to volunteer us for this?" Hunter cast a sideways frown at his younger brother as he grabbed one of the shovels leaning against Luke's truck. "Really? I thought you'd want to spend as much time with your girlfriend while she's here as you can."

"Honor looks right at home, don't you think?" Luke, the poor besotted sap, wore his heart on his sleeve. One hundred percent in love with a woman who would one day let him down, shatter his heart and leave him in irreparable pieces. Not that he wanted it to happen to his brother—Luke was a good man— but wasn't that love's inevitable course?

"I won't deny she's a nice lady, but love is a rocky road." He opened the tailgate, breathing in the woody smell of the fresh sawdust. "How are you going to make a long-distance relationship work? She lives in California."

"Not anymore." Luke drew in a breath, taking his time. Looked like he was about to drop a bombshell as he propped one arm on the truck bed, gathering his words and maybe his courage. "See, here's the thing. I'm driving back with her tomorrow."

"You're *what?*" He dropped his shovel. "Tomorrow? To California? Are you kidding me?"

"I've thought this through, Honor and I've talked it over and it's the right thing to do."

To be honest, he wasn't sure about her driving all the way

by herself, but he didn't have to let Luke know that. He rescued his shovel. "What about the milking?"

"I hired Cal, you know, one of Milton's milkers? He's going to fill in for me, and before you say it, I told Brandi we'd pay her to help out at Millie's. You can train her tonight."

"You decided all this by yourself?" He bit back his grin. "Exactly when did you become boss over me?"

"I got caught up in the moment. Saw a solution and took it especially because you were over at Millie's climbing on her roof. Cal drove by on his way to see me and told me all about how you two were getting along."

"That's the problem with living in a small town." Everyone always knew your business. His gaze arrowed across the rolling lawns to the kids playing soccer. Easy to spot Millie's boy—flyaway black hair, glasses, scoring a goal to the glee of his team. Likable, just the way she was.

It hurt to look at that kid. To think of her betrayal. It wasn't exactly a betrayal, a little voice in the back of his brain reminded him. He'd been terrible boyfriend material. She'd wanted more, and he'd refused to give her an engagement ring. Of course she'd gone on with her life. The fact that she'd been able to move on so fast and easily still wounded him, no matter how hard he tried to get over it.

"You need to drop by and do a quick roof repair." Tough to talk with his teeth locked together, so he forced his jaw to relax. "The chimney needs flashing."

"That's going to be hard to do, because as soon as I finish tonight's milking, I'm packing for my trip."

"It's a good thing." Tim, their minister, strolled up with a grocery sack tucked in one arm. He came from the direction of the smoking grill, where the first round of hamburgers smoked and sizzled. Most folks were busy spreading out blankets on the shady side of the church grounds and adding their contributions to the food-laden picnic table next to the grill. "A man has to follow his heart."

"Yeah, Hunter." Luke grinned wide, pleased to have an ally. "A lady like Honor only comes around once in a man's life. I don't intend to let her go."

"Are you going to marry this girl?" He shot a glance over at Honor Crosby, the woman who had hooked his brother's heart. On the other side of the lawn, he spotted her handing Mrs. Hoffsteader a cup of lemonade, apparently having fetched it for her. Hard to find a single thing wrong with that. Honor was clearly a nice lady.

"That's my plan." Luke took an economy-sized bag of wrapped mini candy bars the minister handed him. Tim offered a second bag to Hunter.

He took it, ripping open the top. "How long are you going to be gone on your California trip?"

"Just long enough to rent a truck, pack up Honor's things and drive back. Well, we'll take a few days to meet her friends and family."

"Sure." Maybe being saddled with the sole responsibility of running the dairy was a good thing. He'd have less time to see Millie, or to bump into Millie or to find her climbing that rickety ladder he wanted her to stay off and thereby wouldn't be obligated to stop and help. Now this was a plan that could work.

"Take all the time you need." He liked this more and more. He upended the bag into the sawdust and watched the candy fall. "I can keep things covered here."

"This is sure a change of tune. Thanks, bro. It means a lot to have your support. Not sure where it's coming from, but thanks."

"Guess I've warned you off enough." Not that he was optimistic, but if anyone deserved to find the real thing and have it last, it was Luke.

"Speaking as a happily married man, I'm glad you're doing this, Luke." Tim, a thoughtful and quiet man, gave a nod of approval. He pulled out a large baggie of change from his grocery bag. "You and Honor should grab all the happiness you can."

Hunter hopped into the back of the truck, took the money bag from the minister and emptied it in the sawdust. Glinting pennies and sparkling nickels, dimes and quarters tumbled into the wood shavings. Time to get this unloaded because his stomach started growling. The aroma from the barbecue grill carried on the breeze, reminding him it was past lunchtime.

He dug in with his shovel, sensing something else on the wind. The squeals and shouts of kids in the heat of a soccer battle raced closer. Their feet drumming, their shouts rising and then the *thwap* of a ball as it slammed one of the kids in the face. A black-haired kid, who held his hands to his nose. Blood oozed bright and crimson between his fingers.

It was Millie's son.

Chapter Seven

Brooke's car pulled to a stop curbside with a perfect view of the church grounds. The cats were safely hiding beneath Millie's dad's back porch, with comfortable beds made out of old blankets for them in the nearby carport and plenty of fresh water and kibble, so she had hopes of a better night's sleep.

"You have no idea how you've saved me," Millie told her friend. "Huge. Big time."

"My pleasure. It's a win-win because you get help with your mice problem and the cats get a safe place to live and someone to watch out for them." Brooke cut the engine, unbuckled and swung open the door. "So, what's up with you and Hunter?"

"Nothing. Not one thing. Why would there be? He's the same man. He hasn't changed." Millie climbed out into the sunshine. Did she sound unaffected? Did she come across like she'd never given Hunter a second thought? She hoped so. She squinted into the sunshine, searching for Simon on the busy church grounds. "He and I are neighbors, that's all. *Temporary* neighbors."

"Right. How's your dad—"

That was all she heard because she'd found her son standing in front of a dark-haired, wide-shouldered man who was down on both knees. Hunter. What were they doing together?

She launched onto the lawn, leaving Brooke behind and the door wide open. Halfway across the lawn she noticed a few drops of blood on Hunter's hand as he tipped her child's head back and pinched the bridge of his little nose. Her poor boy.

"You took that blow like a man." Hunter's gruff compliment rumbled kindly, carried to her on the breeze. "That had to hurt."

"I'b tuff."

"So, I see." Hunter dabbed at Simon's nose with a tissue, mopping up the little bit of blood. A travel-sized box sat on the grass next to his knee.

"I hafta take care of by bob."

Faster, she told her feet, but time had screeched to an inexplicable stop like it did right before doom happened. Was she the only one who noticed they shared a high forehead, sloping nose and a carved chin?

"Your mom's blessed to have you taking care of her," Hunter dabbed at drying blood, wiping it off Simon's fingers with his free hand. "Sounds like you're the man of the house."

"Dat's right. Ab I still bleedink?"

"Simon!" Millie skidded to a stop, adrenaline kicking through her veins. "Thanks, Hunter, but I can take over."

"Good, because that's about all I know. I'm no medic, but I'd say this is minor. He'll be scoring goals as soon as lunch is over." A hint of a grin, a nod of encouragement and he released his hold on Simon's nose. "Keep your head tipped back, okay? You play an awesome game of soccer, buddy."

"Danks, neighbor." Simon glowed at the compliment, responding to Hunter in a way that made the fear coiling in her stomach ratchet a notch tighter.

"No problem, kid." Hunter rocked back on his heels, rising to his six-plus feet. His shadow fell across her, blocking the sun's warmth.

When his gaze locked on hers, she shivered. Did he know? Did he suspect? Had there been an unspoken instinct he'd felt when he'd gazed into Simon's eyes and recognized his son?

But thankfully Hunter said nothing. Good news was the bleeding had stopped. "How are you feeling, kiddo?"

"Okay. I'b sorry." Simon's apology shone in his eyes.

"By glasses."

That's when she realized he wasn't wearing them. She smoothed a shock of hair off his forehead. "It's okay. We'll get another pair."

"I found the doctor." Brandi jogged into sight, pale with worry. "Millie, I'm sorry! I watched him like a hawk, I promise you, but it happened so fast."

"It would have happened if I'd been here instead." Goose bumps broke out on her arms, aware of the man watching her. He'd retreated to lean against the pickup beside his brother, arms crossed over his chest. His dark eyes shuttered, making it impossible to guess what he was thinking.

"Let me take a look." Dr. Moss tromped up, his gray hair wind-tousled. Still the same doc with his plaid shirts and friendly smile that put anyone at ease. "Millie, I haven't seen you in ages."

"Aren't you retired by now?"

"Sure, but duty calls. Hi, there." The older man knelt in front of the boy for a quick examination. "I used to treat your mom when she was little."

"Cool."

The weight of Hunter's gaze raked over her. Was it her imagination or did she feel his condemnation? It took all her courage to meet his gaze boring into her. What was he going to do? What was he going to say? Miserable, she bowed her head watching the doctor check for a broken nose, shake his head and pat Simon on the shoulder.

"You'll be fine. Take it easy until after you eat. Millie, he's clotted just fine. There shouldn't be any problems, but if that bleeding starts up again, you know where to find me."

"Thanks, Doc." Her skin prickled with awareness as Hunter

launched off the side of the truck toward her. Every movement he made shot through her like judgment.

"Mbomb?" Simon danced in place, pure little-boy energy. Nothing could keep him down for long. "Are you mbad? When we get to Grandpa's house, I can glue 'em."

The kid worried too much. She smoothed down his tousled hair, not that it would do any good; that shock of his cowlick stuck straight up again.

"We'll drive into Bozeman when we get a chance and get a new pair. No worries." She swallowed hard, aware of Hunter taking the broken pair of glasses from Brandi and disappearing around his truck. If only she could forget the image of Hunter kneeling before her son, taking care of him with kindness warming his words.

That was very fatherlike. Never in her wildest dreams had she been able to picture him as father material. Back then, he'd been sometimes cold, often quick to shut down his emotions and push away those who cared about him.

"Millie?" Footsteps rasped beside her in the grass. When she looked up, Jerry from the volunteer fire department gave his Stetson a hitch. "See your boy's all right. That was quite a goal you scored there, young man."

"Danks." Simon's eyes glowed. "I got lucky. Got in a good, clean shot."

"You sure did. My son Jonah is over at the barbecue waiting for you. If it's okay with your mom?"

"Absolutely." She squeezed Simon's shoulder. "Have fun, kiddo. Stay where I can see you."

"Wait." Hunter strolled into her line of sight, his jaw clenched tight as if in anger. He held out Simon's glasses, repaired with a strip of adhesive tape he must have found in Luke's truck. "Now you can see where you're going."

"Thanks, Hunter." Simon's smile went up in wattage two hundred percent. "I like to see my food before I eat it."

"That's a good plan." Strain snapped along Hunter's jawline. "A word of advice. Hit the dessert table right away. If you wait, you'll miss the best stuff."

"Got it. Are you comin', Mom?" The boy took off, walking backward, only a few drops of blood on his shirt a clue that he'd been a soccer casualty.

"I'll be right there soon." She waited until her son, Brandi and Jerry were out of earshot before she dared face Hunter. She tried to ignore the rat-tat-tat of her pulse in her skull and faced him head-on and honestly, the way she wished she could have ten years ago. "I really need to explain—"

"Forget it. I know what you're going to say." He jammed his hands into his pockets, pacing away from the truck, where Luke stood in the bed, shoveling sawdust into a pile on the ground. "I'm guessing you never figured on seeing me alone with your son."

"That's putting it mildly."

"The kid was hurt. Whatever you think of me, I'm not going to stand by and do nothing, especially for a child." A muscle ticked along his iron jawline, a sign of his struggle to hold his emotion.

Here it comes. She steeled her spine, bracing for the first blow. They were alone, just the two of them, huddling at the edge of the grass where tall trees cast them in shadow. "Hunter, maybe I should have—"

"I need to talk to you about the dairy." He squared his shoulders, all business. "Luke's leaving town for a week or so with his girlfriend."

"This is news." The change of subject surprised her, but she went with it. "And you're actually letting him go?"

"Don't see how I can stop him." Hunter's grin could still make her heart thump.

"Oh, I get where this is going. With Luke gone, you'll be shorthanded milking your herd, so you won't be able to help Milton and me. It's not a problem." The words rushed out, driven by relief. "Don't worry. The milk check should come next week, so we'll be able to hire back—"

"No." He leaned in, towering over her, so close she breathed in the scents of sawdust and hay clinging to his shirt. "Luke had the idea of training Brandi to come help you out. She needs the income for college, so you'd be helping her out."

"That's not what I expected you to say, so give me a minute here. I'm a little speechless."

"Don't have to say anything." He swallowed hard, but that didn't do a thing to dislodge the wad of emotion apparently stuck in his throat. "Don't even thank me. Truth is, I wasn't always good to you when we were together. I regret that."

"I regret a lot of things, too." She bit her bottom lip, looking forlorn. That just went to show what a rotten boyfriend he'd once been. Hurting her had never been his intention. Truth was, he'd been so determined to be tough and not to give in to love that he hadn't realized what he was doing, unable to see how much he'd hurt her.

He could see it now. He'd spent his entire life pushing people away so no one could get close. Shouldn't be a big surprise that it worked. There was no do-over button he could push. His only option was to try and do better. He grabbed the shovel leaning against the side of the truck. "I'm not that fond of kids."

"I know, you've told me many times."

"But I like yours. He's a lot like you."

"Really?" Worry crinkled across her forehead, like maybe she expected him to say something harsh about her child.

Not going to happen. It wasn't that he didn't like kids; more like he was afraid he would be a bad father, the way his dad had been for him. "Sure. He's got your sense of humor. Your dark hair. That can't-stop-me attitude. Your love of team sports."

"I guess so." Her gentle gaze found his and held, looking deeply into him. Sympathy flitted across her face, as obvious as if she'd said the words.

She felt sorry for him? What for? Or was it because she

could see all the ways he hadn't changed? The barricade around his heart stood fortress-strong, as immovable as ever. That's the way it would stay.

"Mom!" A distant voice traveled across the grounds. "I got a plate for you."

"I'd better go." She darted away, eager to leave. "See you around."

"Maybe, maybe not." He shrugged, her look of sympathy lingered, getting to him, even when he joined Luke in the truck bed. Sawdust flew, the pile on the ground grew and he kept sneaking glances across the lawn at Millie, sitting with her son and his sisters. At Millie, laughing and beautiful.

Sympathy for him? Ridiculous. There was nothing to feel sorry for. He was right where he wanted to be in his life. Single was exactly the way he wanted it.

"Millie, it's a good thing you've done, coming back for your dad." Lee Paulson, a neighboring rancher, moseyed up to the picnic table. Time had put more lines in his face and a little gray in his hair, but his brown eyes were still good-humored. "Not that Whip deserves it."

"He's dying. It's time to put our differences aside." She poured lemonade into her plastic cup. "Thanks for coming to help put out the fire."

"Not a problem. We're neighbors. We're both dairy farmers. Helping out is what we do around here. Just glad we could knock it down before the whole structure went. Of course, Hunter was the one who saved the day."

"I'm trying not to think too hard on that," she quipped. Hunter's good deeds toward her were adding up. She grabbed Lee's cup from him and filled it. "I hear your Ethan and Natalie are in high school."

"Yep, they're all grown up. To think you used to babysit for 'em. They're around here somewhere. Probably playing baseball with the youth group kids."

"If I don't run into them, tell them hi." She handed him his cup.

"Will do. See ya around." He tipped his Stetson and ambled away.

Nice to see him again. There were good memories in this valley, too, and even better people.

"I didn't believe the rumors, not at all, not until I saw you with my own eyes." A red-haired woman took a brownie from a baking dish and tucked plastic wrap back into place. Cissy Larson, they'd grown up together. "You really are here. I thought you were gone for good."

"No kidding, but plans change." She glanced at the loose cluster of kids in front of a makeshift starting line. Simon had paired up with Jonah, waiting for Brandi to tie their legs together. His nose was just fine, although his glasses sat a bit askew. "It's that never-say-never thing. I said never to coming back and here I am."

"You should have heard the tantrum your daddy threw when you left." Sympathy glinted in Cissy's caring gaze. "He had to hire two men to do the work you did for him for free. I couldn't stand to look at him after I heard that. I'm trying to feel Christian charity for him, but it's not easy."

"Believe me, I know. How have you been?"

"Good. I married Billy a few years after you left. I'm Cissy Taylor now. We have three little ones. The baby is sleeping with her daddy." Cissy nodded across the grounds to a green plaid blanket and an older version of Billy, the high school football player, holding his sleeping daughter in one arm. "The preschooler is racing around keeping Grammy on her toes, and our oldest is gearing up for the three-legged race."

"So's mine. He's the one in the blue shirt."

"Millie, he looks just like you. Those cheeks. Those big beautiful eyes. Remember how you used to wear those reading glasses?"

"I still do." A sigh escaped her. So, people saw what they

expected to see. No one but her father had known she'd been pregnant when she'd fled town. "Your little girl is the one in the purple shirt."

"How did you guess? It wouldn't be the red ringlets, would it?"

"She looks just like you. Gorgeous."

"You're the same, Millie. So *good* to have you back. Oh, the baby's waking up." Cissy raised her hand in a just-a-minute sign to her husband, taking a few hesitant steps. "Don't think we won't talk about Hunter either. Can you believe him? Never married. Some say he's been pining for you all this time."

"Pining? For me?" No way. Impossible to imagine it. "He's the one who ended everything."

"That's not what everyone says." Across the way, Cissy's baby started to cry. "Now I really have to go. We'll talk later. I'll call you."

Millie watched her girlhood friend scurry away, remembering there had been good times spent in this town.

"Get ready!" The minister's voice boomed above the happy sounds of conversations and laughter ringing across the grounds. With toes up to the masking tape starting line, a row of paired-up kids bobbed and danced, eager to be on their way. "Get set! Go!"

Off they went, staggering awkwardly. Simon and Jonah found their rhythm and pulled into third place. Cissy's girl and her partner went tumbling, laughing as they hit the ground. Cheers rose, encouraging everyone on.

"Hey, your kid's pulling into second." Hunter's baritone. Hunter's gait on the grass sidling up behind her. He seized the pitcher's handle. "I checked on your dad's truck. It's blocked in worse than before. Too many folks ran out to make a quick run home or to the store and parked on the street."

"And here I wanted to give your keys back." Her attention remained firmly on the race. Simon and Jonah were neck and neck with the leaders, trying to pass, but the finish line loomed ahead. There wasn't enough time. The race was over.

"Mom! Second place!" Simon's happiness lit him up.

"Yay! Woo-hoo! Good job!" She cheered, proud as her son politely congratulated the first-place winners.

Other parents called out congratulations, too, parents she recognized because she'd gone to school with them. Anne Roland, who'd apparently married her high school sweetheart, James, whose son was accepting a third-place prize. Kathi Olenz standing hand in hand with her husband; they'd dated in school, too.

Everywhere she looked were families. Hunter was the only single man with no family ties and no one to love. Did he like being alone? Were there times he regretted his solitary life? Again, the image of him kneeling before Simon, pinching the boy's bleeding nose, flashed into her mind. But a moment of kindness didn't change things.

"See ya around, Millie." He saluted her with his glass of lemonade, walking away.

Chapter Eight

"That was fun. So totally fun." Simon bounced in the passenger seat of the borrowed truck and popped a bite-sized candy bar into his mouth.

Yes, the sugar was definitely at work. "I'm glad you had a great time, kiddo."

"And Hunter's truck is supercool." He eyed the controls to the sound system and ran his fingers over the plush upholstery. "Did he really used to be your boyfriend?"

"Long ago, yes." And that's all she wanted to say on the subject. "You scored a lot of candy in the penny hunt."

"And lots of candy money." Simon's hand covered his pocket, where his treasure gave a muted jingle. "Hmm, I wonder what I'll buy."

"Something good, right?" She wheeled into the driveway, the groceries behind the seat rustling as they shifted around. She'd stopped on the way home, took twenty from her meager savings account at the ATM and tried not to think about their precarious finances.

"Right, or maybe ice-cream bars." Simon opened the door and hit the ground with a two-footed thud.

It did her good to hear him so happy. She opened the door, let the country air breeze over her and hauled a sack of groceries off the floor. Simon circled around to her, arms out, and she handed him the lightest bag.

"So, where does Jonah live?" He tromped alongside her.

"The farm on the other side of the river." She spied a shadow hunched on the porch swing, the home-care nurse looking wrung out. She knew just how Dad could make a person feel. "Simon, please put the bag in the kitchen."

"I'll take both, Mom." He hefted the second sack from her, clomped up the steps and wrestled open the screen door. Once he was inside, the homecare worker rose from the swing.

"I'm sorry." The lady who'd introduced herself as Rosa when she'd arrived in the morning slipped her hands into her pockets, looking worse for wear. "I'll get back to work."

"It's okay. Everyone needs a break. Especially from my father."

"He's a difficult patient." Rosa squared her shoulders. "But it's my job to deal with him. I only needed a little fresh air."

She likely needed more than that, judging by the strain on her face. Millie wondered what her father had said or done, then again, did she really want to know? "Why don't you take a few more minutes? I know what he's like."

"My shift is almost over, so I should get back." The woman slid past her, walking quickly to return to her duties. "Caitlin will be the next shift nurse. I'll leave some notes for her so she's prepared."

"Thank you, Rosa." Whatever Dad had done, she prayed it wasn't bad enough to drive away the nursing care he needed. She followed the nurse's aide into the house, stopping to glance toward the kitchen to check on her son. He was dutifully putting away a gallon jug of milk into the fridge.

"It's about time. I've been waiting." Whip's scolding tone boomed through the house, obviously aimed at Rosa. "Get your wide butt to the kitchen and fetch me some juice."

That man and his cruel tongue. Millie pounded down the hall. "Simon, go outside and play. Now."

"Okay." A few beats more and the back screen snapped shut, meaning he was safely out of earshot. She rounded the corner and skidded to a stop at the mess her father had made of the room. What had happened here?

"I'm sorry, Millie." Rosa picked up a piece of a shattered mug on the carpet. "He did this when I was buttering his toast. I came back from the kitchen to this."

"This is why you needed a moment on the porch. Completely understandable." Millie blew out her breath, taking it all in. The chicken noodle soup dripping down the wall, noodles stuck to the frame of the television set. The remote control in pieces. The broken dishes, juice glass and orange stain on the rug. Books from the nightstand lay hazard and open on the floor, spines broken and pages bent.

"Stupid, lazy woman, are you deaf?" Red flushed Whip's face. "Go get my juice."

If only there was a pill to make him nicer. All the prayer in the world couldn't help him because behaving this way was Dad's decision. She gently took the shards from Rosa. "Why don't you pour both of us a glass of iced tea? I'll be out in a moment."

"If you think that's best." Rosa pursed her lips, saying nothing more as she slipped from the room.

"Where did you find that one?" Whip demanded. "Someone ought to light a fire under her butt. She's slow and as dumb as a rock—"

"That's enough." Millie gathered the last chunk of what used to be a coffee cup handle, overwhelmed by the mess. She pushed off the floor, wishing she was back in Portland with such force that the room in front of her blurred. "Stop treating Rosa that way. I can't take care of you by myself and run the dairy. It's too much for one person."

"You don't want to do any work, you mean." His craggy face wreathed with rancor. "You always were lazy, girl. Good for nothing."

He was dying. What was the use in arguing? An argument was what he wanted to start and she wanted to avoid. Keeping her mouth tightly clamped, she left the room. Whip's temper flared again and he spewed a string of curse words, each more offensive than the last. She closed the door, muffling it, and joined Rosa in the kitchen.

"I upped his pain medication to the highest allowable, but it did not seem to help." Rosa held the pitcher in one hand and the refrigerator door in the other. In went the pitcher, the door swung shut. "I know he is in pain."

"Yes, but mostly he's always been like that." She glanced out the window searching for Simon. There he was, sitting on the back porch step. At least he'd been out of earshot for the worst of Whip's tirade. "If you want to leave, I totally understand. I'll explain to your supervisor."

"No, I want to stay. This assignment is close to home, which is nice for a change. Usually I wind up driving all the way to Bozeman." Some of the strain slid off Rosa's face as she took a sip of iced tea. "I can handle it."

"If you're sure. The thing to know about my dad is that he says what he thinks will hurt the most. Which means his words are just a weapon he's throwing, nothing more."

"I'll try and remember. I've had patients like him before." Rosa set down her glass. "You haven't put your groceries away yet. Let me help."

"Not your job, thanks, and I'd rather you rested. You'll need it for when we have to go back into that room." Her father's muffled curses continued to emanate from the hallway. He had everything he needed but a target for his bitterness. "I'm going to make banana bread. It's not much, but I want to do something to thank the men who came over last night to help. We had a small barn fire, nothing serious, thanks to them."

"Oh, I love to bake. I have two girls, five and three, and I bring them into the kitchen and we measure flour and cream butter and have the sweetest time."

"It must be nice to have daughters, although I wouldn't trade my Simon for the world." The one great treasure in her life she thanked God for every day. Her gaze found him automatically. All she could see was the top of his head bob as he checked on the kitties hiding under the porch. She set down her glass. "Okay, I'm ready to face Dad. I'll take him his juice."

"Better get a cup that can't break."

"My thought exactly." Millie thought she felt the Lord's touch on her shoulder, the reassurance she needed to keep going.

Seeing her father through the end of his life wasn't going to be easy. But it was the right thing to do.

"Thanks for helping clean up." The minister opened his car door in the parking lot, where the sun's heat bounced off the blacktop, cooking them both.

"My pleasure." Hunter dived into his pocket for his keys and came up empty. Millie had them, but she hadn't given him a set in return. No matter. "Let me know if you need help setting up for the next one."

"Will do. Are you doing all right with Millie back in town?" Concern and an invitation to listen softened the man's voice. Tim was a good guy, but there was no reason for him to be concerned.

"I'm great. Why wouldn't I be?" He tried to sound casual, backing toward the street. "Have a good one, Tim."

"You, too."

Alone again, he had time to think. His self-revelation remained at the back of his mind, as irritating as a pebble in his shoe. Fine, so he kept a distance from everyone, letting them in only so close. So, nothing was wrong with that. It was a free country, and it was his choice. The thing was, he'd never thought to look at it from Millie's view. She'd been young and vulnerable when he'd pushed her away ten years ago, and he'd hurt her. He'd only been trying to protect himself, but that didn't change the pain done to her. Not that it excused her behavior, but he understood why she'd run straight into another man's arms.

"Hey, there you are!" Brandi looked up from her paperback. Sitting on the shady grass, with her platinum hair tied back, she looked as sweet as pie. Hard to believe she would be graduating from college soon, all grown up already. She closed her book. "Ready to go?"

"As soon as I can find the spare key." He yanked open the unlocked driver's door.

"It's in the ashtray." Brandi bounded up, swiped away bits of grass and hopped over to the truck. "Millie told me before she left."

"That makes it easier." He gave the ashtray a hard yank to reveal the key. He had a lot to get done before the sun set. "I doubt Luke remembered his promise to drop the flashing off at Millie's. Did he say anything to you? His mind is mush lately."

"No. Love will do that to you." Brandi buckled in. "Why are you scowling?"

"I'm not. Why bother? There's no use to it. Luke has fallen into the trap and no one can get him out."

"I'm inclined to agree with you about romance in general, but every once in a while—" she paused while the engine rolled over with a roar "—the fairy tale happens. Not to me, but to some people. I'm thinking this time it's happened to Luke and Honor."

"Humph." Because the minivans had cleared out and he had the entire length of the street, he put the truck into gear and pulled away from the curb. The engine backfired, echoing like a gunshot along the quiet street. The air-conditioner gave a hot puff, so he rolled down his window. Air whooshed into the cab, ruffling bits of hay and grain and sending hayseed flying. A crackle of paper caught his attention, but it was Brandi who snatched it from midair.

"Oh, it must be Millie's. A to-do list. I'll keep it for her."

"Give it here." He grabbed it. Sure enough that was Millie's elegant script on the back of an empty envelope. A long list—correct that, an overwhelming list. Not that it was any of his business, but did that stop him from folding it into his shirt pocket? No. He was troubled by the reason why.

Brandi's phone chimed. She whipped it out of her pocket and bent over the screen, smiling at whatever the text said. Probably from one of their sisters. Her thumbs tapped out an answer, keeping her busy while the small town rolled by and turned to ranching country. Cattle grazed, fields of wheat and hay and corn baked in an unrelenting sun and the Wilson dairy rolled into view. He pulled into the driveway and parked next to his truck.

"Hi." Simon popped out of the grass, his glasses askew. "You have a cool pickup."

"Thanks." His boots hit the ground. "Did you try the sound system? It rocks."

"No. Mom wouldn't let me touch anything." Simon grinned, wide and easily, just the way Millie did.

He couldn't hold a grudge against a child; that wasn't right. It wasn't Simon's fault his mother had chosen another man. "That's a mom for you. What are you up to?"

"I was trying to make friends with Shadow and Smokey, but they didn't want to."

"They haven't had much reason to trust people before this. Just give them time." He slammed the groaning door shut, the impact made rust crumble off into the grass. How much longer the truck lasted was anyone's guess. "So, are you having fun around here?"

"No." Simon shrugged. "Grandpa has the only TV and he doesn't share."

"Sounds just like Whip." Hunter glanced over his shoulder, nodded to Brandi to follow. "There used to be an old tire swing on the maple tree outback."

"That's what Mom said when we first got here, but when we looked, there was just the tire leaning against the tree."

"Maybe I can find some rope in the barn. We'll see what I can rig up."

"Really? That would be sweet." Simon fell in alongside him, working to keep up with Hunter's longer gait.

He shortened his stride. Okay, maybe he liked the kid. "We have an extra horse that came with the dairy when Luke and I bought it. Mrs. Hoffsteader used to keep him for her grandkids to ride, but they grew up. Why don't you ask your mom if it would be okay for me to bring over Sundae?"

"Really? Honest? Do you mean it? Like I could ride him and everything? I'd take really good care of him. Honest. I know I can talk Mom into it. I'm pretty good at that."

"I'm sure you are." It really was hard not to like this kid. "I'll throw in a bag of grain and bring over a truckload of alfalfa. How's that? But you would have to take care of him. I'd show you how."

"Okay. Maybe you could show me some other stuff. You know, like how to feed the cows and do the milking. I know I could do it." He pushed up his taped-up and slightly crooked glasses. "Mom said she worked in the barn when she was younger than me."

"She did. I'd like to help you out, but the thing is, I know your mom doesn't want you to work the way she did." They'd crossed the road and stepped into the barn, so his words echoed a bit in the rafters. "Besides, your mom has me and other neighbors to help out. You don't need to worry about it."

"That's why I'm here," Brandi chimed in from inside the office. "I like to make myself useful."

"Impossible." Hunter winked at her. "There's no use for you."

"So I've been told." With a grin, she plopped into the desk chair to pull on her boots. "Hey, what are you two up to? Try and stay out of trouble, you hear?"

"Hard to say. There's no telling what Simon and I are up to." His boots thudded on the concrete as they entered the spotless milking parlor, empty for now. Milton hadn't arrived yet. He took a moment to pull out Millie's to-do list. *Number one, batteries in the smoke detectors. Number two, haystack has got to go.*

That didn't surprise him. Those were on his list, too.

"Hey, that's my mom's." Simon studied him from behind lenses. "Why do you have it?"

"I want to do a few things for her." Judging by the look of the kid, he wasn't going anywhere soon. May as well accept it. "Do you want to help?"

"Sure!"

"Then let's head around the corner to my place. I could use help loading up my truck. Okay?"

"Okay."

Looked like he had a little partner. He pulled out his phone to text Millie that he was taking off with her kid.

"It's good to know you had no problem going out and having fun, and all with a clear conscience, when I'm laying here dying." Whip hit mute on his newly repaired remote, currently held together by electrical tape, and squinted at her. "Have a good time?"

"I stayed for Simon's sake." She wrung out the rag in the sudsy bucket and ignored her cell's chime. Probably Hunter letting her know he and Simon were back. "Would you like more juice?"

"What I want is for this cancer to go away. I feel like cr—"

"Stop swearing, Dad," she interrupted, scrubbing the wall with all her might.

"Oh, you find that offensive, and yet it doesn't bother you having that kid out of wedlock?" He snorted, amused by that. "Not surprised. That's a good Christian for ya."

Her father, the man who believed there was no God, did and

said exactly what he wanted to without conscience or concern for anything else. Her jaws locked together and it took all her effort not to rise to his bait. Not exactly easy. Sure, he was in pain and had to be afraid, but that couldn't excuse the things he said. She tossed the rag in the pail and grabbed the handle. Enough was enough. Maybe it'd be easier to come back when he was sleeping.

"You know Sara Thomas's girl? You used to babysit her." A spiteful grin twisted Whip's hard mouth. "She started running around and got herself a brat out of marriage. She grew up to be just like you."

Another word bomb meant to devastate, but did he really think his twisting of the truth could hurt her? Not when she knew what had really happened. She marched from the room, ignoring his snort of pleasure and closed the door. She'd had all she could take of him for a while. She glanced at the kitchen clock on her way to the sink.

"This should take the sting out of him." Rosa counted out Dad's round of medication, the pills clacking on the tray. "At least for a little while."

"It's almost time for you to go home. I'm guessing you can't wait to get out of here."

"I won't lie to you and say differently." Rosa smiled beautifully, a lovely woman with soft brown curls and melted chocolate eyes. "I promised my little ones pizza tonight. Going to pick it up on the way home."

"Does the diner still make to-die-for pepperoni?"

"Yes, and they've added cheese bread to their menu. If you pick up a pizza for your boy sometime, don't forget to get an order. It's amazing."

"Good to know." She upended the bucket with a splash and gave it a good rinse. "Every now and then, I get a craving for cheesy bread."

"Who doesn't?" Rosa found a plastic glass in the cupboard and plopped it onto the faded counter. "Someone just drove in."

"Okay." She dried her hands, listening to the clunk of a car door slamming shut. "Maybe it's Milton, although it's a little early for milking and he usually parks at the barn. I'd better go see what's up."

Curiosity drove her through the house. Three trucks were lined up in the driveway. She spotted her dad's truck first, next to Hunter's parked in the shade of the house. When did he get here? Although with the way Dad had been carrying on, she wouldn't have noticed a meteor crashing to earth in the neighboring field.

"Hi, Millie." Cal, the owner of the third truck, tipped his hat. "I would have parked at the barn, but there was no room."

"It's okay. If you've come about your paycheck, I still can't make good on it." The screen door clicked shut behind her as she stepped into the heat and sun. "I'd pay you if I could."

"That's not why I'm here." The ranch hand, in his mid-thirties, dressed in a simple white T-shirt and worn jeans, gestured across the road. "Hunter rounded up a few of us to help out."

"What?" She hopped down the steps, rounded the lilac bush blocking her view and saw pickups parked end on end, crowded around the front of the barn. Voices carried as truck doors shut and her neighbors called out to one another.

"Whip has worn out every bit of goodwill folks have for him," Cal explained. "But it's different now. You're the one needing help. We're here for you, Millie."

Emotion burned in her throat. She blinked, unable to believe her eyes. Hunter strolled into sight from the barn, his hat tilted at a jaunty angle. His granite features softened into a welcoming grin as he greeted his friends and neighbors.

He'd done this. How was she going to keep from liking him now?

Chapter Nine

"I totally have the hang of this." Brandi stomped around the carousel in her barn boots. "Hunter, go on with you. I can handle it here."

"Forget it. I'll leave when you finish the last cow. Everything has to be cleaned—"

"Milton can show me that, right, Milton?"

"Right," came an answer from behind the second carousel.

"See?" Brandi waved him away with a wink. "We've got it covered, and you've been up since 4:00 a.m. Go. You're not wanted here."

He took one look at her smile and shook his head. Sisters. He didn't want her to see his soft side, so he put on an extra scowl and stormed out of the parlor.

"Aw, c'mon, Mom." Across the barn, Simon's distant voice caught his ear. "I can do it, I know I can."

"That's not the point. You're not working in this barn. I did enough of that for both of us when I was your age. Scoot on up to the house. Don't you want to play in the creek?"

"I wanna be where the action is."

A few steps more brought him to the main aisle where he could see Millie, sweeping the slab of concrete where the haystack used to be. Half the winter's hay was gone, broken down and hauled away for compost by the neighbors whose numbers were dwindling. They'd gone home to milk their own cows.

"Hunter, I'll stay for the cleanup." Cal marched out of the storeroom, hefting a fifty-pound sack of grain on his shoulder. "The last group of cows are going through now."

"Yeah, I know." The milking had gone fast with all three carousels full and enough workers to man them. He'd worked hard and fast, moving cows in, getting them milked, detaching the clusters, moving them out, and he'd hardly taken time to look around until Milton had shouldered in and replaced him. He didn't have to ask to know Cal had worked hard, too. "Thanks for being here."

"It's for Millie, and you're paying me to. Glad to be working for you, boss." With a grin, Cal ambled off.

So, the barn work was covered, but there were other chores to do. He pulled Millie's list from his pocket, stepped into the office and hunted down a pen. He crossed the first two items off her list, studying the next one. *Roof.*

Considering the look of the building thunderheads outside, that was a good idea. He crossed the road, breathing in the muggy air. Grass rustled in a rough wind as he fished in the back of his truck for his tools.

He didn't know how long it would take for Millie to figure out what he was up to. The storm threatening to roll in would be nothing next to her irritation when she did, but it would be worth it. A man could only carry a weight on his conscience for so long.

How are the cats? Brooke's text lit up her phone screen. Millie leaned one shoulder against the barn's door frame and tapped out an answer. So far so good. Still hiding under the porch, as far as I know.

"Hey, Millie. I'm headin' home." Jerry tromped down the aisle, his boots sloshing from the cleanup work of the cement slab where the haystack used to be. "I've got cows of my own, or I'd stay longer."

"You didn't need to stay at all, so thank you. You need anything, you call me. Got it?"

"Right." With a grin, Jerry took off. He hopped into his two-ton, the pickup glinting in the rapidly disappearing sunshine. Big clouds had moved in to dominate the sky, veiling the golden ball of the sun. Looked like a hard blow was coming.

Her phone chimed with Brooke's answer. Sorry I had 2 leave the picnic early.

No problem. How R things at home? Millie wrote.

Good. I'm at Colbie's right now, helping with her mom.

It's what family does. Wasn't that why she was here? She crossed the long stretch of lonely road. I'd love 2 get together sometime. But when? I have no free time.

We'll play it by ear.

OK. Have a good evening, my friend, Millie texted.

U, 2.

She slipped her phone in her pocket, looked up, and there was Hunter walking on the roof. Really, hadn't he done enough? She grasped the aluminum ladder he'd obviously brought from his farm, grappled up the rungs and landed on the roof. She picked her way across the shingles. "The last time I checked, this wasn't your house."

"True, but I promised you flashing and because Luke is busy packing for his California trip and those clouds mean business, I thought I'd do it."

Oh, that crook of a grin could still melt her knees. Proceed with caution, she thought, and she wasn't talking about the roof. "Haven't you done enough around here?"

"Depends. I'm trying to butter you up." He fished a nail out of his leather tool bag slung low on his hips and bent to work, his dark fall of hair tumbling across his forehead. *Whack, whack, whack* went his hammer and drove the nail home. "If there's any chance of that. You'll have to tell me."

"It depends on what you want." She crouched beside him, wishing she had a hammer, too. She hated watching when she could be doing.

"I was going to have Luke talk to you about it, but he has other plans. I wanted him to do this for you for a reason." He drove in another nail. *Bang, bang, bang.* "I didn't want you to wonder if I was playing on old feelings."

"You made it clear there were none."

"I wasn't exactly honest with myself." *Bam, bam, bam.* "You are always going to mean something more to me, Millie. I'm always going to want your happiness."

"I see." The gleam of emotion in his violet-blue eyes surprised her, a show of emotion she'd never seen in him before. Was it possible that the man of stone had mellowed a tad over time? Boggling to think about. "Happiness is what I want for you, too."

"Which is why I'm going to chase all the bats out of the attic for you."

"Wow, that's a mighty impressive feat. You're braving bats for me?"

"Not so brave. They don't bother me." He shrugged in a casual, masculine way that said confronting an army of winged creatures was no big deal.

"And all because you want something?" Hard to believe. She watched him hammer in the final nail. "That's not like the Hunter I used to know. He was a straightforward guy."

"I see that grin." He arched one brow, more handsome than

ever. "I have to have a good reason for being here, so don't order me off your roof."

"As if you would follow my orders."

"Exactly." He moved over a few feet and drilled a nail through the curling-up end of a shingle. "Have you given any thought to the hay growing in your fields? It needs to be cut soon."

"No kidding. I'm trying not to think about it, frankly, because I'm still ticked at Dad's harvesting job. Putting up damp hay. He knows better."

"He did it because he didn't want to sell it to me." He stood and hooked his hammer in his belt. "Around late June I realized he was looking sick and knew of his trouble meeting payroll, so I offered him good cash for the grass standing in his fields. He refused."

"So that's why he did the haying himself." Now she understood. Her father had a stubborn streak, too. "So you're here trying to get on my good side so I'll sell to you?"

"Can't hurt a guy to hope."

"You keep hoping." Why play easy to get? "Maybe I should wait for a better offer."

"Are you trying to torture me?"

"A little."

"But you'll let me have the hay?" Pleasant wrinkles crinkled around his eyes, doubling the effect of his smile.

"Sure. I don't see why not." She left the obvious unspoken. The farm and cows would have to be sold when her father passed. No need for winter feed. "By the way, you didn't have to butter me up. I'd have sold you the hay anyway."

"I know, but I needed a reason for you to let me help you."

"That was my suspicion. So, are you coming down?" She inched down the sloping roof.

"I see a few more shingles needing fixing." A flash of lightning snaked across the sky behind him.

"Hunter, I think you'd better—" *Boom!* Thunder rattled like cannon fire across the angry sky. "Forget about them. This roof has been like this for a long time."

"You're getting wet."

"Right, because it's raining."

"Oh, so, that's what this wet stuff is." He grasped her elbow, his grip strong and supportive. "C'mon, let's go. You first."

"There you go being gentlemanly again. You don't have to."

"I wasn't. I figured if you slipped and hit the ground, you'll be there to break my fall."

"Think again, buddy." Raindrops pelted like liquid bullets, plopping on her nose, her head and the shingles beneath her feet, making them slippery. "Maybe you should go first. The ladder looks slick."

"It does." Iron strength, steely muscles. Impossible not to notice as he held the ladder. A white-hot bolt blazed across the sky and thunder shook the house. "Wow, that storm means business. Hurry up. I'm not going to let you get struck by lightning."

"I hate to break it to you, but you're not in control of that." She hoisted herself onto the rungs and her boot slipped. Oops. She clutched the ladder but he was there, his strong hand banding her forearm, holding her safe, determined not to let her fall.

"Easy, now. You're okay. I gotcha." His gaze found hers and locked.

Captive, she couldn't break away. Time froze. The sound and fury of the storm silenced. His violet-blue depths pulled her in, forcing her to see him. To really look into him at the man he'd become. Mountain-strong with rain dripping off his hat brim, far from the same boy she'd fallen for. Time had changed him more than she'd let herself see.

"I'm all right, Hunter." The words sounded foreign, not like her own at all. She didn't feel like herself, shivering hard and not because of the cold rain. "You can let go."

He did, holding the ladder secure as the wind buffeted it, making it rattle. The weight of his gaze was a touch against her face as she went down hand over hand until her toes touched the ground. Don't look up, she told herself firmly, resisting the pull of his presence.

"Okay," she shouted above the swish of wind-driven rain. "Come on down."

"Looks like Milt took care of things. The barn's closed up against the weather." His baritone cut through the thunderclap, easy and light. "Is he still working without pay?"

"Yes. He's a good employee. More than that, really."

"Right, he's a friend. What he's given this dairy, you can't pay him for." *Thump, thump, thump* went his boots on the rungs. "That's true friendship."

"I worry what's going to happen to him when Dad passes." Her troubled sigh said it all as he dropped down beside her. "He deserves a big cash bonus, but I'll be stretched to make good on his back pay."

"Doesn't surprise me." He hefted the ladder away from the house before it fell down, and laid it along the rhododendron bed. "The land is mortgaged to the hilt, isn't it?"

"The cattle, too." She led the way onto the covered porch, her jeans and blue T-shirt drenched, her hair a dark raven tangle. She braced her hands on the weather-beaten rail and gazed out at the barn across the way. "This was an original homestead. It's been in our family for four generations."

"And it's the end of the line?"

"Yes. It will be a miracle if I can sell it before the bank takes it."

"If there was a way to keep it, you wouldn't want to stay here and run the dairy?" He leaned in next to her and watched the rain fall like a gray sheet off the porch roof. "You know how to do the job and you're good at it. And considering you're unemployed, this place might be a blessing in disguise for you."

"I wouldn't do it even if I could." She didn't explain as she swiped the rain dripping off her bangs. She looked pretty in the gray, stormy light.

"Lots of difficult memories here." He bumped her gently with his shoulder. "Understandable. You wouldn't want to live in this house where you were so unhappy. It's where your mom died."

"And where she was miserable." A wisp of hair blew into her face, a soft tangle against her cheek. He brushed it away, trying not to notice her satin skin, warm cheek and the emotional closeness he couldn't deny. Millie'd had it tough here, and still did.

"Not sure I want to raise Simon with those memories hanging around." She shrugged her slender shoulders with an oh-well gesture, tossing him a half smile as if to lighten the mood. "Would you really want us as neighbors?"

Seeing Millie and her son in town, at church, out in the field when he drove by? His heart was getting stronger. "Maybe I could stand it."

"Good to know." Her half grin broadened into a breath-taking full smile that scrambled his senses. "So you might stay?"

"I think it would be better for Simon if we didn't." She didn't elaborate, simply watched the lightning snake across the underbellies of black clouds. When thunder hit, it rattled the window panes. "Thank you, by the way."

"Uh, judging by the sarcasm, I'm afraid to ask for what."

"Offering to lend Simon a horse." She didn't really sound angry. "Without your asking me first?"

"Ah, so there's the problem." He took off his hat and shook off rain water. "I got caught up in the moment. The words were out and I couldn't take 'em back. I figured you wouldn't mind. You like horses."

"Not the point."

"Sure." He studied the hat in his hands. "Sundae's a gentle guy."

"I'm sure he is."

"You'll like him."

"I'm sure I will." She pierced him with a look. "Do I have to tell you this isn't a good time to have the expense of a horse?"

"Sundae comes with his own grain barrel and alfalfa. All he needs is a grassy field, and there happens to be one behind your house."

"You've thought of everything, haven't you?"

"I try. No grass grows under these boots."

"So I see. Let me remind you who is in charge here." Light, breezy, more beautiful than words could say, she faced him, she made the locked doors around his heart buckle. She was not only the Millie he'd known, but also someone stronger. She tossed her tangled hair over her shoulder. "This might be hard for you to accept, but you don't rule the world."

"Never thought I did."

"Next time you get a brilliant idea about anything that involves this dairy, me or my son, you run it by me first." Tough, gorgeous, funny. "Got it?"

"I hear you loud and clear, ma'am." He liked this new Millie. A lot. "You know I don't like being told what to do, right?"

"Deal with it, big guy."

"Then I guess I'd better ask you this before I get into big trouble again. The chances are there might be bats trapped in your attic, thanks to the flashing I just put on. Now, I don't want to assume anything, but I'm thinking you might want me to chase 'em out?"

"Absolutely. Don't let me stop you. Do it now. Right now. Why are you just standing there? Hurry."

"I thought you might say that." Mischief brought out the purple flecks in his eyes. "Hey, any chance you'd like to help?"

"No way. As if. Ew." She shuddered, trying to get rid of the creepy-crawlies trickling across her skin. Getting cozy with a bunch of bats? Not gonna happen.

The screen door banged open behind her and Simon stood in the doorway, his dark hair soaked with rain. "Hey, Mom?"

"Were you out checking on the cats?"

"Yep. I wanted to make sure they weren't scared of the thunder." The boy hopped onto the porch, his wet sneakers squeaking. "Shadow and Smokey were okay, though. They're dry under the porch."

"It was good you checked on them." Hunter spoke up, warm and kind.

"I used to be afraid of thunder." Simon balanced on the top step, letting the rain pour over him.

"Really? Do you need to get wetter?" She would never know what drove the male brain. "In the house, dry off, and I've got to think about supper."

"I already preheated the oven, you know, for the pizza." Simon yanked open the screen door, water flying off him in big droplets. "Hunter, you could stay. It's the frozen kind, but it's pretty good."

Did she really want the man staying a moment longer than necessary? Maybe. He'd been almost fun, and it was this side of him she'd once fallen hard for. No chance of that these days, so why not let him? "If you can stomach it, we'd love to have you stay. After all, you are ridding our attic of bats."

"I'll think about it."

"Bats?" Simon perked up, eyes wide. "Really? Can I help, Hunter?"

"Sure, why not?"

"It's this way to the attic. C'mon, I'll show you."

"That's just what I need. Help with the bats." Hunter's granite features gentled, much to her surprise. What had happened to the man who'd told her he wanted nothing to do with kids? That he didn't like being in the same room with them? "Guess I'll see you later, unless you've changed your mind? Three people chasing bats are better than two."

"Not funny." She stood in the doorway, watching man and boy trail across the living room, similar gaits, similar stances their shoulders braced identically as they disappeared around the corner.

She'd made the right decision long ago, hadn't she? She listened to the echo of Hunter's voice in the hallway. Deep and low, rumbling with softness and warmth. What if she'd been wrong?

Chapter Ten

"There's another one!" Simon's excited squeal bounced around the rafters as something dark and winged dived out of the curtains and flapped around the attic. "Don't hurt him!"

"Wouldn't even." Hunter swiped his fishing net through the air, caught the little creature and carried the drooping net to the open dormer window. Rain splattered the sill and hit his face as he stuck the pole out into the gale, turned the net inside out and gave it a slight shake. The bat clung with its feet to the web, holding on for a moment, getting his bearings.

"He's real weird-looking." Simon clamored up and leaned over the sill. "Will he be okay?"

"Sure. He'll find somewhere to hang low until nightfall. Then he'll have to figure out another home."

"'Cuz he can't sleep here, not anymore. It weirds Mom out."

"Women don't generally like creepy-crawly and winged things loose in their houses."

"But bats just eat bugs, right?"

"Right. They're good to have around in the country." Finally, the bat let loose, spread its bony wings and sailed off on a strong gust.

"Think there are some more?"

"Why don't you go see?" Hunter shook the rainwater off

the handle of his fishing net and something flapped danger-
ously close to his head, soared into the gray clouds and disappeared. Guess that answered that. There were definitely more
bats in the attic.

The wind changed direction, breezing lightly against his
nape, sending tingles down his spine. Those charges of awareness felt sweet as a summer day, and he didn't have to turn
around to know Millie was near.

"Hey, Mom. We've found five bats—"

"Five?" Going pale, hand flying to her throat, she glanced
around. "They're gone, right?"

"And they're real cool. They aren't scary at all, but really
weird-looking, and they don't hurt people." Simon pushed his
crooked glasses up his nose, gleaming with excitement. "If we
catch another one, I'll show you."

"Uh, sounds great, but I really don't need a look. Honest.
I ventured up here because I figured you boys might want to
know the pizza is almost ready. Take a break and come wash
up."

"Good, 'cuz I'm starvin'." Simon clomped across the floorboard, still looking for bats. "Aren't you, Hunter?"

"I'm still debating, kid." He winked, not sure if staying
would be a wise move with Millie looking so pretty. She'd
combed her hair into a sleek dark fall that tumbled over her
shoulders. She'd changed out of her wet clothes and into an
old high school T-shirt that said in cracked letters Prospect
Wildcats. Time-faded denim shorts hugged her lean legs as
she whirled away from him, lithe and breezy and confident.

"Well, make up your mind, bat hunter. I'll just go down
and take the pizza out of the oven." She brushed against an
old bureau, the attached mirror rattled and a small black shape
launched from behind it, winging straight at her head. She
shrieked. "Hunter!"

He was already across the attic to rescue her, net in hand.
She ducked, shrieking again at the creature circling her head.

One swipe and he netted the creature. "Got him. Don't worry, you're safe."

"I am?" She opened one eye.

"Would I lie?" Not on his life. "Want to take a look?"

"Not even." Her mouth curved upward, crinkling in the corners.

He remembered what it had been like to kiss her. Sweet, sweet, sweet. Like Christmas candy and sugar plums and angel food cake all wrapped into one. His chest ached just as sweetly.

"He probably misses his family." Simon tripped across the floorboards hands out. "Can I let him go?"

"Knock yourself out, kid." He handed over the long metal pole, the handle awkward for the boy, but he managed. Tromping over to the open window, he leaned out and gently gave the net a shake.

"Looks like you two are having fun up here." Her tender blue eyes gazed up at him, catching him like a lasso, reeling him in. "Not my kind of fun, but still."

"We're having a blast." Did he want to be reeled in by Millie? No. He meant to take a step back, but his boots stayed stubbornly rooted to the floor. "Looks like we're done here."

"Then you'll stay for supper?" A silent question in her eyes. She wanted him to stay.

Truth was, he did, too. Panic kicked through him. He was already too close to her. Staying would only complicate things. "Thanks, but I've got stuff to warm up at home."

"You mean you cook?"

"I had to learn if I wanted to feed myself. Luke's better at it, he's usually the one fixing dinner for us, but now that he'll probably wind up marrying that California girl, I'll have to go back to figuring out the stove." Humor. It was his only defense. Better to talk about mundane matters and not what was happening inside him. "Remember, if you need anything, you can ask me."

"That's the last thing I want to do."

"I know, but whether you want to lean on anyone or not, you aren't alone. Got it?" Why his hand reached out, he didn't know. His fingers brushed a lock of hair near her eyes, just to touch her.

Tenderness he didn't want rushed upward like a summer breeze, impossible to stop. Tenderness. What was wrong with him? Feeling like this was what he had to avoid. He jerked away, forcing his feet to carry him back a few steps when it was the last thing he wanted…and at the same time exactly what he wanted.

"Thanks, Hunter. I know this isn't easy for you." Her hand landed on his, her touch an electric shock that zinged through him. His nervous system froze, his brains scrambled and his soul reeled. Look at the power she had over him. One touch and he cared.

No way could he let that happen again. "It's not so bad."

"Good to know." Millie's chin bobbed down, her hair curtained her face, as if she wanted to hide her feelings from him.

He wanted to hide his from her, too. He rescued his hat from a stack of cardboard boxes. He was no longer the head-strong, angry young man he'd been, but he was still afraid of loving anyone, especially Millie.

If he were honest with himself, then he had to admit it hurt. Big time. He hadn't realized how much he wished he could have changed for her.

"Here's your net." Simon thrust the handle at him. "That was fun."

"You were a fantastic assistant. Next time I have bat problems, I'll give you a call, partner."

"Deal." Simon grinned wide, so like Millie.

"See ya around." He headed down the steps. There was no other choice. He couldn't stay and risk getting closer to her. His nape prickled under the weight of her gaze; he could feel her watching him, but he didn't look back. His boots hit the carpet in the hallway and he pivoted, one eye on the door, but a familiar voice barked at him through the open doorway.

"Never thought I'd see the likes of you hanging 'round here." Whip coughed, propped up by pillows, the remote control clutched in a skeletal hand. Meanness shone from his gaze as he gave a crooked, cruel grin.

"Howdy, Whip." Best to keep on walking. He heard Millie's footsteps on the stairs behind him, so he headed for the door. Rain dripped off the eaves and blew on the wind, but the storm wasn't loud enough to drown out what was going on inside the house. Whip, calling to Millie. "Get your fat butt over here and wait on me, girl."

"How many times, Dad? I've told you. Don't speak like that in front of Simon." Millie's answer was patient, firm but never cruel. That wasn't Millie.

No, the blame was on him. Every drop of it. He'd been the one to drive her away and he was doing it again. *Lord, You know how sorry I am for that.* He hung his head, clipped down the steps and let the rain beat him.

Finally, Dad was asleep. Millie tiptoed across the floor, the carpet fiber soft against her bare feet, and listened to the even, shallow wheeze of her father's breathing. Propped up, head back, he hardly made a bump in the covers. The glow from the nightlight shadowed him, hid his yellowed skin and the shocking protrusion of bone.

I'm not sure there's anything You can do for him, Lord, but please try. He was her father. Growing up in this house with his yelling and tantrums followed her like phantoms as she slipped down the hall to peer into her childhood bedroom. Simon slept soundly on the far twin bed, turned away from her, his cowlick sticking up like a reminder of the man who kept infiltrating her thoughts.

Just try not to think about him. The day had been long and her head hurt too much to really analyze why he was doing so much for her. She poured a tall glass of lemonade in the kitchen and plopped into a chair at the table, staring out at the dark night. Unpaid bills sat in neat stacks nearby, and both the dairy's and Dad's personal checking accounts stared up at her, both down to the last pennies. How she was going to get them through the week, she didn't know. Her savings account was pretty much tapped out.

Things are going to turn around, right, Lord? She gazed at the inscrutable sky, midnight-black and fathomless. Flashes of distant lightning flashed the underbellies of faraway clouds. It had been a night like this when she'd fled this farm intending never to come back. The memory became vivid and she could feel the bunch of fear in her throat and the tremor of her hands. She'd just taken a pregnancy test and was afraid of the changes to come in her life and of Hunter's reaction, but she'd gathered her courage and she sat down on the front step next to him. The far-off thunder reverberating like doom in the night.

Tell him, she'd thought, dragging in a mouthful of air. Just say the words.

But did they come? No. She hedged, already knowing the answer. How many times had Hunter hinted he was not a marrying man? Not that it had stopped her heart. "So, I was talking with Mrs. Hoffsteader's granddaughter today. She's engaged."

"Huh." Hunter gazed at the sky, watching the flash and bang of the storm. Any sign of softness in him retreated. He sat spine straight, an unyielding silhouette against the blacker night. "Engaged? That's crazy. I feel sorry for her. What's marriage? Nothing but a ball and chain for a man and misery for a woman. Look at my parents. Look at yours. There's not one thing on Earth that would ever make me do something that stupid."

"Nothing?" She hated hearing the thin, desperate hope in her voice.

"Nothing. Never." Hard, biting words. His wall had gone

up. The caring man disappeared, leaving behind bitterness. "You know how I feel about this, Millie."

"But it doesn't always have to be that way, right? I mean, there has to be—"

"Don't do this." He hung his head, elbows planted on his knees, looking like a man in pain. He gentled his words, but the iron rang in them, uncompromising. "You know I'm never going to give you an engagement ring, right?"

"But what about kids?" She picked at the frayed hem of her denim shorts, unable to look at him. *Tell him about the baby. You can do it.*

"I don't want 'em. You know that. Me and kids? Isn't going to happen."

"You never want a child? Ever?"

"Me, want a kid? Not under any circumstances. I'd jump off a cliff first." Bitterness dripped from his words, and she knew he had reason. His dad had been unreliable; he'd run out on the family leaving them destitute. Hunter was hurt over it. That's what he was reacting to. "If you've suddenly got the itch to settle down, get married and raise a family, we're done here. I'm gone."

Hot-headed, just turned twenty-two, he launched to his feet and stalked through the puddles in the driveway. His truck started with an angry roar and sped off, leaving her alone in the dark. Alone with unshed tears in her eyes and a baby on the way he didn't want. How could she tell him now?

As the memory faded, she blinked and found herself in the present, alone in her father's kitchen. A shadowy movement on the other side of the window caught her attention. It was one of the cats crawling out to take a look around. He slunk along the back rail, eyes glinting in the night as he stared at her through the glass. Alarmed, his tail bushed, his back arched and he bolted, likely back to safety beneath the porch.

"Millie?" A faint, wet cough echoed through the house. "Millie?"

"Coming." She pushed away from the table covered with bills and worries, left her lemonade sitting untouched and padded down the hall. The nightlight's glow outlined her dad sitting up against his pillows, something glistening on his face and hands. Blood.

"Looks like you have a little problem." She swiped a couple tissues from the bedside table. Alarm roared through her, but somehow she managed to keep it out of her voice. "Let's get you cleaned up and to the emergency room."

At least Hunter was out of her mind. If only she could keep him there.

He couldn't get to sleep. Tossing and turning frustrated him, so Hunter kicked back his covers, shot out of bed and paced down the hall. Emptiness echoed around him, greater tonight than it had ever been before. Every rustle, every breath, every footfall reverberated in the darkness, gaining strength as if to remind him of his loneliness.

Lonely is better than misery. That had always been his motto, but tonight? It didn't come close to comforting him, so he yanked open the door. The deck floorboard felt cool against his bare feet. He leaned on the rail, letting the night air breeze over his face and ruffle his hair. Felt good after a long, hot day. Thick clouds blocked out all light from moon and stars, so he waited for his eyes to adjust to the dark.

A comforting moo rose from the nearby field. No mystery who it could be. One of his favorite cows, retired from the milk herd and enjoying her golden years as a pet. "Hi, Betty. How's it going?"

Another reassuring moo. She made a dark lump in the soft grass. Only a slight rustle told him she must have laid her head back down and closed her eyes.

He should be sleeping, too, if only he could get rid of the unsettled jumble sitting behind his rib cage. That moment in Millie's attic stayed with him, jabbing him like a sharp blade that wouldn't relent. He'd disappointed her. She'd wanted him to stay and eat supper with them. After everything he'd done to her, she was offering a truce. Why couldn't he accept it?

Because he cared for her. Distance was safer. He rubbed the heel of his hand against his sternum where it hurt the most. Funny how a decade could go by and you could ignore what troubled you. You could set it aside, forget it and go on with your life. But one look from her and there it was, worse than it had ever been.

It was the same look she'd given him that night before she'd left town. Back then, he hadn't understood why she'd brought up marriage and family. Didn't she know him? Angry, he'd stormed away, betrayed by her sudden interest in a wedding ring when he'd been honest from the start. She'd been afraid of commitment, too, but something had changed or she wouldn't have brought it up, and he soon found out what: another man offering her a promise of marriage, one he obviously fell through on once he got her in a family way.

The memory rolled back, vivid and real until it was all he could see. He recalled the honeysuckle blooms bright yellow against green vines climbing up one side of the porch. The cushions Millie's mom had made with the cheerful yellow check against white siding. The flutter of Millie's long, dark hair on the wind as she bowed her head, shielding her face from him.

She'd always been a wee bit of a thing, lean and coltish, petite, but she looked smaller somehow in a white T-shirt and denim shorts. Her bare toes curled around the edge of the step, her shoulders slumped. Her vulnerability had touched him, made him stop, made him long to go back to her and set things right.

But an engagement? Was that what she wanted? His molars had clacked together, gritting his teeth with anger. Not really anger, but it was a good cover for the mess of feelings the thought of a marriage gave him. He heard his mom's sobs of disappointment, the fights, Dad's drinking. He'd been a boy, standing in the hallway at night, listening in, desperately unhappy. That's the way families were, right? One big lie.

He'd yanked open his door and dropped behind the wheel, the hood of his pickup pearled with rainwater. The sight of Millie tugged at him, that woman had a hold on his heart, and if he went to her he'd lose the rest of it. What did he have to give her? The same misery? What if he was no better than his dad? Spending the night arguing with her and then listening to her muffled cries when the fighting ended, the distance between them greater than before.

That wasn't what he wanted to give her. So he'd turned the key, the engine caught and he drove away. What he couldn't tell Millie, who he trusted more than almost anyone, was that he liked the idea of a happy-ever-after with her. But he didn't believe in dreams. Love was for fools and saps. He was neither, so it didn't explain why driving away from her felt wrong. Instinct shouted at him to go back.

He couldn't. Come morning when he went to talk things through with her, Whip took pleasure in telling him she was gone. Bitterness overwhelmed him, knocking the strength from his knees and the softness from his heart. He shook his head, dispersing the memory, letting the night breeze blow it away and bring him back to the present.

Lights flashed to life in the darkness near the barn, headlights on the road going to town. Curious, he zeroed in, recognizing the old-model Fold pickup, too far away to see the driver but the engine's backfire said it all. Whip's truck. Millie had to be behind the wheel. Whip was too incapacitated to drive.

Was everything all right? Worry trickled through him. Not your business, he told himself. He watched the truck motor by, disappearing first behind the barn and reappearing on the other side. A few brief moments and it disappeared again around the corner. Her absence tugged at him, the same way her presence did, a physical pain right behind his sternum.

It wasn't tenderness aching in his heart. He refused to allow it. There was nothing weaker than love. It shattered in an instant, it withered with time and died without warning. He'd never been able to let himself love Millie, and that would never change. He would be a fool if he tried.

Chapter Eleven

Dawn was a pink-and-gold explosion across the eastern sky. Millie took a bracing sip of hospital coffee and kept watching her son sleep on one of the waiting room couches. Covered with a blanket a nurse's aide had fetched for her, hands tucked beneath his chin, he looked lost in good dreams.

She rose from the couch, careful not to make any noise. Aside from the desk nurse, there was no one around, but she didn't feel alone. God's presence accompanied her as she studied the parking lot below. A newspaper truck pulled up to the hospital's portico, slipping out of sight beneath the roof, a reminder that life went on, relentlessly moving forward with news to report and deliveries to make.

Her phone chimed a merry little tone, not loud enough to wake Simon, thankfully. She rescued her cell from her pocket. Likely it was Milton or Brandi, wondering where she was for the morning milking.

Surprise. Hunter's text stared up at her from her screen. Saw U drive by last nite. How's Whip?

Still unstable. Her fingers felt stiff from being up all night and from dread, but she managed to tap out an answer.

I'm sorry.

Not UR fault. She hit Send, smiling a little. She took her coffee cup off the windowsill and sipped in caffeine. This would be easier if Hunter wasn't a decent man.

Don't worry about the milking. Milton's on it.

I knew he would B. Simon shifted in his sleep, sighing, but he didn't wake.

I let Brooke know UR in Bozeman. She'll check in on U. Gotta go. His text popped on her screen, but it was what he didn't say that mattered. He hadn't asked about how she was doing or how she felt. Wasn't that Hunter, though, always shying away from feelings? He liked sticking to the facts and problems to be solved. He had no use for touchy-feely stuff.

Emptiness ached within her. She tucked her phone away, trying not to let it bother her. As if she needed his shoulder to lean on. The last time she'd tried, it had ended in disaster. She eased down beside her son, watching him sleep. Really, Hunter had never been there for her in the ways that mattered.

Another chime interrupted her thoughts. She dug out her cell just as a doctor appeared in the hallway. "Ms. Wilson?"

"Yes." She whisked by a snoozing Simon and faced the doctor, cold with fear. "How's my dad?"

"Stable for now, but his organs are shutting down." Dr. White's sympathy schooled his craggy features, worn by time and experience. Gray tufts of hair stood up on end. Clearly he'd had a long night, too. "He doesn't have much time left."

She nodded, her tongue tying. Beneath all the sharp words and the unhappiness he'd tried to make of her childhood, there did lurk some affection. She hadn't felt it in a really long time, not since she'd been old enough to realize what kind of man her father really was. "Is he comfortable?"

"We're doing our best. He's scheduled for tests this morning. You might want to go home and get some rest. It will take most of the day." He plunged one hand into the pocket of his white coat. "I'm done with my shift, but Dr. Ames will call you with the results."

"Thank you." She took the card he offered her. Sad. Buried somewhere inside her was the little girl who'd loved her dad.

"Mom?" Simon blinked, sleepy-eyed, peering over the back of the couch. "Is Grandpa gonna come home with us?"

"I don't know. Maybe not today." She tried to purge last night's trip to the emergency room from her mind. Dad coughing blood. Simon's worried eyes as he handed tissues to his grandfather. Her fears they would reach the hospital too late.

She smoothed a tuft of her son's dark hair. "You did an amazing job last night. You were a big comfort to your grandpa."

"It had to be scary to be like that." He scrunched his forehead, wrestling with a question. "Mom, is he gonna go to heaven when he dies?"

"I honestly don't know." One thing was for sure, Whip wasn't worried about it. "Your grandpa believes you live and you die and that's it. There is no heaven or hell. There is no God."

"How can there be no God?" Concern bunched up on his button face, as dear as could be.

"I think Grandpa closed his heart up so tight through the years, now he can't feel anything real at all. Even God." She smoothed those wrinkles away. "C'mon, let's go hunt down something to eat."

"Okay." He slipped off the couch, lurching a bit from tiredness.

Only then did she remember her text message. She glanced at her phone, surprised it wasn't from Milton or even Hunter.

Feelin' hungry? Brooke wrote. Follow the direction below & you'll find pancakes, eggs & sausages. Not 2 mention service with a smile.

"There you are!" Brooke bounded down the steps toward the curb, dressed in jeans and a pink smock with cartoon cats on it, looking ready for her job at the vet clinic. "I've been keeping my eye out for you. You look exhausted."

"What gave it away? The bags under my eyes?" Not to mention the disheveled hair, the wrinkled clothes from her attempts at sleeping on one of the waiting room couches and the huge yawn she tried to hide with her hand. She closed the truck's door with a mighty shove, thankful she had a wide berth at the curb. Plenty of space whenever she needed to leave.

"Are you kidding? You look great." Brooke wrapped her in a quick hug. "I wish I could look that good after a night without much sleep."

"You flatterer. Not at all sure what I'm going to do with you." She hiked her purse strap higher on her shoulder, keeping an eye on Simon as he drew in the loose gravel with the toe of his sneaker. "Can't believe you invited us over. It's early, and you must have to leave for work."

"Not quite yet. Hi, Simon. Any chance you like blueberry pancakes?"

"Definitely!" Wide grin, dimples showing, Simon turned them full-wattage on Brooke. "Is my stomach growling or what?"

"I can hear it from here. You'd better go on ahead and feed that monster. Go on." Brooke's gentle manner shone like the fresh morning sun as she waved the kid down the walk. She turned to Millie. "Come with me. How's your dad?"

"Hanging in there. I was afraid last night that would be it, but he's hung in there. He still might."

"It's good you got away from the hospital. Recharge, get something nutritious to eat, get in a nap. I'm giving you my apartment key. You and Simon can hang there for a while. Both Bree and I are at work all day, so you might as well make yourselves at home."

"That's great of you, Brooke."

"It's nothing, really. This might not be the time, but how are things with Hunter?"

"Weird."

"Well, of course, given that it involves my brother." Brooke rolled her eyes, leading the way up the porch steps, next to a wheelchair ramp. Colbie and Lil's home, Millie surmised as she tripped up the steps. "Other than weird, how's it going?"

"Why are you asking?" She slid her gaze sideways, stopping on the porch because a cold hand gripped her stomach. Something was wrong. "You're not hoping we'll get back together, right?"

"Right. Then again, he isn't as gruff as he first appears. Time has mellowed him."

"I noticed." Hard not to. She pushed down the memories, images that tugged at her with unprecedented force. The caring in his eyes, the gentleness in his voice, the way he'd chased bats with Simon. "He's mellowed, but he hasn't changed."

"I keep hoping maybe you can change him."

"Sorry, not interested." She shrugged, wishing she could give her friend a different answer. Simon had disappeared through the screen door, which slapped shut behind him. A lazy breeze stirred fragrance from nearby rose bushes. "Maybe you can find someone else for him."

"Oh, that's not likely." Brooke swung open the screen door. "After all these years, Hunter only has eyes for you."

"No way, because he hates me for leaving. I'm pretty angry at him for letting me go." There, that was the truth, out after all these years of shoving it down. She stepped through the screen door and Brooke followed her in.

In the nearby kitchen, sausage links sizzled, a stack of pancakes sat in the middle of a dinette table where Colbie uncovered a butter dish for Simon. The boy plopped down in a chair and looked at the food hungrily.

"This is really nice of you." So tired, her feelings felt right at the surface. "This beats a restaurant hands down."

"It was Hunter's idea." Colbie smiled, pretty with her cap of dark hair and sweetheart's face. "Good to see you again, Millie. I can't believe this boy of yours. How old is he?"

"Nine." Simon licked his lips hungrily, his eyes on the food. "Did you make faces in the pancakes?"

"Monster faces," came a voice from the behind the cabinets. Bree, Brandi's twin, carried a plate of omelets from the stove. "Faces are my specialty at the bakery I work at. I get to put them on cookies and muffins. Total fun."

"Cool." Simon grinned up at the twin and the impressive omelet platter that slid onto the table. "Can I say grace? Can I?"

"Eager to get eating, are we?" Colbie sparkled with humor as she rescued a full carafe from the coffeemaker. "I'll take Mom her plate. She's still in bed. Go ahead without me."

"Do you need help?" Brooke asked.

"Nope, I've got it covered." Colbie took a plate from the counter and whirled down the hall, out of sight.

A loud growl drew everyone's attention. Simon shook his head. "I told you I was hungry."

"That was your stomach?" Bree plopped into a chair. "Hurry. This kid needs food."

"He needs something." Millie ruffled his fine, baby-soft hair as she settled into a chair beside him. Such a good kid.

"Dear God." Simon folded his hands together, bowing his head. The cowlick in the back stuck straight up, visible for all to see. "Thank You for our daily bread. We are grateful for every cup and plateful, and please love my grandpa even though he doesn't love You. Amen."

"Amen." A lump stuck in her throat. Taking a swallow from the juice glass next to her plate couldn't dislodge it. The boy had a good heart, so like his father's, when he wasn't busy protecting it. Suddenly sad, she grabbed the platter Brooke handed her and forked monster-faced pancakes onto Simon's plate.

"Hunter, haven't seen you in my store in a long time." John Denton stepped into sight from the back room behind his store counter. "The church had a good picnic on Sunday."

"They always do." He unfolded Millie's list. "Looked like your family had a good time."

"Our daughter won the potato sack race. Wild times, my friend, wild times." John's humor rang as warmly as his smile. "What can I do for you?"

"How much for that little TV in front?" He leaned against the scarred wooden counter, tucked the envelope into his pocket, trying to act like this was no big deal. Just doing errands for a neighbor.

Yeah, tell that to his heart. It skipped every third beat, a telltale sign he was on hazardous ground. Did he retreat, change his mind and return her list? No. He hauled out his wallet and thumbed through the wad of bills.

"How does twenty bucks sound?" John offered.

"Like there's something you're not telling me. It works, right?"

"Yes, just fine the last time I turned it on. You helped my parents during the wildfire last year. It was their crop you helped save. Wouldn't feel right to make a profit on you."

"As long as you're sure." He counted out two tens and waved off a receipt. "Thanks, John."

"Not a problem. Say, I happened to notice you spending time with Millie."

"No, don't even say it. Nothing is going on." He tipped his hat in thanks, turned on his heel and snagged the thirteen inch off the display. "See you around, John."

The bell overhead jangled as he escaped onto the sidewalk. He opened his truck door and tucked the television onto the passenger side floor.

"Hey, Hunter." A familiar voice—the minister's voice—called out. "You're an answered prayer."

"Me? That's unlikely." He straightened up and shut the door.

"I just heard about Whip. I've tried calling Millie, but no one's home. I don't have her cell."

"I do." He whipped out his phone and scrolled down the screen. "Has there been any news?"

"Only that he's in stable but serious condition. How is Millie holding up?"

"How should I know?" He tapped out a text. "Millie and I are civil. We aren't exactly what I'd call close."

"Are you sure? There aren't some old feelings still there?" That was Tim, always trying to fix what was broken.

"I don't have those kinds of feelings, trust me." His heart banged against his ribs. What he felt was new, things he'd never been able to feel before. Only a sappy man would go around admitting it to anyone, including himself. He hit Send, and Tim's phone chimed, muffled by his pocket. "There's her number. Give her a call."

"Will do." Tim headed down the sidewalk with a wave.

Hunter tugged the list out of his pocket to double check it. Looked like he had everything. The ride through town went quick, and he'd pulled into the Wilsons' driveway in no time. The lazy country day, the cows grazing in the fields and the empty horse pasture close to the house resonated with lark song as he went in search of the extra key. Still above the doorframe, like always. That made it easy to get in, haul in supplies and the TV and get to work.

He'd do the same thing for any neighbor, he rationalized while ripping open a pack of 9 volts. He hauled a chair from the kitchen and opened the smoke detector in the hallway. No battery. He inserted one, winced at the squawk and hopped down. On to the next task.

The truth followed him around the empty house like a whisper, one he couldn't keep denying. Millie wasn't just any neighbor. For the tenth time, he took out his cell, pulled up her number and his thumb hesitated over Call. He didn't do it, but he wanted to.

How telling was that?

* * *

Why did she keep checking her phone? All evening long, everyone had called—Tim, Brandi, Milton, Cal and even Mrs. Hoffsteader, everyone but Hunter. Why was it his name she wanted to see on her missed-call list?

Millie dropped her cell into her purse, grabbed the truck key and opened the door. The last dregs of sunshine flirted with the tops of the trees crowning the hill behind the house. The day had whizzed by in a haze of sleep deprivation, discussions with doctors and sitting with her father, who was more ill-tempered than usual. Wrung out, she hopped out of the truck, thankful to be home.

Hunter ambled out of the shadows, a hammer in hand. His tool belt slung low on his hips, his Stetson shaded his face. "Hey, you're back."

"And not a moment too soon." She kept her voice low, so as not to wake Simon napping on the bench seat. "Don't tell me you're fixing the roof again."

"The roof? Haven't even climbed up there. Honest." He raised his fist to cover his heart, hammer in hand. The strong line of his jaw softened with the hint of a grin. "You've had a long day. My sisters helped you out?"

"Immensely. They made us breakfast, gave us a place to grab a few hours of shut-eye and a shower and there was their friendship." Her phone chimed with another text. She held up her phone. "There's Colbie now."

"They're good at that. Those sisters of mine are the friendly sort." Grass whispered beneath his work boots as he tread closer. "I was never good at relationships."

"No kidding." They smiled together, the long evening shadows cloaking them. "What are you doing here anyway?"

"You know me, up to no good."

"I do know you, which is why I'm asking."

"I just finished walking the fence line. Nailed in the last new board. It's ready for the horse I promised Simon."

"Good timing." She glanced over her shoulder, watching her son sleep. It was after nine, past his bedtime. "He couldn't keep his eyes open on the drive. This is rough for him."

"And for you."

Was that sympathy in his voice? A note of caring? "I can handle it, but I worry about Simon. This isn't the summer I want for him, full of doctor's appointments, hospital waiting rooms and seeing his grandfather decline."

"He'll be all right. He has you to make sure of it."

"That sounds strangely like a compliment."

"Meant it to be." Warmth, kindness, strength. He moved in, stood beside her, gazed out at the field. "You're a good mom."

"Just trying to be half as good as mine was." A lark flew by and landed on the porch rail, tweeting a merry tune.

Life, so vivid and bright and magnificent, surrounded her, yet the sadness from the hospital remained, clinging stubbornly. She wasn't sure why, but the feel tonight of shadows in the air and impending darkness made her remember the night her mother died of an aneurysm. It had been sudden, without warning and final. One minute she was doing the supper dishes and the next she'd tumbled to the floor lifeless.

"When your mom looks down at you from heaven, she's proud of you." Hunter winced, shook his head, took a few steps back. "Think that's my quota of touchy-feely for the year."

"I'm totally shocked you have a quota at all." She blinked, trying to clear her blurry eyes. Did she want him to know he'd touched her deeply? No way, no how. "You really have changed, Hunter. There's a crack in those iron walls you keep around your heart."

"Don't let that get around. The rumor would spread and the next thing you know, my reputation is shot."

"Your secret is safe with me." She bumped his arm with her shoulder, like old times. He tipped his hat back, revealing a tender gleam in his eyes as he folded a stray lock of hair behind her ear, the way he used to.

She pressed her cheek against his hand, just slightly, unable to stop herself. His gentle touch. It soothed her heavy soul and she longed to step into his strong arms and cuddle against his chest, to lean on him.

"He's sure sound asleep." Hunter broke the moment, turning away. "Want me to carry him in?"

No. That was what she should say. "That would be nice."

With a tip of his hat, Hunter moved away like a part of the coming night. She followed the shadows up the grass to the porch steps and turned the key in the dead bolt, her every sense attuned to the man. The pad of his step, the squeak the truck door made when he opened it, the rustle of blanket and clothing as he gathered the boy into his arms.

She propped the screen door open, tumbled into the entry way and stared at the TV set up in the living room. It was a sleek, slim-screen model, but hooked up and ready to go on a stand brought down from the attic. She sniffed and smelled carpet cleaner in the air. Sure enough, the carpet looked slightly damp. The screens were fixed, there were mousetraps set in the kitchen, the smoke detector blinked overhead, alive once again.

"You did this, didn't you?" She accused him the moment he appeared in her line of sight.

"I found your list. Couldn't help myself." Hunter swung through the open doorway, Simon in his arms. "Are you mad?"

"Pretty much."

"Fine, let me have it. I can take the hit." He didn't look worried. "Where do you want him?"

"My old room, end of the hall, the bed near the window." The words grated up her throat. Overwhelmed, exhausted, she leaned against the wall, fighting the burn behind her eyes. She could cope with disliking Hunter, she could handle never seeing him again. But his kindness? No, it was too much. It was the one thing she couldn't handle.

Chapter Twelve

The last time he'd seen Millie that exhausted had been after her mother died. Troubled, he fumbled through the dark room, stubbed his toe on the foot of the bed and bent to lay the sleeping bundle on top of the covers. Slack with sleep, the boy snuggled into his pillow, lost in dreams.

Weight settled on his chest, compressing his ribs. What would have happened if he hadn't driven Millie away back then? What if he'd realized she'd really been asking him to open his heart and love her? If he had, maybe he would be a father by now, putting his son to bed. Not that he could imagine it. Him, a father? Not likely. But maybe it wouldn't be so bad. It was a cozy feeling, watching the boy sleep and hearing Millie's footfalls in the hallway, knowing she was near.

"Thanks, Hunter." She moved silently, brushing past him. "Sure." He walked away, snapping out of it. What was he thinking? Marriage and family were a misery he didn't want. He left her to cover Simon with a light blanket and turn on the fan. The weight on his chest grew, making it hard to breathe. He tugged the envelope from his pocket, every item checked, and set it face up on the coffee table. He'd done what he came to do. Time to go.

"Hunter?" The moment his boots hit the porch steps, her

voice called him back. She stood behind the mesh screen, biting her bottom lip. He saw the crinkle above the bridge of her nose and knew what it meant.

"You're unhappy." He unbuckled his tool belt. "What did I do wrong?"

"Just about everything."

"That's nothing new."

She stalked out onto the porch, gilded by the last long rays of sunlight, framed by the bright crimson and purple of the encroaching sunset. "I wondered where my list went. How did you get it?"

"Found it in your truck the day I drove it."

"And you just took over without asking me?" She stormed down the steps, a formidable force for so small a woman. Lips pursed, gaze narrowed, slender hands fisted.

"Uh-oh. You look a little mad." He lowered his tool belt into the back of his truck. "I was just trying to help."

"You can't walk into my life and take over." Her voice cracked.

Poor Millie. Time to face it. He cared. He always had. Always would. "I thought I could stand by and mind my own business, but I can't take seeing you unhappy."

"Well, you've made it worse. Having you here like this, pitching in the way you used to—" She didn't finish, ducking her chin to stare at her toes. A muscle ticked along her jaw line. "Look at me. Unhappy."

"Yeah, I see. But it was my only option. You're overwhelmed trying to handle everything. No one, not even super Millie, can do this alone." He added the extra lumber leaning against the fender into the truck bed. "You might not want help, but you need it."

"Fine, maybe you're right." The last sunlight bled from the sky, cloaking her, and slid away to leave her in shadow. "But does help have to come from you?"

"Yes. Some habits are tough to break." He grabbed the last

board and tossed it in. "Apparently, I'll always be here for you, given the chance."

"No, no, you really aren't." She lifted her chin, stalking toward him, hardly aware of anything but the upset driving her. "Sure, here you are taking care of things for me. But you don't get it. All this does is remind me of all the times you were never there for me."

"Hey, I was always there for you."

"You do all this, but what I really need—" She winced, realizing what she'd almost said. She didn't need him.

"Hey, Millie." His fingers beneath her chin forced her to meet his gaze. "What can I do for you?"

"Nothing, not one thing." She felt like an idiot, so angry at him for being thoughtful and neighborly. "You're being a nice guy and I want to throw something at you."

"No doubt I deserve it. Let's see what's around. There are some rocks, a couple of sticks in the flower bed. The hammer from my tool belt."

"Stop trying to make me laugh. You're being so wonderful and I—" Was it guilt tearing at her? Or the fact that his chest looked so strong, the safest harbor she'd ever known? She wanted to be tougher than this. She needed that harbor again, wanting to rest, just to rest, in his arms for one brief respite. For one moment, to close her eyes and listen to the beat of his heart and let his comfort surround her.

Need him? That would be the worst mistake.

"Millie." As if he read her mind, his arms folded around her, drawing her against his warmth. His voice rumbled in her ear. "It's all right. Just relax. It's going to be okay."

It really did feel that way. She pressed her cheek against his cotton tee and rested against him. At last. It felt like coming home to the place she'd always belonged. She let her eyelids drift shut. The steady thump of his heartbeat filled her ear, his muscled arms held her tight as if nothing—not one thing—

could hurt her. Weary, she drew in his strength, felt the fan of his breath in her hair and held on.

Never wanted to let go.

Night fell softly, the shadows darkened and an owl hooted in a nearby tree. She felt his lips against the crown of her head, a tender and chaste kiss, and the gathering of his muscles told her he'd had enough. Gently he pulled away, he was the one who always pulled away. She rocked back onto her heels, standing on her own steam, separate from him, feeling oddly bereft.

"Guess I'd best get home." Caring. It shone in his eyes, deepened his voice and extended the closeness between them, a closeness neither of them wanted.

"It is getting late." She bit her lip, holding back the obvious. They'd tried that before, it had failed. For all the ways he'd changed, he remained uncomfortable with emotional closeness. Would he treat a son that way, too? There for him in all ways except the ones that really mattered?

"Is there anything else I can do before I leave?" The warmth in his tone had never been like this, but he took a step back, pulled his keys from his pocket, leaving. Always retreating.

Just stop wishing he'd keep holding you, Millie. She wasn't ready to let him go. How sad was that? The worst mistake she could make would be to fall for him a second time. "No, go home. I'm just really tired."

"Then go to bed. Get some sleep. Don't worry about the morning milking. Brandi, Milton and Cal have it covered. I think Jerry's pitching in again." He pulled his keys from his pocket, his silhouette black against the night. "You'll probably be heading to the hospital tomorrow?"

"First thing." Stars blinked to life and spilled a silvery glow across the yard, lighting her way to the porch. "I'm thinking about asking Brandi to stay with Simon tomorrow, do a little babysitting. What do you think?"

"I'm sure she'd love to. I'll let her know."

"Hunter, you're doing it again."

"Doing what?" He planted his foot on the running board, hesitating, wondering what he'd done now.

"Forget it. Probably impossible to get you to stop." A half smile closed the distance between them, turning yards into inches. The power she had over him boggled.

"Okay. Whatever I did, I'm sorry." He rubbed the back of his neck. "Maybe it's best to apologize up front."

"Good strategy."

She stopped on the porch step, awash with starlight, surrounded by darkness. Tenderness ached within him with a force he could no longer deny, a force he'd never known before. It was a power that held no regard for the barriers around his heart. Ridiculous, feeling this was. He wasn't foolish enough to go down that road with Millie again. Love was for saps and fools. Love failed you. It always let you down. End of story.

But for the first time in his life, he didn't want it to be like that.

"Good night, Hunter." Something that sounded strangely like affection knelled in the soft notes of her alto. Affection? No, that couldn't be right. Millie had never really loved him. How could she care about him now?

"See you tomorrow." He had to fight his instincts to go to her and protect her from the world. He gritted his teeth, held his ground and popped into the truck. "I'm praying it's a better day for you."

"Thanks for everything you've done. The list. Everything."

"My pleasure."

She lifted three fingers in a little wave. His instincts shouted at him to go back to her, but he had to do what was right. Giving in and caring for her would be a colossal disaster, even if she seemed utterly solitary, sweet Millie without her smile.

Just be smart and drive away. He closed the door, plugged in his key and rolled down his window. Her back to him, she opened the screen door, stepped into the light and disappeared from sight. The door closed, the living room lights blinked on and here he was, hurting over her.

Lord, help me. He sent a prayer heavenward because he needed fortitude. Getting himself to stop caring for Millie would take Herculean willpower. Maybe even a miracle.

He backed around and nosed his truck down the driveway. The lights snapping on through the house filled in his rearview. He thought of Millie. The scent of her lilac shampoo clung faintly to his shirt and like a key turning the lock on his heart, he could not stop the click. Maybe it was inevitable.

Hunter. Why couldn't she get him out of her mind? Millie's fingers gripped the steering wheel, yanking hard to manhandle it around a curve in the road. She blinked against the too-bright sunshine, her eyes were sensitive from a bad night's sleep.

Again, Hunter's fault. He'd been the reason she'd tossed and turned, praying for sleep. Morning had come and even well into the day, the brush of his kiss in her hair and the security she'd felt in his arms still dogged her. It had followed her around all day at the hospital, talking to doctors, listening to test results and now on the drive home. Hunter.

Why couldn't her gray stuff come up with something else to dwell on? There were certainly plenty of other things to worry about. Namely, her passenger in the truck, which would be her father.

"Bet this is a disappointing day for you." Whip leaned propped up against the locked door, halfway sitting and lying down. "Having to bring me home like this. You were probably hoping that'd be it for me."

"Of course I don't want you to die." Honestly. She gave the truck more gas, watching the speedometer needle zip upward. It had been a long day. "Why would you say something like that? To upset me?"

"Upset you? Girl, you're too sensitive. I'm saying it because it's fact. Don't think when I'm gone that you're getting the farm. That's why you really came back, didn't you?" Cold blue eyes glittered. "What? You don't have anything to say? Not even a tear of disappointment?"

The last turn in the road never looked better. Relief poured through her. If only this drive would end. "I know you're not feeling well. Maybe you should close your eyes and rest."

"Not feeling well? I'm dying." A spiteful grin tugged at the corners of his mouth, turning his hollow face skeletal. "I know that's something you can't face. You pretty it up with fairy tales of heaven and a kindly Father. You're weak-minded. That's why you're after my money."

Bite your tongue, Millie. Don't say what you think. The man is coming home to die. She wrestled the truck off the road and bumped up the driveway, as she was going a tiny bit too fast. She hit the breaks, experienced a mild case of whiplash, and gave thanks from the bottom of her heart. They were home. Hallelujah.

"Hey, Millie!" Brandi looked up from her paperback, where she rocked back and forth on the porch swing. "Simon and I got your dad's room all ready. Fresh sheets, new batteries in the remote. Even have lunch in the oven."

"You are a gem. Thank you." Her sneakers hit the ground and she choked in the powdery dust rising up from the driveway. "That was beyond the call of duty."

"I like to stay busy. I couldn't help myself." She plopped her book on the cushion beside her. "It's my nature."

"So I see. Did you mow the lawn?" She blinked, realizing how short it was, glittering green and neatly trimmed.

"No, Hunter did yesterday, but we watered it this morning, didn't we, Simon?"

"Yep." He stood up clutching his handheld video game. He thumbed up his glasses, the adhesive tape holding them together beginning to fray. "We went into the shed to find a hose. Things are living in there, Mom."

"Great." She shivered, making a note to either scare out

whatever creatures had taken up residence or never to go in the shed at all. The latter sounded like the best deal. She rescued her purse from the seat and tugged out the brand-new glasses case. "Here you go, kiddo. Try to make these last more than a month."

"No guarantees." Simon loped over. "Hi, Grandpa."

Nothing but a grunt by way of an answer. Dad must have run out of steam. Being mean looked mighty exhausting.

"We'd better get him in." Bracing for more verbal abuse, she circled the truck with Simon dashing companionably ahead of her.

"Look! It's Hunter." A grin split the boy's face as he went up on tiptoe to wave.

A pickup lumbered up the driveway, towing a horse trailer. Sun glinted and sparkled off the windshield as the truck stopped. Dust flew, the door opened and an artery strummed in her throat at the sight of the strapping man hopping to the ground. *So* not prepared to see him again.

"Oh boy!" Simon took off, feet drumming. "I thought you'd ride him over or something."

"Not if I wanted to bring all his things." Hunter tipped his hat, his gaze sharpening when he spotted her. "Hope now's a good time?"

"Sure. As good as any." Why did her voice crack like that? Because she couldn't stop remembering last night tucked in his warm arms, that's why. Was he remembering it, too?

"Is that Whip in the truck with you?" He ambled closer, slow and easy, like a man who wasn't affected by why he'd held her last night. As stoic as granite, his gaze collided with hers. "Why isn't he at the hospital?"

"I got tired of arguing with him." She shrugged. "So I gave in and brought him home."

"Don't trust those places." Whip's mouth compressed into a sour line. "They're full of doctors."

"I see." Hunter strode closer, his dark piercing gaze unwavering. "Millie, you look exhausted. Worse than yesterday. Didn't you get any sleep?"

"I had a lot on my mind." How did she tell him he was the cause?

"Let me get Whip inside for you." He spotted the folded-up wheelchair in the truck bed. He seemed grim, as if he realized her father could no longer walk on his own steam. "Why don't I bring over some lumber and make a ramp. If I have your permission."

"That would be a big help." She ignored the quirk in the corners of his mouth. She was too tired to get upset at him doing more for her. In truth, she really needed help.

"Good. I'll do it as soon as we get the horses settled."

"Uh, horses? As in two of them? That wasn't our agreement."

"Sure, but you don't want Sundae to get lonely, right? Wouldn't you like to spend time with Lena again?"

"Lena?" Her pulse stalled as he eased close.

"Yes, your old horse." His hand cradled the side of her face, his palm sun-warmed and slightly callused. So tender. His touch telegraphed comfort that words could not convey. The power of it burrowed into her heart, hooking deep.

"I can't believe you still have her." The horse he'd bought for her.

"Couldn't bring myself to part with her." He dragged in a breath and steeled his chest. "Don't go reading anything into it. I tried, but I never found the right home for her."

"Right." She didn't look as if she believed that. Her gaze softened, maybe seeing too much of him.

That was close enough for now. He pulled away, full of emotions he'd be a fool to analyze. Best to get Whip in the house and settled. Concentrate on getting things done so he wouldn't have to run into these feelings again.

"Okay, Whip." The window was partly down, giving him a view of the top of the man's head. He was partially sitting against the door, propped with a pillow and covered with a blanket. Not a good sign if the man was cold on a ninety-six degree day. "Careful now, I'm opening the door."

"Did I ask you to help?" Whip's tone could cut metal.

"No, but someone has to." He opened the door carefully, catching the old man, who was apparently too weak to hold himself up. Another not-so-good sign. Millie must be taking this hard. He thought of his own dad and wondered how he'd feel if the man were dying. What if time were running out for the chance for his father to change?

"Do you want this here or on the porch?" Millie asked, and he didn't need to turn and see what she meant. She'd taken charge of the wheelchair.

"On the porch." He gathered Whip in his arms, ignoring the wince of sadness at the man's fragility and carried him up the steps.

Millie bounded ahead, carrying the chair, and set it on the shady porch. He couldn't help noticing her quick and graceful movements, and concern tucked into adorable crinkles in her forehead.

"Don't think you're worming your way back into this family," Whip growled, settling into the seat. "I'm not gonna change my mind."

"Not expecting you to." He reached for the grips, but Millie beat him to it, taking charge of the chair.

"My back thanks you, Hunter." She gestured toward the stairs.

"No problem." The pull of her gaze roped him in and made him care. Things had gone too far. He was no longer sure he could control it. "You need anything, holler. I'll be nearby getting the horses settled."

"Look at Simon." The kid had climbed onto the trailer's tailgate, chatting away to the horses. Appreciation chased some of the weariness from her face. "You've done a good thing for him."

"I liked to ride at that age." He clomped down the stairs. "Couldn't get me off my pony. Luke and I rode from sunup to sunset in the summers."

"Strange. I can't picture you actually enjoying anything."

"Ha, ha." His smile crinkled his eyes. Talk about attractive. A little zing gripped her heart. It would be crazy to fall for him again. Nuts. Bonkers. Looney-tunes.

"Get me in the house," Whip spat out with a frown. "I'm tired of waiting while you two flirt and lust."

"Dad, that's a horrible thing to say. Honestly. You're not even close." Face flaming, she whirled the chair toward the door and didn't look back. "And in front of Hunter, Dad? You have a terrible mind."

"You're awfully defensive." Once he found a nerve, Whip liked to push. "Don't go getting yourself in trouble again, girl."

It was tempting to walk away and leave him there helpless in his chair. To make him realize that she didn't have to help him. She could have stayed in Portland. In fact, she was sorely wishing she'd done just that. It took all her self-discipline to keep going. With her teeth clamped shut, she aimed the wheelchair down the hall. He's dying, remember, she told herself. Be kind. Don't rise to his bait.

"One brat is bad enough." His bitter frown grew, apparently unhappy he wasn't getting a big enough reaction. "Not that I mind the kid so much. At least he can carry on the family name."

As if that was the important part of having a grandchild. She'd left the door open behind them and the sounds from the yard blew in with the wind. Simon's dear voice full of excitement as he chattered away about the horses. Love flooded her heart, and it gave her strength to keep going. She angled the chair into the bedroom and brought it alongside the bed.

She got him into bed, took off his slippers and handed him the remote. His TV roared to life, drowning out all sounds from outside. She could no longer hear Simon's voice.

"Get some rest, Dad." She hesitated at the doorway, wishing, just wishing. That he wasn't in pain, that he didn't take pleasure from hurting others, that he could be different.

Everyone had good in them. Her father's had faded over time, becoming less and less, until it was impossible to see. It was the choices a person made that determined the value of their heart. Whip had chosen himself over others so many times now there seemed to be no good left.

I do feel sorry for him, Lord. She left the room with a prayer in her heart. *I don't know what can be done for him, but please do what You can.*

The music of Simon's laughter drew her to the living room window. Sunshine blazed, green trees rustled in the breeze and her son trotted across the newly mown grass, lead rope in hand. A black-and-white pinto followed him eagerly. A beautiful animal, mustang-strong, with lithe legs made for running and a thick white mane. So good to see him happy, conversing away with the man at his side.

It was hard to tell what dominated her heart as she watched Hunter swing open the gate, holding it while boy and mustang headed into the pasture. Love for her son, that was surely what this must be and not affection for the man who spotted her at the window and gestured for her to join them. All the denial in the world couldn't change the hint of gentleness in his violet eyes, an openness in him she'd never seen before.

Like a lasso to her heart, she was caught. Trapped by an invisible tie too strong to fight.

Chapter Thirteen

Didn't look like she intended to come out of the house. Hunter tried to deny the tick of disappointment, but no good. It washed over him, the sorry sap that he was. He swung the gate shut, holding it in place.

"Hey, Hunter!" Simon's face scrunched up as he worked at unclipping the lead from Sundae's halter. "I think he really likes me. How cool, right?"

"Right." He croaked out the word. His thoughts slid right back to Millie. Probably a smart move to stay in the house, safe from whatever this was building between them. Good choice. He should applaud her for it, for saving them both.

Happy, boyish laughter cut into his thoughts. The mustang liked the boy, nibbling his hair, lipping his shirt to give it a tug, seeming to take delight in making the kid giggle. A curl of fondness settled behind his ribs. Now that was just plain crazy caring for Millie's son.

"Hey, here's Lena." Brandi sauntered over, lead rope in one hand, rubbing the mare's silky nose with the other. "I'm sure going to miss riding you, girl. Totally the best part about hanging out on my brothers' ranch."

"What? I thought I was the best part." With a wink, Hunter swung open the gate.

"Of course that's what I meant. What was I thinking?"

Brandi unclipped the lead and patted Lena on her sleek, white neck. "Go on, girl. Check out your new digs."

The mare ambled through the open gate, long tail swishing. Head up, ears pricked, she surveyed the large field full of tall grass and dotted with wildflowers and nickered her approval. Sweet girl. He patted her neck as she walked by and closed her in. His knees buckled when he caught sight of a slim, dark-haired woman crossing the lawn toward them.

Millie. So she'd decided to come out. His throat snapped shut, his palms went damp, and he stood there like a fool.

"Couldn't resist coming to see my girl. My long-ago girl," Millie corrected. Her gaze found his and filled with a message only he could understand. There were no words, just feelings. He couldn't ignore them if he tried.

"She missed you." It wasn't what he meant, but at the glint of recognition in her blue depths, he knew she understood. He'd taken care of Lena all this time for her. Not a day had gone by when he hadn't.

"I missed her. We had a lot of fun together, didn't we, girl?" Lena nosed in between them, nodding her head, nickering excitedly. "All our trail rides. Snuggles in the field. Rides to the diner for ice cream. Good times."

"Good times together." Picnics in the forest, horse rides to town, moments reading in the haymow, walks in the rain. It was the past he saw, but also a possible future. His heart squeezed with the force of the wish. Could it come true? Why did he want it so much, he who did not believe in love?

"Hey, lunch is out of the oven." Brandi's call from the porch sailed to them. "Want me to keep it warm?"

"We won't be long." Millie's elegant fingers trailed up and down the mare's nose. "Will you stay this time?"

"Might as well." Didn't want to seem over eager. Didn't want her to think he was softening. It was the only protection he had. "Gotta eat sometime, right?"

"Right. Can't have you feeling faint in the pasture when there's more work to do."

"Honey, I don't ever feel faint."

"Too macho. Sorry." She rolled her eyes. "My mistake."

"I should think so. I'm tough as nails and don't you forget it." He wished it were the truth. He wanted it to be because then he'd be tough enough to stop the wash of affection rising up and to keep his hand from covering hers. Smaller, much smaller, compared to his own, but touching her felt right. The connection charged through him with the power of a thousand suns lighting up the dark places in his soul.

How had she gotten past his defenses? He didn't know. The walls were down for the first time in his life.

"I think the hose is still out so we can fill the water trough." Unaware of his feelings, she squinted into the sun swept field. "Or, Simon, did you and Brandi put it away in the shed? The shed with crawling things in it?"

"More crawly things?" He leaned in so close he could see the light blue threads in her irises. "I can check it out."

"No, I'm pretending they're mice and once the cats start prowling around, they'll take off for a distant part of the field."

"Whatever gets you through the day." He didn't know how it happened, but his lips grazed her forehead. Quick, brief, silken wisps of her hair tickled his nose and caught on his jaw as he pulled away. One look at the surprise on her face made him take off in search of the hose. "Crawly things don't bother me. How about you, Simon?"

"No, sir!"

"Want to come help me?"

"Yeah!"

He kept going toward the house, feeling the tangible sensation of Millie's gaze. How was he going to hold back his feelings now?

"Looks like they are getting along, right?" Brandi plunged her hands into battered oven mitts, motioning out the kitchen window.

"Right." Millie fumbled with the plates. They clacked together and she almost dropped them on the counter. Totally clumsy, proof of how much Hunter was affecting her. His faint rumble of baritone and Simon's muffled answer sailed in through the open window over the sink. There they were with Simon leading the way, hands clasped around the green garden hose. Hunter followed, carrying the heavy coil, unwinding it as they headed toward the big metal tub in the sun field.

Looking at him, she could almost believe nothing was out of the ordinary. As if he hadn't kissed her. She almost didn't believe it herself. It was a total shock.

"They're two peas in a pod, aren't they?" Brandi set the casserole on the table. "So alike, you can barely tell them apart."

"What?" Her knees gave out. The plates hit the counter with a deafening clatter.

"Shadow and Smokey." Brandi gestured toward the back window. "Look at them. They must be feeling more comfortable here."

"Yes." The cats. Jolting panic subsided. What a relief. Sure enough, two fuzzy faces peered in from the other window. Curious green eyes watched every movement inside the kitchen. "I know they're wild, but they look like they want to be friendly."

"Maybe it's just a matter of trust. Maybe they were pets at one time. They could have been abandoned or abused and wound up alone in the wild." Brandi pulled off the mitts and hung them next to the oven. "They seem to like it here. Hi, guys."

Realizing they'd been spotted, alarm widened feline eyes, the cats streaked away, diving for cover.

"Maybe I can entice them with a little milk." Brandi yanked open the fridge. "I'm going to win them over yet."

"Go for it." Millie grabbed a bowl from the cupboard and handed it over. But where was her brain? On Hunter's kiss. What had it meant? Was it a friendly kiss or was it more? Absentmindedly, she set the plates around the table, hardly noticing Brandi pouring milk and carrying the bowl outside.

Hunter could be sweet. Today he'd been open and genuine with his emotion instead of closing up and pushing her away. The touch, the kiss, the feeling of being close to him made her see him anew. Tough as iron, yes, but had he finally learned how to open his heart?

She peeked out the window, drawn to the sight of father and son. Sunshine kissed them, the man with his Stetson at a jaunty angle and the boy with a wide grin radiating happiness. Simon slid the hose over a fence rail, Hunter moved in to check it and twist the nozzle. Water sparkled in an arc into the tub. The horses pushed in to investigate. They lipped the nozzle, they nudged the hose and nibbled Simon's hair.

Hunter's hand lighted on the boy's shoulder, a natural touch. He bent down to speak, Simon nodded and they both smiled identical smiles.

Now that the decision was made, she needed to find the right words. Maybe the Lord would help her with that.

"The poor things ran like the wind when they saw me." Brandi waltzed in, platinum ponytail flying behind her as she grabbed the milk pitcher from the counter and kept coming. "Your son will tame them in no time, that's my guess. He has a way with animals I think."

"I do, too." Millie ripped her gaze from the window, hearing a car pull up in the driveway. "Sounds like Dad's nurse is here. I'll get her settled. You may have to start eating without me."

"Are you sure?" Brandi set the pitcher on the table. "I could help, so you could get done quicker. You have to be hungry, too."

"I'll be fine. You have to refuel. You've been running after Simon all morning."

"He did keep me on my toes."

"Tell me about it." She spied Rosa through the mesh and

held open the screen door for her. "So glad you could come on short notice."

"Hey, that's what I'm here for. I'm sorry to hear the news is all." Rosa lowered her voice, her lovely face gentle with sympathy. "I have been praying for him."

"Thank you." If anyone needed prayers, it was her father. She felt a prickle on the back of her neck. Hunter was close and coming closer. She knew it before she glanced over her shoulder and spotted him through the window with Simon at his side. "Come in and get settled. Have you eaten?"

"No, I didn't get a chance, but that smells wonderful."

"Doesn't it? But I can't take credit, not even close." Aware of Hunter and every step bringing him nearer, she bolted toward the hallway. "Brandi made it."

"It's true. I have a talent with tuna and noodles," Brandi chimed in. "Hey, Hunter. Hi, Simon."

"Hi!" The boy trudged across the floor, feet pounding. "We had to get another hose from the shed so it would be long enough, and we saw what was living in there. Boy, was it great."

"I'm afraid to ask." Brandi shivered. "More bats? Rats? Snakes?"

"Raccoons!"

"As far as I could tell, it was just one family of them." The low boom of Hunter's voice drew her attention, freezing her in place. He swept off his hat and raked a hand through his dark hair. Humor looked good on him. "Shouldn't be hard to encourage them to move on."

"How are you gonna do that?" Simon asked, plunging his hands into the stream of the kitchen faucet.

"We'll lure them out with food and board up the hole they're using for a door." His attention focused on her standing in the hallway. His penetrating blue-violet eyes seemed to shrink the room. He'd been good with their son. It mattered so much to her. Affection welled up, brimming her soul in a sudden surge.

"Millie?" Dad croaked from his bed, awake from his nap. "Get your lard butt in here."

Reality intruded, as it always did. She followed Rosa into the bedroom. She had to fight her growing feelings for Hunter with all her might. Falling in love with him could only end in grief.

The kiss to her forehead, nothing but a display of emotion, troubled him. All through the meal, even though Millie stayed with her father, he kept reliving it. While he carried his empty plate to the sink and helped Brandi clear off the table, the experience stuck with him. The sweetness of being close to Millie dogged him, refusing to let go.

"Look, Brandi." Simon went up on tiptoe, gazing through the window. "The cats drank the milk. They are gonna figure out that we want to be friends with them."

"Yes, they will." Brandi's cheer matched the sunshine tumbling through the windows, but it couldn't pierce the bubble that seemed wrapped around his head. A Millie bubble—all he could hear was the dulcet murmur of her voice down the hall, the comforting lull of her words, the whisperlike pad of her gait.

He'd kissed her. He'd done it automatically and without thought, as if it were the most natural thing in the world. He'd made a big mistake this time and it wasn't only the kiss.

"Our old neighbors had a cat, and I used to take care of Roger when they went on vacation." Simon scooped the empty glasses from the table, dutifully carrying them to the sink. "He purred real loud, like a motor, when you scratched his chin. We had to move to come here. Shadow and Smokey are sorta mine now, too, right?"

"Right." Brandi tugged open the fridge putting things away.

Hunter tried to pay attention, but his senses were sharpened to what was going on down the hall where Millie was. Sounded like Whip was giving both Millie and the nurse's aide a hard time. Footsteps padded in their direction, but it wasn't Millie. He knew her gait by heart.

"I've been sent out to eat before you put lunch all away." The home-care nurse swept in.

"Dig in, absolutely." Brandi snared a clean plate out of the dishwasher. "What would you like to drink? Juice? Milk?"

"Water, and you don't need to wait on me." She flushed a little, passing him by to fill a water glass for herself.

"Hunter?" Simon called to him. "Can I go down and pet Sundae again?"

"Sure, kid. He's yours for as long as you're here." Really, really hard not to like that boy. He listened to the drum of steps, the slam of the screen door and reached for the serving spoon to fill Millie's plate.

Family life. He'd never thought much of it, and always tried his best not to. Inevitably it pulled up memories of his childhood, Mom's disappointment, Dad's failures and the chaos that made everyday life difficult to navigate. But it had been pleasant talking with Simon over tuna casserole. The kid was funny, and Millie made any house seem like home, even if she wasn't in the room.

He shook his head, surprised at himself. He was getting soft, wanting what he didn't believe in. That didn't stop him from wanting.

Brandi was busy making the nurse's aide comfortable, so he grabbed a paper napkin and Millie's fork from the table and veered down the hallway. No sound came from the room. When he shouldered through the partly closed door, Whip lay sunken and motionless in bed, as if asleep.

"Hey, what are you still doing here?" Millie, face pinched, clutched the wooden arms of the chair where she was sitting. "I thought you'd be home getting ready to start haying."

"That can wait another day." He lowered his voice, doing his best not to look at Whip. It was sad what that man had to show for his life and sad that it was almost over. "We still haven't talked price for the hay."

"We don't need to. Sending Brandi and Cal over to help, fighting the fire, finishing my to-do list, being good to Simon. No, I owe you."

"Impossible. I've been keeping a running tab."

Her smile, even a sad one, could put hope where there'd been none before. She rose from the chair. "Is that for me?"

"Yeah." He jabbed the plate at her, embarrassed by his softer side. "Take it to your room and eat. Rest, maybe sneak in a nap. I know you'll be up watching him tonight."

"A little alone time sounds nice." Worry and exhaustion marked her face. Her lovely, lovely face.

"Then do it. Don't worry." He'd better play it smart and not kiss her again. "I'll sit with him until Rosa gets back."

"I shouldn't." Her stomach growled, and she blushed. "Oops. Okay, maybe I should eat."

"Do you think?" Gently, so gently, he moved over to her and held the door. Fine, so he wouldn't kiss her but he couldn't stop his hand from reaching out to cradle the side of her face. A man could get lost in her big blue eyes.

"I don't know what I'd do without you." Caring shone from within her, not just appreciation, not merely gratitude, but something bigger. Something pure and grand and true. "Just forget it, okay?" He couldn't hide the love in his voice, didn't try.

She slipped from the room, leaving him unguarded and overwhelmed with too many feelings to sort out.

"Still sweet on her?" Whip croaked, cracking open one eye. Slitted, that light shade of blue shone cold. He spoke between heavy breaths, hampered by an oxygen mask. "Didn't you learn your lesson last time, boy?"

"You'd better rest, Whip." What he felt for Millie…he swallowed hard, unable to complete the thought. He didn't do love. He'd always fought loving her. But this time around was dif-

ferent and he was fighting a losing battle. Not that he'd admit
it to Whip. "Take it easy. You don't look so well."

"I'm dying. It's life. You live, you die." He sucked in air,
wheezing as he fought to speak. "There is one thing I'd like
to get off my chest before I go."

"You're turning red, Whip." A little alarming to see the man
struggling hard to breathe. "Let me get the nurse."

"He's yours." Whip's clawlike grip clamped around Hunter's wrist, clinging tight.

"What are you talking about?" Did he mean Simon? He
shook off Whip's hold. "I'm not going to let you mess with me."

"She kept it secret. Kept him from you." Menace twisted the
man's gaunt face. "You don't believe me? Ask the boy when
he was born. Eight months and two weeks after that girl ran
away from here, disgraced."

"There's no proof he's mine." It couldn't be true, his brain
couldn't process it. A hum filled his ears. Pain roared through
him. He hated lies. "You've done what you've set out to do.
Hope you're proud of yourself."

"Yep." Whip's grin twisted, apparently pleased that as weak
as he was, he still possessed the power to hurt.

It had to be a lie told by a dying man. His feet hit the hall
carpet without remembering leaving the room. The affection
he felt for Millie was gone and the anger came back. He felt
torn up, remembering her long-ago betrayal. Whip was lying,
taking pleasure in spreading unhappiness, just like always.

"Hunter." Millie stood stock-still, frozen in the middle of
her bedroom doorway. Jaw dropped in surprise, she stared at
him, her silent apology so sincere no way could he miss it.

Whip wasn't lying. The boy, Simon, really was his son.

Chapter Fourteen

"Hunter. I'm sorry." She was slack with shock, unable to believe what her father had done. "So, so sorry. You shouldn't have learned it this way."

"I should have known." His teeth clacked together. A muscle bunched along his jawline. "Simon is mine."

"Y-yes." A terrible ripping sensation traveled through her, rending her in two. No way could she look him in the eye. His boots were braced, planted on the carpet like a man ready to fight. His powerful hands balled into tight, white-knuckled fists, proof of the fury he held back.

"I'm sorry." She'd say it a hundred thousand times if it would make a difference. Oh, the pain carved into his face broke her heart. How did she make it better for him?

"Sorry?" Fury lined his face in deep furrows. "You think an apology can fix this?"

"I wish it could." More than he could possibly know.

"With you it's one lie after another. Remember you told me about Simon's father? How he didn't help out, how he didn't want Simon?" he bit out through clenched teeth. "Why didn't you tell me then?"

"I didn't know if I should." Honesty was all she had. She drew herself up straight, bracing for the rage she rightfully deserved. "Although what I told you was true. Simon's father didn't help out. He didn't want kids."

"I was twenty-two and I was an idiot." He jerked away, wrath radiating from him as he stalked to the door. "I had a messed-up childhood, no different from a lot of people's, but I let it affect me."

"Affect you? No, it was more than that. How many times did you tell me marriage was stupid? That it was a—"

"A ball and chain for a man and misery for a woman. I know, I said it a lot, but we're talking about a child here. You were carrying him and you kept him from me."

"I did." There wasn't an excuse big enough to justify what she'd done. "I denied you your son and Simon his father. You should hate me for that."

"Hate you? You just don't get it, do you?" He slammed through the screen, his boots pounding on the porch boards. The door smacked the side of the house with the force of his temper and ricocheted, banging shut. The sunshine didn't dare touch him as he raged down the steps. "You took something from me you can never give back."

"I know." Tears burned in her eyes, blurring her vision, but she refused to let them fall. She pushed through the door. "I wish I could."

"Those coupons in the grocery store. Handing back crackers because you couldn't stretch your budget." He fished his truck keys out of his pocket. "That's the life you gave my son? Squeaking by as a single mom. That was better?"

"Hey, I've done a good job providing for him." Except for the last nine months, but plenty of people had been affected by unemployment lately. That wasn't her fault. "I work hard to make sure Simon has everything he needs."

"Everything but a father." Bitterness twisted his granite features and he turned away, as if he couldn't stand to look at her. He yanked open his truck door and strain rippled across his shoulders. Vibrating with anger, he hopped onto the seat.

"I need to go. Wrap my head around this. Tell Simon I'll be back tomorrow."

Beneath his anger lurked an equally powerful pain. Pain he would never share with anyone. That wasn't Hunter's way. Never show weakness. And love? That was definitely off-limits.

She wrapped her arms around her middle, hating that she wanted to comfort him. Now that he knew the truth, he was going to hate her forever.

"Find someone else to fix things around here." He rolled down his window, not meeting her gaze. The engine roared to life. "I'm done."

Bitter words, his wounded heart shining in his eyes. A hurt that looked too deep to fix.

Please understand, she tried to tell him, hoping he could read it in her, but he drove away. The strength left her knees as she watched his pickup speed down the driveway, leaving behind a cloud of dust. Only then did she put her face in her hands and breathe.

"Mom?"

A tentative voice cut through her grief. She lowered her hands, blinking hard. Simon. How could she have forgotten about him? "Hi, kiddo. How are the horses settling in?"

"Okay, I guess. They're eatin' grass." He plopped down on the porch step beside her.

Calm down, she told herself. Simon was what mattered here. "Do you like Sundae?"

"Yeah, a lot." His face scrunched up in thought. "Is Hunter really my dad?"

"You heard that, huh?"

"Yeah." He shrugged. "He was really angry."

"Angry at me, not you. Never you, sweetheart." She slipped an arm around his shoulders, pulling him close, holding him. His little-boy scent, his hair tickling her chin, the cozy-close feeling of her son. Priceless. It was an experience Hunter had never known. "How are you feeling about this?"

"Okay, I guess." He blew out a sigh, troubled. "He didn't want us?"

"He didn't know about you. I told you when you were little he just wouldn't be in our lives, right?" She prayed with all her heart that Hunter could be the father her son deserved. "He's coming over tomorrow."

"Yeah, he told me when we were setting up the hose for the water trough. He's gonna teach me how to ride. I won't do it if you don't want me to."

"I want you to be happy. That's all that matters." It was why she'd left this house in the first place, so she wouldn't raise her child anywhere near Whip. It was why she'd left Hunter, so Simon would never have to face his cold rejection. "For the record, I think you should give your dad a chance. You both deserve to see what can happen."

"Okay." He paused, bit his lip, considering things. "I really like him."

"Me, too." They smiled together, just like always. Some wounds could be mended, but others? No idea. She glanced down the road, where the dust cloud lingered, hovering in the air like the ghosts of the past that would never leave.

"He has a cowlick just like mine. I noticed when he took his hat off to eat with us." Hope lit him up. "I've been kinda wondering anyway."

"You have? You could have said something to me."

"He has dimples, too. And when you said you used to date him." A shrug of his shoulders, a tentative grin. "I just started hoping. A little. You know."

"I see." Maybe she should have been worried about his figuring out the truth instead of everyone else. "Are you sure you're okay?"

"Yes, Mom." He rolled his eyes and shoved off the step. "I kinda like it here."

"Me, too." She watched him go, kicking at the dandelions in the lawn as he went. At least he seemed to be handling things okay. That was all she could ask, considering.

"Millie? Your father wants to come sit in the sunshine." Hinges squeaked as Rosa eased open the screen door. "I wanted to check with you first."

"As long as he feels up to it." She stood, feeling wooden and hollowed out, like nothing would ever be the same again. She looked toward the hillside, the trees hiding any view of Hunter's property from sight, but she knew he was there, somewhere. Was he still hurting? Down deep, was he glad at the news?

There was no way to know. She followed Rosa into the house, praying for the strength to deal with her dad.

How could she deceive him like that—again? He still couldn't believe it. Hunter tossed a wrench into the toolbox, the rattle echoing in the barnyard. He leaned against the tractor's fender, staring into the greasy engine. His mind took him right back to Millie standing on the porch with her arms wrapped around her middle, looking beautiful and adorable and sincerely sorry.

Sorry? What good did that do? His hands fisted, he squeezed his eyes shut, grimacing against building indignation. She'd kept the fact of her pregnancy from him, ran to another man and what? Wound up alone when he discovered the truth? Was that how it played out? He had no idea how a woman's mind worked. He opened his eyes, stared into the engine compartment instead of actually doing his work.

As long as he stayed angry, he wouldn't have to look at other things. Like how hard it must have been for her on her own. How lost and alone she had to be after he'd pushed her away. He clamped his molars together so hard his jaw ached. No, he couldn't start feeling sorry for her. She stole his son. Not one word, not one call, even a letter would have done it. She could have told the truth. She hadn't wanted to. That was what he had to focus on. Once again, Millie's deceit.

"Hey, boss." Cal strode over, boots crunching in the gravel. "Looks like you're about to do some maintenance. Your brother hired me just to help with the milking, but now might be a good time to point out I'm a decent mechanic. If you have work I can do, I'd be happy to turn this part-time job into a full-time one."

"Maybe that's a good idea." He liked Cal, and he was a hard worker. "I'm not getting anything done here. I'm not in the mood."

"You look like something's up. Anything I can do?"

"Woman trouble." That ought to explain everything. It was crazy, here he was a decade later, torn up over the same girl. Hadn't he learned his lesson last time? He frowned, trying to remember the saying. Fool me once, shame on you. Fool me twice, shame on me.

There wouldn't be a third time. He'd make certain of that.

"Yeah, that'll do it. Women. They can really mess you up." Cal winked and plucked a socket wrench from the toolbox. "Then again, they're usually worth it."

"Right." Bitterness flooded him and he stalked away. He couldn't move fast enough to outrun his feelings. Not this time. They stuck with him, locked in his chest, refusing to let him go.

The two late-season calves blinked their sleepy eyes as he paraded by. They stirred from their naps curled up in the soft hay and bleated, their baby moos echoing in the empty barn.

"Go back to sleep, little ones," he told them quietly. "It's just me passing through."

When he hit the end of the barn, he stood in the sunshine, out of steam. He didn't know where to go. He sank down on a boulder, just right for sitting, and rubbed his forehead where tension drilled like nails through his skull.

Millie. He'd never left this valley. If she'd wanted to hunt him down, she could have. He'd been right here, a land owner, living his life, building his business with his brother, living the only dream he could count on. The decent thing—no, the moral thing, would have been to tell him he had a son.

A son. He blew out a breath, overwhelmed. Simon and his fistful of wildflowers. Simon and his bloody nose. Simon's excitement over the horses. Each thought pulled up a memory and an image of the boy, making an invisible lasso cinch around his chest and squeeze tight. It pulled tighter until his entire rib cage felt ready to shatter.

Simon, his son.

Something bumped his hat brim, knocking his hat askew. "Betty, is that you?"

The cow answered by seizing his Stetson at the brim with her teeth.

"Come to keep me company, did you?" He twisted around, not surprised to see her leaning over the fence, waving her prize in the air. "Think you're pretty sassy, don't you, stealing my hat?"

Chocolate brown eyes sparkled at him full of love. Hard not to get on his feet and pet her.

"You're nothing but trouble, girl, you know that?" He rubbed her behind the ears, just where she liked it. "Don't know why I put up with you."

She batted her long curly lashes at him, confident of the reason why. Betty had figured him out long ago.

"Just don't let it get around," he grumbled. "It would ruin my reputation for sure."

He leaned back against the fence rails, more tangled up inside than ever. At least his initial anger had dialed down to a background simmer.

Now there was a new one. Millie had roped him in again. He should have known better, but no, he just had to help her solve her problems. Why? Maybe it was time to be honest. He'd done it because he wanted to see her smile. He wanted to be near her. His feelings for her, that was the problem. And that kiss he'd given her—he squeezed his eyes shut, ignoring the sunshine on his face and the soft plop of his hat falling into the grass. Despair overwhelmed him. If this was what caring got you, he wanted nothing to do with it.

Betty lipped his shoulder, offering sympathy in the only way she knew how.

It had been a miserable afternoon. She couldn't escape it. As the stepladder wobbled on the carpet, Millie splayed a hand on the living room wall to steady herself and risked going up on tiptoes. Her fingers wrapped around the old curtain rod, she wiggled it loose from its moorings and dust rose in a nose-stinging cloud. At least a bat didn't come out, too. See, there were still a lot of things to be grateful for.

And Simon. Always Simon. Her gaze strayed to the boy in the field. Carefree, he tromped through the tall grass along-side the black pinto mustang, exploring Sundae's new home together. Looked like the two had struck up an instant accord. What would happen now? Hunter had changed. Would he want Simon? Would he fight her for custody?

Worry quivered in her stomach. She couldn't make it stop. Maybe concentrating on her work would distract her, not that it had yet. She shook the rod, the curtains plopped to the rug and she choked on more dust. Obviously they hadn't been washed since Mom died.

The oven timer beeped. She hopped down, her feet hit the floor and she scooped up the dusty curtains. She dropped them into the laundry room, zipped to the kitchen and plunged her hands into oven mitts.

The warm, fragrant aroma of banana bread filled the air as she removed four loaf pans from the oven. She set them on racks to cool. That made a dozen loaves sitting on the counter, each one golden brown and perfect. There was enough for each man who'd come to help with the barn fire and to deliver along with the former milkers' paychecks. The milk check had come in the day's mail. Relieved at that, she spun the oven knob to Off, tossed the mitts into their drawer and heard a car in the driveway.

Hunter? Icy skittles zinged through her, leaving her shaking. Was it him? So not ready to see him, she peered through the doorway and spotted a pickup. It wasn't Hunter's. Big relief. Mr. Hoffsteader hopped down, lifted a hand to wave and ambled around the front of his truck. Adorable Myra Hoffsteader waited for her husband to open her door, placed her hand in his and slipped daintily to the ground.

Now there was true love. Millie propped a shoulder against the doorframe, watching the pair. His devotion, her adoration.

Nothing could be more beautiful.

"Millie!" Myra bustled over carrying a covered casserole. "I see you're doing some housework. Can't say this place doesn't need it."

"I'm doing my best." She held open the screen. "Come in, both of you. I'll pour you a glass of lemonade."

"Oh, we just dropped by to give you this." Myra ambled in, leaving her husband to settle on the porch swing. "I wanted to be sure and be the first to bring over a meal. Whip may not be a member of our church, but you and your son are."

"This is very kind of you."

"You're one of us now. We all loved your mother. Janice was such a sweet soul. She'd want us to lend a hand. How is your father doing?"

"Sleeping. His nurse is watching over him." He'd stayed on the porch for about thirty minutes, but it tired him out. His exhaustion concerned her. "We're doing our best to keep him comfortable."

"You're a good girl, Millie." Myra slipped the dish on the counter with a clunk. "Now, put this in the oven at two-fifty for forty minutes. All it needs is a warm-up. My, it looks like you've been busy in here. Your mother's recipe?"

"How could I use anything else?" She grabbed a box of plastic wrap and tore off a length. "I owe a big thanks to a lot of people. Mom's banana bread seems like a good start."

"Where's that boy of yours?" Myra glanced around, as if looking for him. Her bright eyes squinted, her gray curls bobbed.

"He's out with the horses." She nodded toward the window, her hand busily wrapping up a warm loaf. "Hunter brought over a little mustang for him to learn to ride on."

"Wasn't that nice? It must be hard to see Hunter after all this time. I noticed you two talking at the church picnic."

"I can't deny it." She handed over the delicious-smelling bread. "Here. It's best when it's warm."

"You remind me of your mother, dear." Myra took the bundle, breathing in deep, her smile nostalgic. "She used to bake for others, too."

"We used to bake together." So easy to remember her mother's voice filling the kitchen, the pad of her shoes and the squeak of the oven door as she peered in at the baking bread. Of being a little girl, happy just to be with her mom. She walked Myra to the door. "Thank you for the meal. I can't tell you how much it helps."

"My pleasure." Myra beamed. "Now, what I'm about to say might not be any of my business, but can I keep from poking my nose in? Oh, no. No one probably knows what Hunter went through after you ran off, he's the sort who keeps to himself, but I saw. I'm his neighbor."

"I was hurt, too." Myra was right, this really wasn't any of her business, but she didn't want to be impolite. "Thanks again—"

"No, you need to listen to this, dear. I know your son is his. With those dimples, no, there is too much of Hunter in the boy."

"How long have you known?"

"In the grocery store that first day you were back." Myra's sympathy wreathed her gentle face. "That's when I realized what a terrible thing your father had done."

"My father?" That was a surprise. "What did he do?"

"After you left, there was a rumor going around that you had another beau over in Bozeman you were seeing on the side. When you ran away from home, you ran to him." Emotion glinted in Myra's eyes. "Guess who likely started that rumor."

"My dad." It sounded exactly like something he would do.

"I heard him in town confirming it anytime someone would ask if it was true. I'm sorry, honey, was I wrong to tell you?"

"No. I'm glad you did." She patted Mrs. Hoffsteader's hand and opened the door for her. "This explains a lot."

"The rumor about destroyed Hunter. He loved you dearly, Millie, even if he wasn't the sort to admit it." Full of caring, Myra gave her a hug. "I'm not so old that I can't see he feels the same way now."

"No, not Hunter." She could not imagine that. Even with all he'd done for her, and that kiss— She squeezed her eyes shut. *Do not think about his kiss.*

"Are you two gals done shootin' the breeze?" Mr. Hoffsteader ambled over. "That bread smells so good, my stomach is rumbling."

"Well, Millie, guess I'd best get home and feed him." She sparkled, a woman in love. "Call if you need anything, and you think over what I said."

"I'll try." She watched Mr. Hoffsteader guide his wife down the steps and help her into his truck. Some loves lasted, that was clear. Other loves were never meant to be.

Chapter Fifteen

The *who, who* of an owl accompanied her through the dark house. Her reflection stared back at her in the curtainless windows; she hadn't gotten the chance to put them up. The sleeping house echoed around her as she padded into the kitchen. Simon's most recent bouquet of wildflowers sat on the counter.

Not bothering with a light, she snagged the lemonade pitcher from the fridge, fished a clean glass from the dishwasher and poured. She sipped the icy drink in silence, listening to the refrigerator click on and hum. Outside a raccoon prowled the back porch rail, stopped and peered in at her through the window. Hunter had been right about the raccoons in the shed.

Hunter. She couldn't afford to think about him. When she did, her chest felt ready to crack. It was too bad she could no longer deny the truth she'd been fighting. She'd fallen in love with the man a second time, a man who couldn't love her back. Never would.

Her Bible sat in the dark, the white cover reflecting the faintest light as if to draw her closer. She set her glass on the tabletop, slipped into a chair and fingered through the fine, gossamer pages. Those precious words had helped her through every hardship, encouraging her heart and uplifting her spirit.

I never could have made it this far without You, she prayed.
Thank You.

All she had to do was to keep going. Now that the milk
check had come, she'd been able to prepay two of the milkers
for the next week. She'd be able to eke by for the rest of the
summer. She no longer had to accept his help in the barn every
day. That was progress, right?

"Millie?" A weak voice rasped through the dark. "Millie,
are you there?"

"I'm coming, Dad." She pushed from the table. She didn't
like how weak he sounded. When she hurried into the room,
only the nightlight's glow illuminated him. He seemed to
shrink in the last few hours, his face more skull-like than ever
as the night nurse, Sara, finished adjusting his pillow.

Terrible dread clutched her. "What do you need, Dad?"

"I'm cold." He bit the words out as if his being chilly was
her fault.

With a resigned sigh, she grabbed a throw from the chest
at the foot of the bed and shook it out over him. "Better? I can
get another if you need it."

"This'll do," he growled. "Sit down and stay with me. I can't
stand having strangers around."

"The nurses are here to help you. You get that, right?" She
drew the chair closer to his bedside.

"I don't need their help," he rasped out. "I told that doctor
I didn't want them standing around watching me die and figuring out what stuff to steal."

"I'm sorry, Sara," she told the night nurse who rose from a
chair in the corner. As if there was anything valuable in this
house, she thought. Honestly. "Why don't I take over and give
you a break."

"Fine by me." Sara passed by, stopping to squeeze Millie's
hand in understanding, and disappeared down the hall.

Weary, she pulled the chair closer. "Maybe you should close
your eyes and try resting, Dad."

"Should I? If I close 'em, I might not be able to open 'em again." He tried to chuckle but coughed instead. Apparently, he thought dying jokes were funny. "What? Get that look off your face. It's a fact of life. You live, you die. You're weak if you can't handle it."

"You weren't always like this." Seeing him like this, wasting away, brimming with hostility and spite made it impossible to believe there was any good in him. There was once. She dropped into the chair, leaning close. "Remember when I was little and we would go to the town's Fourth of July Days at the park?"

"Haven't thought about it in a long while."

"Me either." She shrugged as the memories unspooled from a different time. Dad had been young and energetic with good health, his hair thick and dark. His laughter had boomed above the cheer of the crowd as she'd knelt in the sawdust, holding up her find. A shiny quarter. "Good goin', girl!" he'd called, while beside him Mom clapped, pretty and sweet in a sundress. Encouraged, she'd kept digging through the pile along with the other kids, discovering wrapped candy and a dollar bill. She ran to her parents with both fists full and handed over her treasures for Dad to hold, so she could dig for more. "It's a good memory. I'd almost forgotten."

"You were a little thing back then." He grunted the words without a hint of emotion, as if that time meant nothing to him.

She hoped it did somewhere and that down deep beneath the hard man he'd become lived a speck of affection.

"I don't know what happened to you, but you used to be cute." His tone softened a hint, but that was all. If he was capable of feeling love these days, it didn't show. He closed his eyes and let out a breath.

He was gone.

"Dad?" She stopped breathing. Icy shock rolled through her. "Dad?"

"Let me see." Sara bustled in to check his pulse and shook her head. "I'm sorry, honey."

"Me, too." Grief clogged her throat. Hot tears spilled down her cheeks. She felt sorry for the stubborn, selfish and cruel person her father had become. She cried for the good side of him, as small as that side had been, for the dad who held her candy, who cheered her on, who had taught her to ride a tricycle.

She didn't know where a soul like Whip's went when his life was done, but she prayed God would have mercy on him.

Cold steel. That's how he had to be. Hunter hopped out of the truck in Millie's driveway, pocketed his keys and adjusted his hat brim to cut the long rays of the morning sun. Distant, that was all he had to be. Civil. Chances were good he could probably do it.

"Hi."

The kid startled him. The boy—his son—popped out of the tall grasses beyond the lawn. It didn't take much to see the hopeful glint in deep blue eyes, so like his own. Why hadn't he noticed it sooner?

Because he'd been too hurt by the past to even consider that Millie's child could be his. He'd seen what he'd expected to—Millie reflected in her son—because he hadn't wanted to wonder about the stranger he'd assumed the father to be.

"Howdy, there." He heard the harshness in his tone, proof his defenses were all the way up and full strength. He blew out a sigh. Not what he needed to be for his kid. "What've you been up to?"

"Filling the water tub to the top." Wet patches all over the boy affirmed he'd been playing with the hose. "Sundae and Lena were thirsty. I wanted to take good care of 'em."

"Looks to me like you're doing a good job. Did you feed them grain this morning?"

"Yep. I carried a bucket all the way from the barn." Simon

marched across the lawn with his glasses sliding down his nose. His dark hair stood straight up as the wind ruffled it.

My son, he thought, feeling it in his heart.

"It wasn't too heavy, and the horses were sure glad to see me comin'." Simon hopped alongside him. "They leaned against the fence and neighed and tried to take the bucket from me when I dumped it in their trough. They were funny."

"Sounds like it." He saw himself in Simon's face. Dimples. The nose. The way he tilted his head to one side when he thought. "When I come back later today, after I cut the hay, I'll make good on my promise."

"Good, 'cuz I really want to learn to ride. Really, really, really. Mom says it's a lot of fun, and I like horses. What's your horse's name?"

"Dakota." His chest squeezed. He'd never much thought of being a father, had always associated it with doom, but clomping up the porch steps next to this little boy just turned him inside out. He prayed he wouldn't mess this up too much. "Is your mom inside?"

"Yeah." Simon hung his head, gave a sad sigh and his feet slowed to a stop on the porch. "She's busy gettin' the house ready."

"Ready for what?" Then it hit him. No home-care worker's car in the driveway. The hollow feeling of loss like a hush surrounding the house. "Did Whip pass?"

A single nod.

"I'm sorry." His hand rested on the boy's small shoulder. Sorrow for his loss and fatherly affection filled him up with way too much feeling. The magnitude was nearly too much to handle. "Are you sad?"

"A little. He let me watch TV with him sometimes. It would have been nice to have a grandpa."

"I know what you mean, kid." People you cared about weren't always what you needed them to be, or weren't good for you to be around. No way did he want to be that for his son. "Do you want to talk about it? Your grandpa dying is a big thing to deal with."

"Nah, I'm good." Simon squared his shoulders in a grown-up way. "But Mom's not."

"Want me to talk to her?"

A vigorous nod. A silent plea.

"Then that's what I'll do." Comforting Millie was the last thing he wanted to do, but he had to deal with her. She was his son's mother. "I'll be out in a bit, okay? Maybe you can show me the cats before I go."

"Okay." Simon lit up some. "I've almost got one of 'em coming up to me. I've got to have a bowl of milk, but still. We're almost friends."

"You keep at it." He ruffled the boy's hair, fighting the affection crowding his rib cage. Trying to stop his feelings had become second nature. Something he had to learn to quit. Resolved, he yanked open the screen and stepped inside the house that felt empty and hushed, proof death had visited.

The carpet muffled his gait as he crossed the living room. A bunch of cardboard boxes still flattened and waiting to be folded leaned against the wall. Others had been made into boxes, half full of picture frames, books and what looked like a serious collection of old Western DVDs.

He caught sight of her in Whip's room on her knees sorting clothes from an open dresser drawer. Lost in thought, she didn't notice him, so he took a moment to notice her. Strain bunched tightly in her delicate jaw. She'd drawn her dark hair into haphazard pigtails. She wore an old white T-shirt a size too large with a streak of dust across one shoulder. Her cheeks seemed hollow and dark circles bruised the skin beneath her eyes. Her movements were jerky as she shook out one of Whip's shirts, studied it and tossed it in a box.

She must have spotted him out of the corner of her eye. Her spine snapped straighter. Her jaw muscles clamped ever tighter.

She didn't look at him as she scooped another shirt from the drawer. "Hunter, I didn't hear you come in."

"Simon told me about Whip." Awkward, not sure if he dared to come closer, so he hung in the hallway. "I'm sorry about Whip."

"Thanks." She hurled the shirt into the box, her tone clipped.

She was holding in a lot of pain. If this had been yesterday and before he'd known the truth, he would have knelt beside her and gathered her in his arms. He would have let her lean on him and hold her against his heart. He'd have let his softer feelings for her rule him.

But not today.

"Hunter, because you're here we should talk." She pushed off the floor, moving slowly. His guess she'd been up all night. "About Simon. I—"

"I don't want to hear it." His words boomed in the hallway, magnifying them, and he winced. Not so hard, Hunter. You have to make this work. "This isn't the time. I'm still too mad to talk this through."

"I see." She bit her lip, that vulnerable little crinkle setting in above the bridge of her nose. "That's wise. It must take some time to adjust to news like that."

"You stole my son from me." Iron control, he reminded himself. "I can never get those years back. It's going to take a long time before I can accept what you did."

Again, harder than he meant. He watched her shoulders sink in agreement. Millie was a good person, and that made this harder because it wasn't black and white. He pulled a check out of his pocket and thrust it at her. "It's nine years of child support."

"No." She held up her hands, backing away. "I can't accept it, Hunter. Not your money."

"Too bad." He dropped the check on the dresser. "You will take it. I don't know what kind of father I am yet, but I'll never be the kind who doesn't support his son."

"Fine, but I can't accept it." She glanced at the amount scrawled across the face of the document. "It's way too much."

"That's your guilt talking." Again, too harsh and it wasn't what he meant. How did he tell her that behind the fury was hurt? "It's what a judge would have made me pay if I'd known. You'll take the money. That's the end of it. Now, I have a question for you. With Whip gone, how much longer will you stay here?"

"Just long enough to clear out the house, help the attorney with the estate and make sure the animals are taken care of. No idea how long that will take. Probably a few weeks." She crossed her arms over her chest, a barrier over her heart, and asked the question she dreaded most. "Are you going to fight me for custody?"

"No, but I want him to stay with me for a while this summer."

"For h-how long?" Air stalled in her chest. She'd never been apart from him, aside for a few sleepovers he'd had at friends' houses.

"For as long as it takes. Face it, when you're done here you'll need to find a new place to live. I'm assuming you still want to go back to Portland. It might be easier on Simon to stay here with me while you hunt for an apartment. Plus this way I can get time to know my son." Not a flicker of emotion marked his face. Cold, controlled anger radiated from him.

Didn't he know her guilt was too much to deal with? Besides, how could she say no? "You want him for just a few weeks, right? Until school starts?"

"Don't worry, I won't fight you for custody." What could have been a hint of tenderness broke the intense force of his gaze. "All I want is to be a part of his life. That seems fair."

"More than fair." Especially for a man who hated her and what she'd done. Hunter really had changed. "It would be good for Simon to spend time with his dad."

"Then we'll work out the details later." He turned to go and hesitated, seeming uncomfortable. "I've always been afraid what kind of father I'd make, but I l-love that little boy. I'll do my best for him. If I fall short of being a good dad, I can count on you to point it out."

"That's a promise." Tears prickled behind her eyes. He had no idea what his words meant to her. This was about Simon. It had always been about Simon.

"You probably have things to do at the funeral home and with the lawyer, huh?" He took a step back, putting more distance between them. "I know this can't be easy for you."

"Keeping busy helps. I have errands to run. Things to do for the funeral." Pictures to go through, flowers to order and decisions to make on the service. "I can't believe he's gone. It's such a shock. I thought there was more time, you know, that he would be here a while longer. But his heart just stopped."

"If it's easier, I can keep Simon busy today for you." Cords stood out in his neck, evidence of his tight control.

"Good idea. Hanging with you might be better for him than tagging along after me."

"Okay." His hands fisted at his sides, his only reaction. "I've got hay to cut. He might like helping me drive the tractor."

"I think he would." This was what their relationship had become. Polite conversation and so much distance between them Jupiter felt closer. Her gaze slid to the wide expanse of his chest, remembering how comforting it had felt to lay her cheek there and feel his arms fold around her.

You don't need him, Millie, she thought, but it wasn't true. She needed him with all the depth of her spirit and every fiber of her being.

"All right, then. Call when you want me to bring him back." Rigid, a controlled force, his indifferent gaze raked over her, betraying no emotion. He pivoted, his back to her, and didn't say goodbye.

Time to admit one more undeniable truth. She didn't just need him. She loved him, the man he had become, and he would never feel the same way. He didn't have it in him.

Chapter Sixteen

"That was cool." Simon bounced through the sunshine, full of pent-up energy. While being cooped up in the air-conditioned tractor for a few hours had been exciting, it hadn't run him down any. "I think I'm a pretty good driver."

"I'd say so." Funny kid. Hunter had let the boy take the wheel, and although some of the cuts hadn't been exactly straight, the boy had gotten a kick out of it. Sharing the time with his son had put a cozy feeling in his chest he'd never felt before. He liked it. He led the way around the barn. "Glad Brandi took over for us. Now come on over here. I want you to meet somebody."

"Who?" Simon skipped along beside him, up and down like a yo-yo. Watching him made the cozy feeling go up a notch.

"It's one of my best buddies." He cut around the back of the barn and slipped two fingers into his mouth. The shrill whistle echoed across the field. Two acres away, a red horse looked up from grazing. The gelding answered with a nicker and a head toss and sailed across the green pasture toward them. "That's Dakota."

"Awesome."

The sorrel gelding really was. A registered American quarter horse with a champion lineage and a big heart, Dakota was one of the best working horses around. The animal loped up to the fence with majestic grace and a flip of his silky mane. His chocolate eyes zeroed in on the little boy. Eager to say hello, Dakota arched his neck over the top rail and lipped Simon's shirt. The boy laughed, the horse snorted and they were friends.

"I like him." Simon tipped back his head gazing up at Dakota's immense beauty. "I'm guessin' he can really run fast."

"So fast he beats my brother's horse every time." Hunter ruffled the boy's dark hair. "Want to help me saddle up?"

"Oh boy. Do I get to ride him?"

"We'll ride him together to your place, how's that? Then we can round up Sundae and start your first riding lesson. What do you say?"

"I say it's a plan. Oh boy, this is really gonna be fun. Can Mom come, too? Her horse is there and everything."

It was incredibly hard to look in those eyes and say no. But how could he say yes? Hanging around Millie was not how he wanted to spend his time.

"We'll have to see. C'mon." He took Dakota by the bridle, opened the gate and led the horse to the barn. He showed his son how to saddle a horse. The boy talked the whole while, watching every step of the process while Dakota stood companionably, lipping the kid's hair every time Simon bounced into range.

He'd saddled up thousands of times in his life, but doing it with Simon changed everything. He wasn't prepared for the cinch of emotion around his chest, banding tighter with every breath. His natural instinct was to shut it down and close it off, but it was too late to even try. What he felt was too great and powerful to stop.

"Are you ready to ride, cowboy?" He slid his boot in the stirrup and swung into the saddle.

"Sure. Maybe we can see how fast he can run, what you do think?" Simon squinted up at him.

"Let's take it one step at a time. Step one is learning to stay on the horse." He took his foot out of the stirrup for Simon, caught the boy's hand and up he went.

"Wow." The kid settled onto Dakota's back. "This is like in Grandpa's movies, except we aren't in the Wild West."

"Well, some folks think there is a lot of the Wild West left in Montana." He gathered the reins in one hand. "Hold on and I'll show you."

In answer the boy's arms snaked around Hunter's waist and wrapped tight. The band around his heart tightened hard and fast with love so forceful that it ached in his chest.

Instead of taking the paved road, he nosed Dakota along the pathway up the hill. Betty mooed as they passed, tail flicking. The roll of Dakota's gait, the clop of his shoes on the earth and the sweetness of riding with his son made it a stellar day. A day he would remember forever. This was the start of his life as a dad.

Simon asked this and that, and Hunter did his best to answer. They followed the path up the hill along a shady grove of trees. Every step the horse took brought them closer to the Wilson property. His anger returned when he thought of Millie.

What had she been doing keeping a secret like that? How many times had she had the chance to tell him the truth since she'd been back? He'd filled in milking for her, fixed her roof and finished her to-do list and not once while he'd been right there in front of her was she honest with him.

Dakota stepped around the trees, onto the Wilsons' driveway and the house came into sight. Hunter's gaze shot to the windows and there she was. Her ponytail swung with the force of her cleaning as she washed the living room walls with a scrub brush. Not the casual swish of someone doing a light cleaning, but the hard, I-mean-business scouring of a woman on a mission.

He closed his eyes, willing the image of her from his mind. He refused to let the softer feelings he harbored for her rule him. Somehow he had to get control of them. Stay angry. Stay in control.

"Mom! Look!" Simon's holler caught her attention. She looked up, set down the brush and came to the sill.

"I see." She smiled out, giving the window a shove to open it wider. Her dark hair escaped her ponytail and framed her face in sleek gossamer curls. "You are quite the horseman."

"Just like my dad." Simon's arms, clasped around Hunter's waist, tightened. "I think I've got the saddling thing figured out, so we're gonna try it on Sundae."

"Sounds like fun."

"Can you come and ride, too?"

"I've got cleaning to do, kiddo. Maybe tomorrow, though. You two have fun. Give me a holler if you need some juice." She adeptly avoided his gaze, Hunter noticed, as she backed into the room.

Not so fast. "Hey, Millie."

"What? Do you need some juice?" She arched a brow at him with a hint of humor.

"No. I'm wondering what you're doing in there." The wall of his chest went tight, his muscles bunching protectively. "It's not your home anymore. It's part of your father's estate. Why are you cleaning it?"

"Because I don't want whoever buys this place to have to do a ton of work before they move in." She shrugged her shoulders in a this-is-no-big-deal way. "Someone from the bank is coming out tomorrow after the funeral. I want it to be presentable for them."

"Right." He clamped his teeth together, struggling with anger that he was beginning to realize wasn't really anger. Because she really wasn't at fault. No, not Millie. She'd never changed. He could see it now. She'd always been sweet and good and strong. All her life she'd done her best for others— her father, her mother and now her son. Millie always did the right thing, not the easy thing.

Maybe it was the way the sunlight caught her for one moment in the house, burnishing her with a soft glow. The image flashed him back ten years to the last evening he'd spent with her. Beneath his defensiveness had lurked a small voice he hadn't bothered to listen to. That was the night she'd tried to tell him the truth, he could see it now. And she was right. He remembered what he'd said when she'd asked if he ever wanted a child. *No way,* he'd told her. *Not under any circumstances. I'd jump off a cliff first.*

He hated how those words must have hurt her. How was she to know that that harsh statement was more about his fears of turning out like his father than anything. That wasn't her fault. He saw the past in a whole new light.

"Time to dismount, cowboy." He offered Simon his stirrup and lowered the boy safely to the ground. Dakota, standing patiently, gave a low-throated nicker, as if calling the child over for another round of affectionate nibbling.

Leather creaked as he swung down. He caught sight of Millie through the windows, emptying a pail of wash water in the sink. Regret hit him so hard that his knees buckled. There were things he needed to say to her, but not with Simon around.

"C'mon, kid. Let's get Sundae saddled." He held out his hand and the boy's palm met his, small and trusting, sealing the bond.

Regardless of how hard she tried not to glance out the window, her eyes betrayed her. She went to throw away the ancient vacuum cleaner's dust bag, and when she walked through the kitchen, she saw him helping Simon with Sundae's saddle cinch. Or when she put out food for the cats, the rich timbre of Hunter's voice murmured across the field. Each time she looked away, places in her heart stinging.

You knew it would turn out like this, she thought, putting the box of cat food kibble back in the pantry. She drew the door shut, her movements echoing in the empty house. She felt empty, too, as if sorrow had carved a chunk out of her. She leaned her back against the counter, staring out at the back porch where two gray heads popped into sight, making sure she was a safe distance from them before scampering to their food bowl.

She took a sip of lemonade from the glass she'd left on the counter. The ice cubes had melted into little slivers. Simon's laughter sailed in through the open window, drawing her attention. Just seeing her boy happy lit her up inside. He was the bright spot in her life and always would be.

But Hunter was something else entirely. He was never going to love her. He'd never let his walls down. She had to be tough enough to close the doors on her heart and pretend she wasn't in love with him. In time, maybe she could even convince her heart of it.

The rumble of an engine drew her attention. John Denton hopped down from the cab of his box truck with the logo from his secondhand store painted on the sign. He waved at her, striding up the walk.

"Sorry I'm late," he called through the screen door she opened for him. "I had a customer who took her time deciding on a purchase and I didn't want to rush her."

"No problem. The furniture isn't going anywhere on its own." She led the way into the living room. "Would you like some iced tea or lemonade?"

"No, thanks." He whipped open the cover of his tablet computer. "Mind if I wander around on my own, or is there anything specific Whip's attorney wanted to get an estimate on?"

"My instructions were to let you look around. Let me pull down the attic stairs for you—"

"I can get it, Millie. Looks like you've been working hard around here." John had a kind smile as he gestured toward the kitchen counter where her glass sat half-full. "Go ahead and finish your break. I'll poke around on my own. You'll hardly know I'm here."

"Okay."

"Looks like your boy is having fun." He passed by the window. "Hunter's turning him into a true Montana boy."

"Apparently. Simon's doing well with his first lesson." It was impossible to miss the boy's wide grin as he sat astride the mustang, riding in large circles in the field.

"I'll say." John nodded his agreement. "He's posting already? He's a natural rider, just like his mother."

"Maybe." She'd gone to school with John, too. She waited until he'd wandered off to start his appraisal in the attic before returning to her work in the kitchen. Time to tackle the dirt ground into the grooves of the linoleum. But when she went in search of the floor cleaner, the bottle was empty.

Maybe she'd run to town, pick up cleaning supplies, deposit her unemployment check that had come in the day's mail and pick up pizza and cheese bread for supper. Not only was it Simon's favorite, but she wouldn't have to take a cleaning break to fix a meal. It was a total win-win. Plus, she could escape the low, resonant notes of Hunter's voice and the sight of him in the field. He did look amazing with the wind tousling his dark hair. His patience with their son got to her.

Just watching made her fall in love with him even more. There was no chance for her breaking heart as she grabbed the truck keys and headed for the door.

He'd lost sight of Millie in the window. Hunter reined Dakota to a stop.

"Good job, Simon."

"Well, I haven't fallen off yet." Simon shoved his glasses higher on his nose. "And besides, Sundae's doin' all the work."

"He's doing all the trotting anyway." He was beginning to see some things differently. The future, for instance. He couldn't picture it any other way than spent riding with his son in a summer's field. "You have a good touch with the reins. Not too tight on the bit, not too slack."

"When can we go fast?" Impossible not to love the kid.

"Trotting isn't fast enough for you?"

"It's a lot of up and down. It's pretty bumpy."

"Once posting is second nature, we'll try cantering." Yeah, he could really get used to spending his days like this. He was beginning to see his life in a whole new way. He had a son. There were things he wanted to teach him, time he wanted to spend with him. A lot of things had become clear that hadn't been before.

His phone chimed, so he hauled it out of his pocket. The message was from Millie.

Heading 2 town. Quick errand, she'd written.

Need any help? He texted back and spotted her skipping down the front steps, her ponytail rippling behind her. She stopped to bend over her phone screen to answer him.

Nope. Bye. She yanked open the old truck's door, and the squeak from the protesting hinges carried to him all the way in the field.

His phone chimed again. Wondering if she'd spotted the problem yet, he squinted at the screen. The message wasn't from her.

We're on R way back, Luke's message read. Should B there in 3 days.

Good. Hunter didn't like to admit it, but he'd missed his brother big time. He tapped out an answer. R U engaged yet?

I proposed on the beach at sunset.

Figures. Hunter dismounted. His boots hit the ground and he resumed typing. How does that ball and chain feel?

Really? That's what U say? Not, congrats. Not, good 4 U, Luke?

He stared at his brother's words. He hadn't meant to let Luke down. He bowed his head, thinking about typing *I'm sorry* when his phone chimed again.

That's exactly what Dad would have said. Luke's message packed a punch. Not that it was true.

Okay, maybe it was a little bit true.

Or a whole lot.

"Hunter?" Simon dismounted and bent to pick a daisy in the grass. "I've been thinkin'. Should I call you, like, maybe, Dad?"

"Is that what you want to do?" Hunter knelt to pick a coneflower and held it out for the boy to add to his growing bouquet.

Vulnerable blue eyes fastened on his. A little nod. It was easy to remember being Simon's age following his father around the farm, wishing for the closeness that his friends had with their dads. He'd hoped that maybe one day his dad would change. That one day he'd stop turning away, stop scolding and finding fault and become a real dad. The kind you did things with, who hugged you and made you laugh.

"Then it sounds good to me." He took off his Stetson and plopped it on the boy's head.

"Okay, Dad." The hat slipped too low and Simon shoved it up with a smile that outshone the sun.

"Why don't you keep picking flowers for your mom, okay? I need to talk with her for a minute." He gave the Stetson's brim a tug to shade the kid's eyes, patted Dakota's neck and climbed through the fence rails. On the way across the lawn he tapped a quick message to his brother.

Way to go. U and Honor deserve a forever happiness. He hit Send and tucked the phone in his pocket. It wasn't easy to change. He might not be an alcoholic ex-con like his father, but he'd learned a lot of things from him. He could hear his dad in memory as crisp as the brilliant day around him. *Love is for suckers, kid. Don't ever be a fool.* He saw where he'd taken on his dad's belief and used it to protect himself from ever being hurt again. Luke was right.

But Millie wasn't going to hurt him. She had never hurt him. He found her in the old rusted Ford, hands to her face, leaning on the steering wheel. He cleared his throat. "Want me to give you a push?"

She jerked, startled. "Hunter, give me a heart attack, why don't you? I didn't hear you sneaking up on me."

"Sorry, couldn't help myself." He propped his forearms against the hot metal door, peering in at her. "I see you in trouble and here I am."

"Why you?" She quirked one brow, trying to make light of it. "Why can't it be someone else, anyone else?"

"Good question. Maybe that's just the way it is."

"Sort of along the lines of what can go wrong will go wrong?"

"Maybe." The corners of his mouth quirked upward. "Want to pop that in Neutral for me?"

"Done." Her heart felt ripped open looking at him, so she looked everywhere else. At the carport behind her, at John's truck ahead of her, even at the steering wheel.

"Great. Make sure the parking brake's off." He shoved away, his presence drawing her like the gravitational force of a black hole, sucking her in, pulling her gaze inexorably toward him. She couldn't stop it. He braced his hands on the hood and pushed. The truck rocked and rolled and she steered around John's vehicle. When she was clear, she hit the brakes.

"Before you go, I have something to say to you." Hunter's shadow fell across her. He towered at the door, more powerful and handsome than ever. "I get why you didn't tell me about Simon."

"You do?" That was a surprise. "I worried you might never forgive me."

"I was pretty hard on you, and I shouldn't have been. I'm sorry."

"It was a shock. You had the right to be angry."

"No, I lost that right long ago. The way I treated you when you came to me asking about an engagement ring and kids, remember? A smarter man might have figured that one out."

"No comment." Whew, it felt good to have that resolved. Off her chest. To know he wasn't going to hate her forever. "Maybe I should have been braver back then."

"You were plenty brave. I was the problem. Hot-headed and turning into my old man." He grimaced, as if that caused him great pain. "Maybe you didn't know I came to apologize the next morning, but you were gone. You shattered me, Millie. Ground me into dust."

"How could I have done that? Impossible." As if she was going to buy that story. Hunter was just trying to make her feel better, trying to fix the broken places in their past for Simon's sake. "I never meant that much to you. You didn't do love, remember? You don't believe in it."

"Like I said, I was an idiot. Just because I wanted to pretend something didn't mean it wasn't true. I was afraid to love you."

"I know." She looked down, surprised to find her hand still folded in his. "I was afraid, too. We were young. We were both doing the best we could."

"I should have done better. That's something I will do from now on."

"That's good for Simon. We're older now. Wiser."

"You, definitely. Me? Maybe." He was all she could see of the world, his dark hair, his violet eyes, the sun in the sky behind him. "I know why you kept Simon from me. I broke your heart and you didn't want me to break his, too."

"Yes, that's exactly it." He did understand. He really did forgive her. Tears filled her throat, making it impossible to tell him what that meant. That after all these years she could finally let go of her guilt and Simon could have the father she'd always wanted for him. "I only wanted him to be loved and wanted."

"He is loved and wanted." Hunter winced. That had to be a hard thing for him to say, this man who shielded his heart forcefully. "And so are you."

"What?" She definitely, absolutely, no way could have heard

that right. It had to be wishful thinking putting thoughts into her head. "What did you say?"

"I love you." His fingers tightened around hers, holding on, as if he never wanted to let go. "You didn't figure on ever hearing those words from me, did you?"

"No. I'm sure I'm hearing things. Maybe from sleep deprivation, overwork or too much lemonade."

"This is strange for me, too." He'd spent a lot of energy protecting what was never in jeopardy. Millie was loyal and true to those she loved. He steeled his spine, gathering his courage. It was time to go all in, to be the man he wanted to be. The man she deserved. No more holding back, regardless of how hard it was. He had to face what he honestly felt for her. "I've had it all wrong. Life shouldn't be spent keeping your heart safe. Life is about loving, about living with your heart."

"Now I know I'm hallucinating. The Hunter McKaslin I know would never say anything like that."

"Sure, go ahead and rub it in. I deserve it. I'm not done yet." He had so many promises to make her, ones he would move heaven and earth to keep, if she would let him. But there were issues to resolve first. "Your father told me a lie, one that kept me from going after you that morning when I'd discovered you'd left. I believed it then, but all I need to do is to look at you, to really look, and I know it was just another lie of his. I'm sorry I wanted to believe it. I know you, Millie. There was no one else, was there?"

"No. Not in all this time."

"For me either. I loved you, I should have trusted in you. That won't happen again."

"So I see." Tears stood in her eyes but did not fall. She looked so beautiful with her hair in pigtails, down-to-earth and all his. His Millie. "Will you stay in Montana? Let me love you. Let me marry you. Let me be the husband you deserve."

"You're *proposing* to me?" Her jaw dropped and she stared up at him in disbelief. "But you don't believe in marriage."

"I believe in you. I'm pledging my life to you." He went down on one knee, cradling her hand in both of his. Nothing had ever felt so right. "I thank God for bringing us back together because I had the privilege of falling in love with you a second time. I got another chance to get this right. To let you know that what I feel for you is great and real and without end. Please be my wife."

"Yes." A tear rolled down her cheek. He was offering her his heart, the one thing she thought he'd never be able to do. She'd be a fool not to accept it. "I love you. Of course I'll marry you. As long as you're sure about the marriage thing."

"Fine, go ahead and tease me. I deserve it." He rose, framed her face with his hands and caught that lone tear with his thumb.

"This is how it's going to be for the rest of our lives," he promised. "You and me, happy."

"Sounds like a dream." Joy filled her like the incandescent summer day, everlasting, eternal and sustaining. One look into his eyes and she could see he felt the same way. He'd opened his heart to love.

"That leaves only one thing to do to seal this proposal." He leaned in, amusement tugging the corners of his mouth.

"A kiss?" she asked.

"A kiss." True to his word, his lips slanted over hers. He kissed her tenderly, making her feel as if she were the most precious thing on earth to him. He made her feel like his dream come true.

Epilogue

One month later

"You so didn't fool me," Brandi said, seated on the backyard picnic table as she cut her slice of wedding cake with a fork. "The minute I saw Simon, I knew he was Hunter's."

"The minute? Please." Brooke shook her head, laughing, and scooped a frosting flower off her piece of cake with a finger. The reception was as casual and comfortable as the wedding had been. "I knew the second I saw that boy. The cowlick, the dimples, the nose. Even the shape of his head."

"You know the shape of my head?" Hunter asked with his mouth half full of cake.

"Hey, I spent my childhood trailing after you, big brother, and staring at the back of your head." Brooke rolled her eyes.

"I know just what you mean," Luke chimed in and slid his arm around Honor's shoulders. Their wedding was scheduled for October in Malibu, where her friends and family lived. It would be a fun trip for all the McKaslins, Millie decided, now that she and Simon were McKaslins.

"Hey! I think I'm being insulted here." Hunter winked at her. "Isn't my wife going to come to my defense?"

"Sorry, defense is your job." She leaned against him to give him a quick hug. "I do the cooking, you do the defending."

"Funny, that wasn't your attitude yesterday when you told me to come help you in the kitchen."

"We were making tacos," Simon explained as he scraped the last of the icing off his plate. "Mom needed help with all the chopping."

Laughter rang around the table, and Millie basked in the happy sound of family. Her family. Life couldn't get any better. She felt ready to burst with joy. True to his word, Hunter had done his best to live with his heart, shower her with love and devotion and be the wonderful father Simon deserved. He'd renovated his house for her and Simon, moved in Shadow and Smokey and bought her father's farm and cows. The McKaslin dairy had expanded so much that they'd hired Milton as foreman. Now all that was left was the happily-ever-after, and she knew it would be.

"I love you, husband," she whispered in his ear, so only he could hear.

"I love you more. Forever and always." His kiss brushed her cheek. Honest love reflected in her gaze, and he'd never get enough of seeing it. Although he'd been married only an hour, it had been bliss. No ball and chain, no misery, only two hearts joined.

The way love should be. It was easy to see their future. Moments spent laughing, working together and raising their son. There would be another baby or two to add to their family one day. Life was good. Overcome by his feelings, he leaned in to kiss his wife's cheek. "Ahs" rang out around the table, but he hardly noticed them.

All he could see was Millie, his heart and soul, his best dream come true. His forever happiness.

* * * * *

Dear Reader,

Welcome back to another McKaslin Clan story. I've wanted to write Hunter's book for a while, since all through the earlier stories in this series I kept asking myself, why does this guy have such a negative attitude toward romance? What makes him tick? Well, in *Montana Dreams,* I got to find that out along with the answers to a few other questions. Will Millie be able to mend things with her dying father? Will anyone figure out who Simon's real dad is? Can Hunter find a way to open his heart and let love in? I hope you enjoy finding out those answers, too, as Millie and Hunter journey toward the love God means for them.

Thank you for choosing *Montana Dreams* and for returning to the McKaslin family with me.

Wishing you love and grace,

Jillian Hart

Questions for Discussion

1. What are your first impressions of Hunter? How would you describe his character?

2. What are your first impressions of Millie? What do you learn about her from the way she treats her father, her son and Hunter? What does this tell you about her character?

3. Hunter believes the best way to protect yourself from heartbreak is not to have a heart. What does this say about him? How is this belief holding him back in life?

4. How does Millie feel about Hunter at the beginning of the book? What influences her? How does this change as she spends time with him again?

5. Why do you think Hunter pitches in and does so much for Millie? What is at the core of his behavior?

6. When does Millie begin to see Hunter differently?

7. What do you think of Millie's relationship with her father? How hard do you think it is for her to take care of him? How does it change her?

8. What are Hunter's strengths? What are his weaknesses? What do you come to admire about him? How do you know he will be a good father?

9. What changes Hunter's mind about love? What makes him believe in love?

10. What values do you think are important in this book?

11. What do you think are the central themes in this book? How do they develop? What meanings do you find in them?

12. How does God guide both Millie and Hunter? How is this evident? How does God lead them to true love?

13. There are many different kinds of love in this book. What are they? What do Millie and Hunter each learn about true love?

KEY WITNESS
Terri Reed

Chapter One

"Evening, Miss Conrad."

Don't look back.

She flew down the stairs to the lobby level. She burst through the door screaming, "Call 911!"

Her frantic gaze sought some way to bar the exit. Nothing was in reach. She flattened her back against the door, prepared to at least slow the killer down when he tried to exit.

But no one came through the door.

NYPD Homicide Detective Andy Howell surveyed the interior of the small apartment, mentally cataloging the scene. Loose papers, couch ripped to shreds, furniture broken. Clues amid chaos. He shifted aside so his partner, Paul Wallace, could take a look.

Andy turned to the first officer at the scene. "What've we got?"

Officer Florez consulted his notes. "One female victim—the apartment's occupant, Sue Hyong, a reporter for the *Village Voice*. DOA at the scene. Looks like blunt force trauma, but won't know for sure until the ME arrives."

A reporter. The computer and layer of papers littering the apartment made sense.

"Murder weapon?"

Florez pointed toward a lamp lying near the victim's body. "Maybe that. Forensics is on their way."

"Witnesses?"

"One. A neighbor, Kristin Conrad."

"Did she hear a commotion?"

"No. Says she walked in and saw a man standing over the dead body. The perp then chased her down the emergency stairs to the lobby."

"So the doorman got a look at him, too?"

Florez shook his head. "Nope. Perp never came out of the stairwell."

Andy's pulse kicked into high gear. The murderer was still in the building?

Chapter Two

Andy's heart pounded against his ribs as the threat of danger to their witness revved his senses to high alert. If the perp was still in the building, they had to secure the witness. "Where's the witness?"

Officer Florez gestured with his hand. "Next apartment over. I have a man stationed with her. But we've already combed the building and came up with nothing. We're widening the search now."

Relieved that the witness was in protective custody, Andy's heart rate slowed. He pulled the center of his attention back to the crime scene. Was this a B&E gone bad, or was this an assassination?

Paul clapped him on the back. "I'll go help search. You do the interview."

"Fine," Andy replied.

But first, he wanted a better look at the crime scene. Taking out his notebook, he recorded his observations. From the amount of damage, the perp had to have been searching for something. Had the victim come home to find him in the apartment, or was she here when he invaded?

He bent closer to the woman on the floor. His cursory inspection showed defensive wounds. She'd fought her attacker.

Good for her. Skin under her nails would provide evidence once they caught the guy. If there was skin…

The ME arrived and Andy moved to the apartment next door to interview the witness. After identifying himself to the officer standing guard, he entered the apartment. Comfortable furniture and splashes of color made the small space cozy and welcoming. Artwork decorated the walls. He glanced around, noting no personal photos.

In the living room, a young woman sat on the overstuffed couch hugging her knees to her chest. Though her arms were bare, her striped skirt covered everything else but the tips of her pink-polished toes. The vulnerability of the pose twisted in his gut, triggering a terrifying memory of his sister the day he'd failed to protect her. For a moment the simple act of breathing was torture to his lungs. He coughed into his hand, forcing the images away. Mentally refocusing, he stepped closer to the woman.

With her head bent forward, all Andy could see was a veil of thick blond hair. "Miss Conrad?"

She lifted her head. Her pale, oval face had dark streaks showing the lines of her tears. Her pink lips trembled. His protective instincts roared to life. "Yes?"

Struck by the vivid color of her bright green eyes, so wide and sad, Andy noted the pupils were dilated with shock. Empathy bounced in his chest like a super ball. "I'm Detective Howell."

She nodded and reached for his outstretched hand.

His fingers closed over her smaller ones, their palms met. Her hand fit snugly within his grasp. Warmth shimmied up his arm. She tugged her hand back, making him aware he'd held on longer than he'd meant to. Reluctantly, he let go.

"I need to ask you some questions," Andy said.

Taking a deep breath, she squared her shoulders and lowered her feet to the floor. With graceful movements, she smoothed out her skirt. He noted no rings on her fingers. Was there a boyfriend that needed to be called?

He frowned.

Now why did he hope there wasn't?

Chapter Three

Wanting to put her at ease so he could get the answers he needed, Andy moved to sit beside her on the couch, but left enough of a gap not to crowd her. "Can you tell me what happened?"

Her voice shook as she spoke. "I was leaving the store where I work when Sue texted me. She wanted me to bring home a package she'd asked me to hold for her. When I arrived at her apartment the door was open…and this man was standing over…her body. He chased me down the emergency stairs."

Her panicked gaze shifted from him to the door and back again. "He must still be in the building!"

The need to reassure her rose sharply. "We've searched the building—don't worry, you're safe. Right now we're combing the neighborhood. If he's here, we'll find him."

Though the worry didn't leave her pretty eyes, her shoulders relaxed slightly.

"Sue's dead, right?"

He nodded.

She closed her eyes tight. Tears streamed down her face. She made no effort to wipe them away.

Her grief touched him, made him want to offer her comfort, but that wasn't his job. His job was to solve a murder. So he forced himself to concentrate on the facts. "Do you still have this package?"

She nodded and pointed to the dining table. On top of the round pine table sat a small box wrapped in brown paper.

"You have no idea what's inside?"

"No. Sue said it was a gift for her grandmother in Seoul. Do you think the box has something to do with her murder?"

"Could be. Do you know what Miss Hyong was working on at the paper?"

"No. I'm sorry. She wouldn't talk about her articles." She hiccuped with a sob. "If only I'd arrived sooner so I could have helped her."

More tears spilled over her long lashes and Andy's gut clenched. The sorrow of others didn't usually bother him so strongly—he had enough of his own grief to deal with. But this woman's pain affected him. Maybe the guilt and grief filling her big green eyes reminded him too much of his own.

He forced himself to stay focused. "Would you be willing to come to the station and look through some mug shots and work with our sketch artist?"

"Yes, of course." She rose, her skirt fluttering about her slender ankles. She was taller than he'd first thought, maybe only a couple inches shorter than his six-three frame. Attraction flared—it wasn't every day he met a woman tall enough to spark his interest.

But there was no place for sparks at a crime scene. Annoyed with himself, he turned his attention back to the box.

Andy carried it with him as he escorted Kristin out of the building where they met up with Paul. "The guy broke into an apartment on the second floor and used the fire escape. But there's no trace of him now. Doesn't look like he stuck around."

"Make sure a patrol is left to keep it that way," Andy said.

He helped Kristin into the back of an awaiting police cruiser and rode with her to the station, making small talk in an attempt to keep her from dwelling on the murder. Though he doubted that would be possible.

Once at the station, he set her up in a room with a cup of coffee and a stack of photo albums containing the mug shots of New York's criminals, the latest and the greatest.

Andy left her there and joined Paul at his desk. "Anything?"

Paul looked at his notes. "Hyong's editor at the *Village Voice* said she'd been working on a story that she was really hush-hush about."

"Seems Miss Hyong was a secretive person," Andy said. He undid the wrapping on the package he'd taken from Kristin. Inside, nestled among cotton batting, lay a small key, like the type used to open a safe deposit box.

So Grandmother was getting this for a present? Interesting. And curious.

What did the key open and who wanted it?

Chapter Four

Kristin's eyes blurred. She rubbed at her eyes to wipe away the fatigue from looking at so many pictures. It didn't work. She'd been at it for an hour, looking at page after page of photos, and still hadn't found the man who had been in Sue's apartment.

Sue. Tears welled in Kristin's eyes. Her temples throbbed. She dropped her face into her hands and tried not to think of the gruesome scene. But the horror of seeing that man bent over Sue's body wouldn't release its ferocious grip.

Kristin did her best to banish the image—that wouldn't help find her friend's killer. The best way for her to be of any use was to keep looking. She dropped her hands back to the book in front of her and resumed searching the photos.

The door opened and Detective Howell walked in. Kristin straightened slightly, embarrassed to be caught slouching in the chair. Her mother hadn't been big on etiquette, but one thing she'd always hated was when Kristin slouched.

Kristin's gaze raked over the detective. She couldn't help but notice that he was tall, broad-shouldered and attractive, even if his suit was ill-fitting and made of cheap fabric. But more than his physical appearance, she'd appreciated the way he'd tried to put her at ease from the moment he'd entered her apartment. He'd been gentle and kind. Even asking if there was a boyfriend or some family member he could call for her. Unfortunately, there wasn't.

She noticed a slight limp on his left leg when he walked. Had he been injured in the line of duty? Was he in pain with every step? A ribbon of sympathy wound around her, making her already tender emotions ache all the more.

The detective smiled, showing straight white teeth. His kind smile softened the prominence of his nose and relieved the hardness of his jaw. He had a face a girl could get used to seeing every day. Heat climbed up her neck. Where had that thought come from?

"Any luck?" he asked.

She dropped her gaze to the book lying in front of her. "No, not yet." She gestured toward the stack of albums to her right. "I still have these five books to go through, though."

"Can I get you some more coffee or hot chocolate?"

"No, thank you, Detective," she replied, appreciating his gracious and generous treatment. "Did you open the package?"

At his nod, she asked, "What was inside?"

He took the seat opposite of her. "A key to a safe deposit box. Any idea where Miss Hyong banked?"

His use of the past tense squeezed at her chest, making her heart throb. She shook her head. "No. I'm sorry I can't be of more help."

He leaned across the table and covered her hand with his. Warmth enveloped her and curled around her heart like a salve to the bruises there.

"And I'm sorry you have to go through this," he said, his midnight-colored eyes tender.

"I just hope you catch that guy." She tried to ignore the way her heart thumped in her chest at his touch.

Something about this man called to her lonely heart in a way no one had in a very long time. She appreciated that he took time—time to listen to her, time to comfort her, time to touch her....

He sat back, leaving a warm spot where his hand had been. "We'll do our best."

"And I better do mine." She pulled another book in front of her and began flipping through the pages. A face jumped out at her.

Fear slammed into her chest. Her breath caught and held as she stared into the eyes of the man who'd killed Sue.

Chapter Five

"Him," Kristin whispered.

"Show me."

She pointed to the image on the page. The man's face would be forever burned in her mind. She shuddered.

Detective Howell pulled the book toward him. "You're sure?"

"One hundred percent sure."

He smiled with approval as he rose. "Good. I'll have an officer escort you home and stay with you until we catch the guy."

Grateful for his consideration, she rose and came around the table. Unable to resist, she placed her hand on his arm. "Thank you for everything."

He placed his hand over hers once again and gave a gentle squeeze. "Just doing my job."

His job. A job full of uncertainty and danger—the opposite of what she craved in her own life. She'd spent too many years never knowing what was coming or where she'd end up from one day to the next. She'd worked hard to put down roots. She couldn't deny her attraction to the detective, but pursuing it made little sense. All she wanted in her life was stability and security—neither of which this man's job could offer if something were to develop between them.

It was a good thing they wouldn't ever see each other again.

As Kristin left the station, Andy felt like a part of him was going with her. Odd. He'd never had such a reaction to anyone before. Let alone a witness. He was usually good about compartmentalizing his emotions and reactions. But not so with Miss Conrad.

He wouldn't be a red-blooded male if he denied she was easy on the eyes. But her looks alone were not what made her special. She'd somehow gotten under his skin with her vulnerability and her willingness to help catch the bad guy.

He shrugged off the sentimental nonsense. He had a job to do. He turned his mind to finding the man she'd identified—Charlie Linder. A two-bit drug dealer with a history—which dated back to his teens—of breaking the law.

Which meant that with a quick computer search, Andy would know the thug's last known address. Just shy of an hour later, Andy and his partner, Paul, stood in front of the Brooklyn Flats apartment building where Charlie Linder resided.

They climbed the stairs to the third floor. A foul odor, like raw sewage, permeated the stifling late summer air and filled the hallway to gagging proportions. The whir of fans echoed off the dank walls. Andy rapped his knuckles hard against Charlie's dark green door.

"It's the police. Open up, Charlie," Paul yelled.

Andy pressed his ear to the door but heard nothing. "Let's get the super."

A few minutes later, the building superintendent—a squat man with a balding head, shiny with sweat—used his master key to open the door.

The smell was stronger in the apartment. Covering his mouth and nose with a hand, Andy entered the living room.

On the floor a pile of garbage spilled out of an overturned trash can.

Andy looked up.

Charlie Linder swung from a knotted rope tied to the living room light fixture.

Chapter Six

The super threw up all over Andy's shoes. Sympathy for the guy twisted in his gut. Seeing a guy hanging from a light wasn't something one saw every day. This was probably only the third such death Andy had seen in his ten years on the force.

Paul hustled the man out. Andy called in for the crime scene techs.

"Looks like suicide," Paul said as he reentered.

"Yeah, looks like. But it's too much of a coincidence. Why would Linder kill himself?" Andy slipped on a pair of gloves.

Paul shrugged. "Remorse for killing the Hyong woman?"

"Doubtful." Andy moved toward the hall. "I'll take the bedroom."

"Kitchen," Paul said and put on a pair of gloves as well.

A few minutes later, Paul yelled for Andy.

Leaving the dismal mess of Charlie's bedroom, Andy hurried to the kitchen where Paul stood in front of the refrigerator.

"Look what we have here." Paul pointed to the interior of the top-door freezer.

Stacks of bound money flanked two large plastic bags of white powder. Andy did a quick calculation—the street value of the stash equaled more than Andy's and Paul's salaries combined.

"Drugs and murder. The two always seem to go together," Andy remarked dryly.

But just how did Sue Hyong fit into the equation?

The killer was dead. Kristin had no reason to be afraid anymore. Except she was still scared. The senseless violence had rocked her illusion of safety. Living in a secure building, knowing her neighbors and being alert to her surroundings couldn't guarantee her well-being. Even the extra locks she'd had installed yesterday at home and at the store didn't bring her a greater sense of security. Yes, she'd made a stable life for herself, one where she felt comfortable, but comfort wasn't protection.

And as she tried to come to terms with Sue's death, the constant need to look over her shoulder only served to tighten her nerves.

At Sue's graveside service, Kristin's gaze traveled through the small crowd, wondering where the next threat would come from. She stood slightly behind Sue's parents as the long black casket was lowered into the ground. Mrs. Hyong's sobs made Kristin's own tears flow more freely. The pastor's soothing voice lifted on the humid breeze that did little to relieve the hot sun beating down on the small group of mourners gathered in the cemetery.

Kristin said a silent prayer of peace for Sue's parents, though she wondered if peace was possible when there was no logical reason for such a tragedy.

The Hyongs had been informed that Sue's death was the result of a random home invasion. No physical evidence suggested a connection between Sue and the now-dead man who'd killed her.

The unpredictability of the crime made Kristin's deep-seated insecurities leap to life. She'd tried so hard as an adult to find the security and stability her parents hadn't provided with their nomadic lifestyle as touring musicians. Between the constant roaming from town to town and her parents' fanatical warnings for her to stay safely out of sight at all times when they weren't with her, fear had been her only friend.

And now, to think that some random intruder could have as easily picked her apartment as Sue's skewed the axis of her carefully plotted life. Was true security and stability ever possible?

As the service ended, a touch on her elbow sent Kristin's pulse skyrocketing. She jerked away and whipped around to find herself staring into the deep depths of Detective Howell's midnight eyes. "Detective. You startled me."

One side of his mouth lifted in a wry smile. "Sorry. And please, call me Andy." His gaze traveled to the now closed-over grave. "I just wanted to let you know I'm still trying to find the safe deposit box that fits Miss Hyong's key. The bank she'd used didn't have a box on file for her."

"That seems odd," Kristin said, wondering what Sue had been hiding. "Why lock up a lock?"

Chapter Seven

"My thought exactly," Andy stated with approval in his gaze.

Kristin's heart did a little bump and roll. Heat infused her cheeks. "So then you are still working the case?"

"Unofficially," he replied and loosened the tie at his neck.

"Why?" A shudder of renewed fear ripped through her. "Don't you believe Linder was the murderer?"

"No, I'm sure he was the guy, I just don't like unanswered questions," he said. "Why had your friend hidden the key?"

"The answer may not have anything to do with her death," Kristin said, hoping that was the case.

"True." He smiled and her fear faded.

She admired his dedication and tenacity. "Thank you."

"You're welcome."

They walked toward the parking lot.

After a moment of comfortable silence, Kristin asked the question burning in her mind. "What happened to your leg?"

Red crept up his neck. "Playing college basketball. Blew out my knee enough to ruin any chance of being a pro ball player—but not enough to keep me off the force."

"I thought maybe you'd been hurt in the line of duty," she said.

His mouth twisted into a grimace. "No, not yet."

She prayed never. "You know, you should come down to the store one day. I'd love to outfit you properly," she said and then realized how rude her words sounded as he arched a dark blonde brow. "Not to say that your suit isn't...well, that you don't dress..." Oh, brother, she was not only swallowing her foot but her whole leg. "Never mind," she finished softly and wished the earth would open and claim her.

His gentle laugh soothed her embarrassment. "It's okay. I have a hard time finding anything that will fit my lanky frame."

"I could," she blurted out. "I mean, I could find you the right fit."

"I'll take you up on that," he said and held out his elbow. "Can I take you home?"

Touched by his manners, and oddly excited by the offer, she placed her arm through his. "I'd like that." She'd prefer a ride with him over public transportation any day, but today especially she needed the sense of security that he seemed to exude.

The ride from the Queens cemetery back into the city flew by as their conversation flowed easily from books to movies to sports and even politics, which they agreed to disagree on.

Soon they were standing at the door to her apartment. She really wanted to invite him in for coffee but something held her back.

Maybe it was the easy way they chatted without that awkward pressure to keep the conversation going, or maybe it was the attraction zinging through her veins. Neither was good for her peace of mind—he was a man who lived a life of risk, where at any moment the unpredictable could happen. She couldn't imagine inviting that kind of fear into her life on a daily basis.

She gave a mental, cynical laugh. On the other hand, hadn't Sue's death shown her how unsecure life could be for anyone?

Shaking away the conflicting thoughts, she smiled at Andy. "Thank you for the ride."

He smiled back, sending her heart knocking against her

ribs. She quickly turned to unlock the door and found it slightly open.

A horrible sense of déjà vu gripped her. She stepped back and bumped up against the hard wall of Andy's chest. "It's open," she whispered.

Pushing her behind him, he motioned for her to move farther down the hall as he withdrew his weapon from the holster beneath his suit jacket. Gripping the gun with both hands, he placed himself near the door jamb as he used the toe of his scuffed dress shoe to push the door wider.

When he disappeared inside, Kristin squeezed her eyes tight and prayed for his safety.

Chapter Eight

❧

"All clear," Andy said as he reemerged from her apartment. "You've had a break-in."

A break-in. Fear shivered down Kristin's spine.

Andy whipped out his cell phone and within ten minutes the crime scene technicians arrived.

The head of the unit, a woman named Barbara Sims, approached Andy. "Walk me through this."

Kristin listened as Andy explained the situation. She was so thankful he'd been here. He'd kept her from freaking out with his calm manner and reassuring words. She stepped closer to him as the technicians dusted for prints and snapped off pictures of her torn-apart apartment.

Thirty minutes later, Sims nodded to Kristin. "You can go in now. Take a look around, see what's missing." Andy followed Kristin through the apartment. Even the kitchen drawers had been dumped on the linoleum floor. Her hall closet stood wide open, her coats lay in a heap on the carpet, the pockets turned inside out. Her bedroom drawers were ripped from their slots and the contents spread across the floor. Her bed had even been stripped, the mattress flipped on its side. Her bedroom closet and the bathroom had received the same treatment.

"I can't tell if anything is missing," she said coming back

into the living room. "I don't have anything of value except the TV, stereo and computer, which are all still here."

"Jewelry?"

She shook her head. "Not worth anything."

"It looks like they were searching for something," said Andy.

Kristin met his gaze and could see he was thinking the same thought she was. *The key.* "This wasn't a random break and enter, was it? This is related to Sue's death. Someone else is involved. Whoever is behind this mustn't have realized I'd turned Sue's box over to you guys. And now they're after me."

After the crime scene technicians cleared out, Kristin and Andy stood alone in the center of her living room.

"I feel so violated," she said and wrapped her arms around her middle.

"That's natural."

She shuddered. "What if I'd been home? Would I have been killed like Sue?"

Andy stepped closer and slid his arm around her, drawing her tightly to his solid chest. "Don't think about that. We're organizing another place for you to stay. You're safe now."

"I know. It's just so jarring...." she said, her voice quiet while she took comfort from his embrace.

"I'll help you put things away," he offered.

"That's kind of you, but I'll be okay," she said and moved away from him.

"You're not okay."

"I appreciate your offer..."

"But?"

She met his gaze. "I like you."

One side of his mouth tipped upward. "I like you, too."

It would be cruel of her to continue to take advantage of his generous and caring nature when she had no intention of having their relationship go any further. Life could be random and unpredictable, but that didn't mean she should or would deliberately embrace trouble. And he certainly qualified as trouble. She wanted a peaceful, steady life. Not one with surprises or uncertainties. Both of which came part and parcel with Andy.

He frowned, his gaze searching her face. "Look. I'm not leaving, so I might as well help."

"Do you intend to stand guard 24/7?" she challenged.

"If need be," he stated, his jaw hardened into a determined line.

She didn't really want to be alone right now anyway, so why was she fighting him?

Chapter Nine

"Okay, if you don't mind helping me with this mess," Kristin said. She pointed to the pile of plastic CD cases strewn on the floor near the stereo. "You can start re-shelving the CDs."

He removed his jacket and rolled up his sleeves. "Any particular order you want them in?"

She was tempted to say alphabetical just to see his reaction but decided *that* would be cruel. "No. Just in their proper case and on the shelf."

As he worked at putting the right CD in the right jacket, he asked, "I can't remember if I asked this already. Did you grow up here in New York?"

She picked up a decorative pillow from the floor. "No, you didn't ask, and no, I didn't grow up here. I didn't move to New York until after college."

"Where's home then?"

"Here. This is home. I grew up an only child and we lived in a motor home. My parents were musicians. We traveled a lot, chasing one gig after another. Not exactly the normal American family life," she said, wincing to hear the note of bitterness coating her words as it sometimes did any time she spoke of her parents.

"You don't get along with your parents?"

She shrugged. "When I see them."

"Which I take it isn't often."

"No, not often. The last postcard I received from them came from Thailand. Their music is still a big hit in that part of the world."

"You lived in a motor home," Andy said, his voice laced with a mix of awe and disbelief. "I don't think I know anyone who's ever owned one. Motor homes aren't exactly made for New York traffic."

"I take it you grew up in the city?"

"Brooklyn Heights. How'd you go to school if you moved around a lot?"

"I was 'homeschooled.'" She made quotation marks in the air. "It was unusual at the time, not the fad that it's become, and it left me feeling very adrift and alone most of the time." She looked deeper into his gentle eyes. "Until I realized that knowing God meant He was with me everywhere we went. It made the moving around less frightening."

Andy repaired the leg to one of her four dining chairs. "But if your family moved around so much, how did you go to church?"

"Once, when I was about twelve, we stopped in a small town in Oklahoma." She smiled, remembering that summer day. "There was this big youth revival going on in the middle of the park and I was drawn to all the activity like a bee to honey." She walked to her desk and gathered the papers. "After that, I'd go to whatever church I could find in every town we stopped in. My parents weren't too hip on the idea but they never stopped me. After college, I moved here, found this apartment and the church down the street. Now I have a community," she said, thinking how blessed she felt to finally have roots somewhere. "Do you go to church?"

One corner of his mouth lifted. "Sometimes. My parents are very devoted. My sister, too."

"But you're not?"

He set the chair at the table and moved to the bookshelf. "I believe."

Something in his tone made her stop. She held bills and other mail in her hand. "But…?"

Chapter Ten

"I believe God exists and that He takes care of those He loves," Andy said.

That didn't explain the note of despair Kristin had detected in his voice. "Tell me about your family," she said, hoping if he opened up a bit, maybe she'd understand what she'd heard.

"My father is a postal worker and my mother a nurse. They've always worked hard to provide for my sister and me. When they worked, it was just Aleesha and me hanging out."

"Is Aleesha younger or older?"

"Younger by four years."

"Are you close?"

He nodded but turned away. Curious about his life and his relationship with his sister, Kristin came over to stand beside him. "Does she live in the city still, like you?"

"No, she left as soon as she could. She's married to a banker in Santa Fe, New Mexico. They have a nice life there. She owns an art gallery."

"Does she have children?"

He swallowed and averted his gaze, but not before she witnessed the torment flashing there.

"No. She can't."

The note of anger and...guilt in his voice compelled her to comfort him. She touched his arm. "I'm sorry."

He stiffened then took her hand and held on. Bleakness entered his gaze. A responding gush of empathy welled up inside of her.

His mouth pressed into a tight line as if he was trying to keep the words from bursting forth. Then finally he said, "It's my fault she can't have kids. I didn't protect her when I should have."

"What do you mean?"

"I was thirteen and mad I had to babysit when all my buddies were going to Coney Island for the day. I didn't want to take her with me so I left her home alone. She was attacked and raped by some door-to-door salesman."

Kristin's heart clenched in shock and empathy. "Did they catch the guy?"

"Yes. After he attacked two other young girls."

Sorrow for the victims burned at the back of her eyes. She squeezed his hand. "You couldn't have known what would happen that day."

"I shouldn't have left her. It was my job to protect her and I chose not to." The self-recrimination in his voice was so finely honed, so well-used, it cut into Kristin for the simple reason she was standing too close to Andy—their usual target.

"And you haven't forgiven yourself," she stated as understanding dawned. "Andy, you were a kid. It shouldn't have been your responsibility to protect her."

"Doesn't matter. It was, and I failed her." He released Kristin's hand.

Hurting for his wounded soul, she asked, "So you think God doesn't love you because of that?"

He pivoted away from her and stood by the window. The setting sun drew streaks of pink and orange across the azure sky visible between the city's skyline. "Look, it's getting late. You're not staying here."

Ignoring his statement, she put her hand on his shoulder. "He does love you, Andy. God wouldn't want you to torment yourself for something that was out of your control. If you had been home, who's to say you wouldn't have been hurt or even killed?"

He jerked away from her. His expression closed, cutting her out of his thoughts. "We've made arrangements to have you stay in a hotel tonight. I'll take you there."

Though it pained her to see his hurt, she relented and contemplated his offer. She didn't want to stay alone in the apartment tonight. The sense of violation lingered and the real fear that the invaders would return loomed. "Give me a minute. I'll pack a few things."

He nodded and turned back to the window.

Heart aching, she headed to her bedroom to gather her things. *Lord, show me how I can help him.*

Would Andy ever be able to forgive himself?

Chapter Eleven

Andy ran a hand over his jaw in disgusted disbelief. What on earth had he been thinking to reveal his failure to Kristin?

He never talked about that day or the torment of regret that rode him hard. But maybe seeing Kristin at Sue Hyong's funeral—clearly mourning the loss of her friend—had shown him how deeply she cared for those around her. And apparently a part of him really wanted to be cared for.

But she was right. He hadn't forgiven himself, and he doubted God had either.

His family said they had, but how could they? He didn't deserve to be forgiven.

Kristin came out of her bedroom carrying a satchel slung over her shoulder. "I'm ready."

Stuffing his private pain back into his own little box in his soul, Andy composed himself. "Let's go." He made a sweeping gesture toward the door.

He drove her to the Hilton in mid-town and paid for a single room. After settling Kristin inside, he stepped to the door. "If you need anything, I'll be right here." Her blond eyebrows drew together in a slight frown. "Right here?" "Outside your door." She lowered her chin. "You don't need to stand guard. I'm sure I'll be safe here."

"Doesn't matter. I'm not leaving." The bad guys who'd trashed her apartment might think she had the key in her purse, or in a pocket. He wasn't taking any chances—much to her relief.

Amusement entered her green eyes. "You are a stubborn man."

One side of his mouth cocked upward. "So I've been told." She left the doorway and returned a moment later dragging the desk chair behind her. "Here. At least sit."

Her thoughtfulness touched him deeply, making him want to pull her into his arms and kiss her.

He stepped back in surprise. Whoa! Not a good idea. *Keep it professional.* She needed his protection, not his advances.

Though standing guard wasn't exactly part of his job description. A fact he chose to ignore.

"Thank you." He positioned the chair to the left of the door.

He straightened and turned back toward the open door, expecting her to still be standing in the doorway. But she'd moved and stood just inches from him. She slipped her arms around his waist and laid her cheek against his chest. Stunned, yet thrilled by her gesture, he wrapped his arms around her, savoring the moment.

This definitely wasn't professional. Kristin felt way too good in his arms, too right. It had been a long time since he'd wanted to hold a woman close, not just physically but emotionally. He was in way over his head. The smart thing would be to arrange for a uniformed officer to replace him. The smart thing to do would be to let Paul take the lead on this. The smart thing to do would be to back off, right now.

But sometimes he wasn't so smart.

She leaned her head back, her eyes wide and full of tenderness. "You are a good man, Detective Andy Howell." Her words were a soothing balm to his weary soul and a bucket of reality to his sanity.

He kissed her forehead and then steered her back to the

room. "Goodnight," he said and firmly shut the door to her room.

And his heart.

Chapter Twelve

A scream jolted Kristin awake.

She bolted upright, scrambled to a sitting position against the headboard and clutched the covers to her chest. Her heart thudded in her ears. Sweat covered her skin. Her gaze searched the dark hotel room for danger. Shadows from the city lights danced at the edge of the curtains.

The scream echoed inside her head.

Sharp pounding at the door sent her stomach plunging with fear.

"Kristin!"

More banging.

Andy.

Desperate to see him, she jumped from the bed and ran for the door. Her fingers scrabbled with the lock until it finally gave way. She yanked the door open.

Tears sprang to her eyes. "Andy."

"Are you okay?" His frantic gaze swept the darkened room beyond her shoulder. "You screamed."

It had been her that had screamed. "Bad dream."

He pulled her to him, his strong arms enveloping her. Tension left her body in a swoosh, leaving her legs wobbly. She clung to him like a lifeline in a storm.

He lifted her face with his hands. His gaze searched her face. "You're sure you're okay?"

Feeling foolish for alarming him, she tried for a smile. Her lips quivered. "I'm sorry. Ever since Sue's murder I keep dreaming about Charlie coming after me."

He smoothed a hand over her hair. "He can't hurt you. I'm not going to let anyone hurt you."

She wanted to believe that. Needed to believe that. "You can't make that promise. That's not something you can control."

His eyebrows drew together in a frown. "I can do everything humanly possible."

"True." She reached up to cup his jaw. "But only God is in control. We have none."

A fact that agitated her stomach to no end.

"Then we'll have to pray for His help."

She dropped her gaze to the front of his wrinkled white shirt and red-striped tie. "I know that, but sometimes, it's so hard to…remember and trust."

Confessing that out loud lifted a weight off her shoulders. She hadn't realized how much she needed someone in her life she could talk to without feeling she'd be judged. Andy wouldn't judge her. She was sure of it.

One corner of his mouth lifted in a wry smile. "Believe me, I understand."

She hurt for him, for the pain he carried because of what had happened to his sister. Kristin cupped his jaw in her hand. "We're quite a pair."

He turned his head to place a kiss in her palm.

Delicious shivers shimmered down her arm to tickle her heart. She met his gaze. The intensity in his dark eyes sent her pulse racing and made her breath stall.

Was Andy as attracted to her as she was to him?

His gaze lowered to her lips. "You should try to get some sleep," he said, his voice low and husky. Good advice. But probably not doable. Not when all she wanted was for him to kiss her. To kiss her fear away.

But that would bring its own danger. Time to retreat. "Good-night. Again."

Once Kristin had relocked the door, she pressed her hand to the solid wood as if she could touch him through the obstacle standing in the way.

Earlier today she'd told him she liked him. But her feelings went beyond like to a deeper caring that scared her.

Did she really have enough faith to trust God to keep him safe?

Chapter Thirteen

Andy had expected Kristin's store to be full of girly frou-frou stuff, and though there was some, she had a very nice men's section with some trendy as well as classic pieces. A nice surprise.

When he had the time, he planned on taking Kristin up on the offer to outfit him. He looked around, eyeing the selections and their price tags. If he could afford it.

She joined him in front of a display where a navy, Italian designer-brand suit hung from a wooden hanger. "That would look divine on you."

He didn't need to look at the price tag to know it was out of his budget.

"I'll bet you're a forty-one long." She pulled a coat from its hanger. "Here, try this on."

Giving in to the urge to do as she instructed, he slipped off his houndstooth sport coat and put on the one she handed to him.

"Perfect," she said. "Look." She steered him to a mirror.

He had to admit the jacket fit like it had been made for him. He turned slightly to see the back. He really liked the coat. Maybe he could splurge just once.

"Hello?" Tony Guzman, one of New York's finest walked into the store.

Embarrassed to be caught preening in front of the mirror, Andy shrugged out of the coat, handed it back to Kristin and took his own jacket back before going to greet the officer.

"Tony, thanks for coming." Andy shook his hand and introduced Kristin.

She pulled Andy aside. "Are you sure this is necessary? Having a uniformed officer in the store might scare away the customers."

"He'll keep a low profile," Andy assured her.

She looked unconvinced.

"Humor me, okay?"

After a moment she gave a slow nod.

"I'll check in later," Andy said before leaving the store.

He headed back to the station knowing Kristin was in good hands. When he arrived, Paul waved a paper in his face. "Here's a list of all the establishments with safe deposit boxes within a fifty mile radius of Hyong's apartment."

"You rock. Let's go." Andy needed to find Sue Hyong's safe deposit box. Because whatever she'd hidden was the key to her murder. And the key to keeping Kristin safe.

After countless banks, Paul and Andy finally found a bank manager of a small savings and loan in the Bowery who confirmed that Sue Hyong had a safe deposit box in their facility.

The bank manager took Paul and Andy back to the vault, motioning to the one registered under Sue Hyong's name. Andy inserted the key into the small lock and pulled out the long narrow box. He set it on the table and opened the lid.

"It's empty," he said, disbelief curling around his words.

"That's odd," Paul said. "Then the key had nothing to do with Hyong's murder or Conrad's break-in. What gives?"

Aggravation pulsed in Andy's veins. "There had to be some reason Hyong secured this box."

He inspected the box on all sides. Nothing. Frustrated, he gave the box a vicious shake. Something rattled inside the box.

Surprised anticipation rocketed through his system. He quickly righted the box. A small piece of plastic slid to a halt in the center of the box.

"Hey, this is what we're looking for," he exclaimed as excitement revved through him. He picked up the square piece of plastic. "It's a memory card for a cell phone."

"Let's get it to the lab." Paul led the way back to the car.

As Paul drove, Andy called Kristin at the store. She would want to know what they'd found.

The phone rang and rang, but there was no answer. Apprehension zinged across Andy's flesh. He tightened his grip on the phone. Why wasn't she answering? Where was the guard?

He snapped the phone closed. "Something's wrong."

Paul switched lanes, skidded into a U-turn and headed toward SoHo.

Chapter Fourteen

Thankful that the light of day had banished the nightmare from last night, Kristin stripped the mannequin in the front window display of her boutique and hummed a tune her parents had written. The lively tune brought back a memory of her childhood. She'd been thirteen, old enough to help set up equipment for the band.

For one moment, she'd stood on the stage staring out at the gathering crowd and excitement had zinged through her. As much as she'd resented the life her parents had chosen for them, she did understand the allure of that rush.

She'd felt that same excitement when she opened the store. And every day since.

Reaching for a new outfit to put on the mannequin, she let her gaze wander to the world outside. A typical summer afternoon. People passed by on the sidewalk, some hurrying with places to go and others meandering, out for a stroll along the trendy street making up the South of Houston area of Manhattan.

A young boy dawdling behind his mother stopped to stare at Kristin. She smiled at the kid. The boy stuck his tongue out.

With a laugh, Kristin turned her attention back to her display. She zipped up the animal-print skirt and was adjusting the hem of the matching top when the acrid smell of smoke assaulted her senses.

Alarm quickened her breath. She scrambled out of the display window, nearly knocking over the mannequin, and rushed into the body of the store.

"Hurry, we have to leave." The young, fresh-faced officer who'd been assigned to stand guard rushed toward her. "The storage room is on fire."

No! This store was her life and she wasn't about to let everything she'd worked so hard for be burned to ash. She pushed past the officer and grabbed a fire extinguisher from behind the cashier's counter.

"Call the fire department." She sprinted to the storage room.

Tendrils of dark smoke curled upward from the space under the closed door like long, grasping black fingers. Adrenaline-laced fear made her fingers clumsy as she struggled to operate the extinguisher.

The officer grabbed the extinguisher from her. "You call 911. I'll do this." Urgency pounded in her blood. She scurried to the phone and fumbled to dial the emergency number. She barked out the necessary information to the too-calm operator.

Anxiety twisted in her gut as flame now licked at the storage room. She stumbled through the growing smoke to find the officer, but the welcome sight of a firefighter dressed in his turnout gear deterred her. He motioned her toward the front door.

"This way," the muffled voice said from inside the mask covering his face.

Relief eased some of the panic tightening her chest. Help had arrived. Impressed by the quick response to her emergency call, she hustled to the door. "There's a police officer still inside."

"We'll get him," the firefighter replied. He took her firmly by the arm and pulled her outside to the sidewalk.

Kristin glanced around as the firefighter rushed her toward the corner and away from the building. There was no fire truck or any emergency response vehicles parked in the street. But the distant cries of sirens drew closer.

Confusion rushed in, quickly chased by apprehension. She dug in her heels, unsuccessfully trying to stop their forward momentum. "Wait! Where are you taking me?"

Chapter Fifteen

The man dressed as a firefighter brutally tightened his fingers on Kristin's arm with bruising force and dragged her to the street where a big black SUV waited. The back door flung open.

Alarm and fear exploded inside Kristin. She screamed, "Help! Help me!"

She twisted and yanked against her captor's fierce grip, but he was too strong. He pushed her into the vehicle and someone roughly shoved a pungent smelling cloth against her face.

She clawed at the hands holding the rag. A wave of dizziness washed over her. Her limbs suddenly refused to move as she collapsed on the seat. Hands pushed and pulled until she was completely inside and the door was slammed shut, the sound echoing inside her head.

She tried to move to see who had her, but her body wouldn't cooperate. The world narrowed to a pinprick of light that quickly vanished.

Paul brought the sedan to a screeching halt next to a fire truck. Andy's heart raced with disbelief. Smoke billowed out of Kristin's store.

Panic clawed at Andy's insides like a caged cat. He jumped

from the car and ran toward the front door. A firefighter grabbed him, preventing him from running into the dense smoke.

"Where's Kristin?" Andy yelled. "The owner?"

The firefighter shook his head.

Fear, stark and breath-stealing, seized him and wouldn't let go.

I can't lose her, not when I've just found her. He wasn't sure where that thought had come from, but there was no time to analyze his feelings. Only one thing mattered—Kristin. "Please, God, please, don't let her be dead."

With a fierce yank, Andy broke free of the firefighter's restraining hands and rushed closer to where two paramedics worked on Tony, the officer assigned to protect Kristin.

Andy knelt down beside the sooty officer. "Kristin? Where is she?"

Tony grabbed at the oxygen mask covering his face and pulled it away to talk. "She got…out."

Andy sagged back on his heels with relief. But he needed to see for himself that she was safe. He bolted, pushing through the crowd. "Kristin! Kristin Conrad!"

Where was she?

"Hey, Mister," a raspy voice called to him. "You lookin' for the shop lady?"

Andy's gaze landed on a disheveled man hunched near the corner waving to him. Hungry for any information, he hurried over. Digging into his pocket for some change, he questioned the man. "Did you see her? Do you know where she is?"

Taking the change like precious gems, the homeless man nodded and pointed to the side street. "Firefighter stuffed her into a big black monster. It took off that way." He pointed south.

Terror squeezed his lungs like a vice. "A firefighter? Are you sure?"

"Yep. He looked just like them others, only his hat was yeller instead of black."

Unsure of the reliability of the man's story, Andy swiftly moved to the firefighter giving orders. Andy flashed his badge. "Hey, any of your guys wearing a yellow helmet?"

"No. Why?"

Gesturing to the homeless man, Andy said, "He saw the owner of the store being forced into a black vehicle by a fire-fighter with a yellow hat."

"Not one of my guys," the chief assured him.

Dread and panic closed around Andy's throat.

Kristin had been kidnapped!

Chapter Sixteen

"Did you find her?" Paul asked.

Shaking his head, Andy choked out the details of Kristin's abduction, though he clung to the hope that the homeless guy had been wrong.

Paul looked around and then pointed across the street on the corner to a bank building. "Let's check if they have a video of the abduction."

Moving in a fog of fear and alarm, Andy ran with Paul to the bank and burst through the double doors. They explained the situation to the startled security guard and were led to the security office.

"Do you have a video feed of the southwest corner?" Andy asked, urging the man to move fast. They were losing precious time. He had to find Kristin.

The officer manning the desk nodded. "Sure do."

"Rewind the tape," Paul instructed.

With a few clicks, the video monitor showed the activity on the street in reverse mode.

"There!" Andy pointed to the images on the screen. Terror slayed his soul as he watched Kristin being forced into a black SUV by a firefighter in turnout gear and a yellow helmet. A mask obscured the man's face as he came around the front of the vehicle and got in on the passenger side. The SUV sped away. The license plate was conspicuously missing. Glare from the sun obscured the other occupants.

Rage cut off the air supply to Andy's brain. Impotent fury aimed at himself for not keeping her safe roared in his ears. For a moment the room dimmed. He struck out at the wall with a fist.

Paul placed a hand on Andy's arm, concern and compassion bright in his eyes. "We've got the memory card, remember? We'll find her."

Andy prayed so.

Forcing himself to function, Andy called in an alert with the model and make of the SUV as Paul drove them back to the station. When they arrived, Andy went directly to the lab tech. "Clyde, I need you to download whatever's on here ASAP."

Irritation crossed Clyde's expression as he stared at Andy through his thick glasses. "I'm busy."

Andy slammed his hand on Clyde's desk. "Now."

Without further comment Clyde took the small memory card and inspected it. "Looks like a two gig for a PDA."

"Can you pull the images off it?" Agitation made his voice shaky.

"Of course." Clyde dug through a drawer and pulled out a larger square piece of plastic. Sticking the card into the square, he then inserted it into a slot on the laptop sitting on the desk.

A few moments later, a video image streamed through the screen and focused on a brick warehouse.

A soft female voice spoke with a slight accent. "Day four of following Charlie. We're on the north side of Queens. Not far from the LIE and BQE. Can't make out the address on the warehouse."

Graffiti marred the exterior of the building. Two huge metal rolling doors stood partially open.

Paul barked out an order to a passing officer. "Get me a

listing of the warehouses in North Queens near the LIE and BQE. Stat."

Forcing himself to breathe, Andy concentrated on the screen. A gathering of men congregated near one door as if waiting for something.

"That's Charlie Linder." Andy pointed to the skinny man nervously smoking a cigarette at the back of the crowd.

"Now we know his connection to Hyong. She must have been doing a story on him," Paul commented.

"But why Linder?" Andy asked. "He was just a street thug."

A black SUV pulled up, sending the gathered men into action. Andy's heart raced.

The vehicle looked exactly like the one that had whisked away Kristin.

Chapter Seventeen

The doors of the vehicle opened and more men exited. One man in particular caught Andy's attention. He leaned closer to the computer to focus on the well-dressed man who stood out from the rest. There was no mistaking the former commander of the United Colombian Auto-Defense militia. His face graced every major law enforcement agency's most wanted list for drug trafficking. "George Mendoza! I thought he'd fled back to Colombia?"

The voice on the video continued speaking, "Oh, no. I can't believe what I'm seeing. Mendoza himself. Oooh, hello Pulitzer for this one. Wait. What are they doing? Oh, no. Oh, no!"

Andy wondered the same thing as the cargo doors to the SUV were flung open and a man, bound and gagged, was dragged out and dropped on the ground.

A collective gasp filled the small lab room as Andy, Paul and Clyde recognized Assistant District Attorney Michael Schomus. The man had been missing for two weeks.

Horror filled Andy as Mendoza approached Schomus with a gun. Mendoza bent down to say something in Schomus' ear, then Mendoza straightened and fired two rounds into Schomus.

The screen went dark. A shocked silence filled the lab.

Nausea roiled in Andy's gut. *God rest his soul and help me to protect Kristin.*

Terror ignited a fiery trail in his chest. What if he was already too late? Mendoza thought nothing of murdering a public official. What would keep him from killing Kristin?

"We've got to find that warehouse," Andy said and headed into the heart of the station.

"He may not have taken her there," Paul said, his voice full of concern and caution.

Trying to compartmentalize his emotions—but failing miserably—Andy rounded on Paul. "It's all we have. Are you with me?"

Paul drew himself up, looking hurt. "Of course."

Andy didn't have time to smooth over Paul's feelings. "We need to get tactical on this."

"Agreed."

Three minutes later they had an address matching the description of the warehouse and in record time they moved out of the station. But it wasn't fast enough.

A howl of pent up rage lay trapped in Andy's lungs as he endured the insufferably long ride to North Queens.

He could only pray they wouldn't be too late.

"Where is it?"

The angry bellow shuddered through Kristin. She shook her head trying to focus on the man yelling in her face. He'd been asking her for some video ever since she awoke. "I don't know anything about a video."

She'd moved past fear and panic into numb horror after the initial shock of being kidnapped and tied to a chair in a dank, smelly room had passed. Sunlight tried to brighten the space but the dingy window wouldn't allow much of the sun's glow to invade the room.

But at least she hadn't been unconscious long enough for the sun to go down. Unless it had simply come back up again....

The man standing before her had hit her twice already. She could feel the tightening of skin over her cheek from the swelling and she was pretty sure her lip was split, if the blood she tasted was any indication.

"I said tell me where it is." He raised his hand for a third blow.

Cringing with anticipation of the pain, she cried out, "Jesus save me."

Chapter Eighteen

The man stayed his hand, his expression turning impossibly harder. His olive complexion seemed to blanch as he stared at her with coal-black eyes.

"God will not save you. There is no God," the man stated harshly. His hand descended for another stinging blow.

Light exploded behind Kristin's right eye. Her head lolled to the side as waves of pain washed over her. "You're wrong," she whispered.

The man spit on the ground. He turned back to the two men standing near the door, he said, "You've searched her house and her store?"

"Yes, sir. Nothing."

"Where could it be?" His frustration echoed off the concrete walls. "If the police get ahold of that video we're done for. Are you sure Linder said this woman had it?"

One of the thugs by the door shrugged his massive shoulders. "That's what he said. Claimed the reporter told him she would give him the video when her neighbor got home."

"Maybe she meant another neighbor, you idiots," the man screamed. "Go back to that apartment building and find me that video. Burn down the place if you have to."

The two thugs exchanged glances before silently leaving the room.

Dismay ran a ragged course over Kristin, rousing her from the pain in her face. She struggled against her restraints, needing to somehow protect her neighbors, her community. The cords at her hands and feet held. Helplessness seeped the fight out of her.

The only way to help the innocent people in her building was to tell the man about the key, so he wouldn't go there and trash the building or hurt anyone else.

"The police," she said. "They have the key."

The man stalked closer. "What did you say?"

"Sue left a key with me. The police have it."

Rage lit his black eyes like embers in a fire pit. He swore, a graphic litany half in English and half in Spanish, then turned on his shiny black Florsheims and exited out the door.

Kristin breathed a sigh of relief. At least he wouldn't be hitting her any time soon. But then a terrible thought entered her mind: they didn't need her any longer. She was as good as dead now.

She closed her eyes tight and prayed Andy would find her, even as despair tried to rob her of any hope. She had no idea where she was. How did she expect Andy to know where to look? In despair, she slumped into the chair.

A noise startled her. She blinked, though her right eye was swollen to a slit.

The door opened again.

Alarm brought her fully upright. She braced herself. This was it. They'd kill her now for sure.

A man slipped inside, a gun in his hand.

Andy.

A cry of joy escaped her sore lips. She'd never thought she'd see him again. And would never have the opportunity to tell him how she felt about him. Love swelled in her chest and tears crested her lashes. "I can't believe you're here."

"Shhh." He worked to undo the ties that bound her. "We're not out of danger yet."

When she was finally released, she flung herself into his arms. "I prayed you'd come."

"I prayed I'd find you." He gave her a tight squeeze. "God answered both of our prayers. Come on now, we've got to go."

He ushered her toward the door, but froze when the man and two new thugs entered the room, weapons drawn and aimed straight for them.

Kristin cringed with dread and resignation.

Now they would die.

Chapter Nineteen

Pushing Kristin behind him, Andy faced Mendoza and his men. The roar of rage for the abuse purpling Kristin's lovely face almost drowned out the voice from his earpiece telling him to back up, to lure Mendoza farther into the room. The only chance of survival that he and Kristin had was to follow the tactical team's orders through the earpiece jammed into his right ear.

Andy stepped back, forcing Kristin to do the same. "You're done, Mendoza. We have the video."

Mendoza moved forward. "And I have you."

"You killed Schomus in cold blood. You'll get the death penalty for that," Andy said, hoping to buy some time.

"Andy?"

Kristin's frightened whisper tugged at his heart. He turned his head slightly so that only she'd hear him. "Trust me. Trust God."

Her big green eyes showed her fear, but she nodded.

"Why'd you kill Schomus? What did he have on you?"

Mendoza laughed. "What makes you so sure Schomus wasn't working for me?"

Andy had only known the Assistant DA in passing, but he'd seemed like a stand up kind of guy. "He wouldn't stoop so low."

Andy pressed Kristin back toward the center of the room to where the SWAT sniper's rifle would have a clean shot of Mendoza and his men.

"You're so short-sighted." Mendoza shook his head with disgust. "You all think just because someone works for the law that they must adhere to the law."

"Schomus wasn't crooked." Andy hoped.

"How do you think I've stayed in business for so long?"

Sick at the thought that the ADA had been dirty, Andy asked, "How'd Linder discover that he was being watched?"

Mendoza stepped closer. "Linder. What a nut job. I swear, sometimes good help is hard to find."

Andy continued, slowly luring Mendoza toward the center of the room. "You didn't answer my question."

"That reporter wasn't careful. One of my men saw her trailing Linder, shooting video of him."

"But how did you discover she'd videotaped you killing Schomus?"

"She was squeamish. It didn't take much to get her to talk," he said, his eyes narrowing. "Enough of this chit-chat. You're wasting my time."

"You'll never get away with killing us."

Mendoza smirked. "Right. And if that was true this place would be crawling with cops. No, I think not. But I might let you live if you get me that video."

The voice in Andy's ears urged him back a few feet further. "You let us go first. Then I'll hand over the video."

Mendoza's eyebrows rose. "You wouldn't be stupid enough to bring it here. Take the girl." He motioned for his men to take them.

The two men stepped past their boss toward Andy and Kristin.

Through the earpiece, Andy heard what he'd been waiting for: target sighted.

Lifting his hand as if in surrender, he closed a fist to signal he was ready. In one swift motion, he grabbed Kristin and pushed her to the ground, throwing himself over her as a shield while the world exploded around them.

Chapter Twenty

Kristin screamed until her lungs hurt. The sound of gunfire filled her head and terror ripped away any hope of survival. Terrified that Andy had been shot, she twisted on the ground, trying to get out from under him in a vain attempt to protect him. But his hard, heavy body pinned her flat.

"Stay still," he ordered into her ear.

The welcome sound of his voice made a sob catch in her throat. Then he pushed off her, pulling her to her feet. Men wearing flack vests and carrying big weapons swarmed the room, surrounding the men on the floor. Mendoza and his two men lay on the ground, injured. Blood stained their clothing and seeped onto the cement floor. Mendoza cursed loudly while his comrades moaned and pleaded for help.

A mixture of relief and shock made her knees weak and the world a bit fuzzy.

"Let's get out of here," Andy said.

Feeling safe with Andy's arm around her, guiding her, she allowed him to hustle her away from the chaos.

Once outside she breathed deeply, taking the fresh air into her lungs and chasing away the horror of the past few hours. As adrenaline left her body, she began to shake as if she'd been stuck in a deep freeze, even though the late summer air was hot and humid.

Andy's arms came around her, pulling her close to his chest. She melted into the comfort of his arms. The hard vest beneath his suit coat jolted her back to reality. She pushed away.

"What were you thinking?" she demanded as residual fear rose. "You could have been killed."

He stared at her a moment with an incredulous gleam in his midnight eyes, before a slow grin spread across his face. "You were the one in danger."

"But you shouldn't have come in there alone. You put your life at unnecessary risk," she stated hotly, thinking of how terribly wrong his stunt could have gone. The very thought made her want to throw up.

Reaching out to tuck some loose hair behind her ear, he said, "Honey, risk is part of the job. There's risk in just walking across a New York City street." He brushed her lips with his index finger. "But today I wasn't doing my job. I was protecting the woman I love."

Stunned speechless, she could only stare at him.

He cupped her face in his hands. "I'm never letting you go, Kristin Conrad. I will protect you until the day I die because I know that God will be watching over us."

Humility and gratefulness spread over her like warm butter. The horror of being kidnapped had been worth the price to bring some healing to Andy's wounded soul.

Not to mention her own. After the terror of the last couple of days, she realized she could never make her life totally safe and predictable. She had to trust that God would watch over them and together they'd have the security and peace that only came from above.

With a sigh of pure bliss, she surrendered to the joy cascading through her veins. Rising on tiptoe, she moved in closer to whisper, "I can't imagine my life without you."

And then she kissed him, showing him all the love in her heart.

* * * * *

REQUEST YOUR FREE BOOKS!

2 FREE INSPIRATIONAL NOVELS
PLUS 2
FREE
MYSTERY GIFTS

YES! Please send me 2 FREE Love Inspired® novels and my 2 FREE mystery gifts (gifts are worth about $10). After receiving them, if I don't wish to receive any more books, I can return the shipping statement marked "cancel." If I don't cancel, I will receive 6 brand-new novels every month and be billed just $4.49 per book in the U.S. or $4.99 per book in Canada. That's a saving of at least 22% off the cover price. It's quite a bargain! Shipping and handling is just 50¢ per book in the U.S. and 75¢ per book in Canada.* I understand that accepting the 2 free books and gifts places me under no obligation to buy anything. I can always return a shipment and cancel at any time. Even if I never buy another book, the two free books and gifts are mine to keep forever.   105/305 IDN FEGR

Name	(PLEASE PRINT)

Address	Apt. #

City	State/Prov.	Zip/Postal Code

Signature (if under 18, a parent or guardian must sign)

Mail to the **Reader Service:**
IN U.S.A.: P.O. Box 1867, Buffalo, NY 14240-1867
IN CANADA: P.O. Box 609, Fort Erie, Ontario L2A 5X3

Not valid for current subscribers to Love Inspired books.

**Are you a subscriber to Love Inspired books
and want to receive the larger-print edition?
Call 1-800-873-8635 or visit www.ReaderService.com.**

* Terms and prices subject to change without notice. Prices do not include applicable taxes. Sales tax applicable in N.Y. Canadian residents will be charged applicable taxes. Offer not valid in Quebec. This offer is limited to one order per household. All orders subject to credit approval. Credit or debit balances in a customer's account(s) may be offset by any other outstanding balance owed by or to the customer. Please allow 4 to 6 weeks for delivery. Offer available while quantities last.

Your Privacy—The Reader Service is committed to protecting your privacy. Our Privacy Policy is available online at www.ReaderService.com or upon request from the Reader Service.

We make a portion of our mailing list available to reputable third parties that offer products we believe may interest you. If you prefer that we not exchange your name with third parties, or if you wish to clarify or modify your communication preferences, please visit us at www.ReaderService.com/consumerschoice or write to us at Reader Service Preference Service, P.O. Box 9062, Buffalo, NY 14269. Include your complete name and address.

When Greta Goodloe is jilted by her longtime sweetheart, she takes comfort in matchmaking between newcomer Luke Starns and her schoolmarm sister. Yet the more Greta tries to throw them together, the more Luke fascinates her.

Read on for a sneak peek of A GROOM FOR GRETA by Anna Schmidt, available October 2012 from Love Inspired® Historical.

***

"So what do you intend to do about this turn of events, Luke?"

"Do? Your sister made her feelings plain last evening. She does not wish to spend her time with me."

Greta sighed heavily. "She does not know what she wants. The question is, are you serious about finding a wife for yourself or not?"

"I am quite serious."

"Then—"

"What I will not do," Luke interrupted, "is go after a woman who has declared openly that she has no interest in making a home with me."

"And what of her idea that you and I should…" She let the sentence trail off.

"That depends," he said slowly.

"On what?"

"On whether or not you are able to put aside your feelings for Josef Bontrager. Your sister believes that your feelings for him were not as strong as they should be for two people planning a life together. Do you agree?"

"Lydia is…I mean…oh, I don't know," Greta replied.

"How can either of you expect me to know what it is that I'm feeling these days? It's too soon."

"If Josef came to you and asked for your forgiveness and pleaded with you to reconsider, would you?"

"No," she finally whispered. "I would not."

Luke felt his heart pounding, and he realized that over the months he had been in Celery Fields, he had taken more notice of the beautiful Greta Goodloe than he had allowed himself to admit. He had learned a hard lesson back in Ontario and he had been determined not to make the same mistake twice.

But if Greta had come to realize that Josef was not for her…

On the other hand, surely the idea that she might be firm in her decision to be rid of Josef did not mean that she was ready for someone new.

***

Don't miss A GROOM FOR GRETA by Anna Schmidt,
the next heartwarming book
in the AMISH BRIDES OF CELERY FIELDS series,
on sale October 2012 wherever Love Inspired® Historical
books are sold!

INSPIRATIONAL ROMANCE
TO WARM YOUR HEART & SOUL

Celebrate 15 years with Love Inspired Books!

Save $1.00

on the purchase of any
Love Inspired® Suspense or
Love Inspired® Historical title.

SAVE
$1.⁰⁰

on the purchase of any
Love Inspired® Suspense or
Love Inspired® Historical title.

Coupon expires November 30, 2012. Redeemable at participating retail outlets in the U.S. and Canada only. Limit one coupon per customer.

Canadian Retailers: Harlequin Enterprises Limited will pay the face value of this coupon plus 10.25¢ if submitted by the customer for this specified product only. Any other use constitutes fraud. Coupon is nonassignable. Void if taxed, prohibited or restricted by law. Void if copied. Consumer must pay any government taxes. Nielsen Clearing House customers ("NCH") submit coupons and proof of sales to Harlequin Enterprises Limited, P.O. Box 3000, Saint John, NB E2L 4L3. Non-NCH retailer: for reimbursement, submit coupons and proof of sales directly to Harlequin Enterprises Limited, Retail Marketing Department, 225 Duncan Mill Rd., Don Mills (Toronto), Ontario M3B 3K9, Canada. Limit one coupon per purchase. Valid in Canada only.

U.S. Retailers: Harlequin Enterprises Limited will pay the face value of this coupon plus 8¢ if submitted by customer for this specified product only. Any other use constitutes fraud. Coupon is nonassignable. Void if taxed, prohibited or restricted by law. Consumer must pay any government taxes. Void if copied. For reimbursement, submit coupons and proof of sales directly to Harlequin Enterprises Limited, P.O. Box 880478, El Paso, TX 88588-0478, U.S.A. Cash value 1/100 cents. Limit one coupon per purchase. Valid in the U.S. only.

52610484

5 65373 00076 2   (8100)0 11809

® and TM are trademarks owned and used by the trademark owner and/or its licensee.
© 2012 Harlequin Enterprises Limited

LICOUP0912

celebrating 15 YEARS *Love Inspired*™

Another heartwarming installment of

←TEXAS TWINS→

Two sets of twins, torn apart by family secrets, find their way home

When big-city cop Grayson Wallace visits an elementary school for career day, he finds his heartstrings unexpectedly tugged by a six-year-old fatherless boy and his widowed mother, Elise Lopez. Now he can't get the struggling Lopezes off his mind. All he can think about is what family means—especially after discovering the identical twin brother he hadn't known he had in Grasslands. Maybe a trip to ranch country is just what he, Elise and little Cory need.

Look-Alike Lawman
by **Glynna Kaye**